THE
MAGIC

LANTERN

THE MAGIC LANTERN

A Mystical Murder Mystery

EDWARD HAYS

Forest of Peace Books, Inc.

Other Books by the Author:
(available through the publisher or your favorite bookstore)

Prayers and Rituals
Psalms for Zero Gravity
Prayers for a Planetary Pilgrim
Prayers for the Domestic Church
Prayers for the Servants of God

Parables and Stories
The Gospel of Gabriel
Sundancer
St. George and the Dragon
The Flaming Pearl
The Ethiopian Tattoo Shop
Twelve and One-Half Keys
The Christmas Eve Storyteller

Contemporary Spirituality
The Old Hermit's Almanac
The Lenten Labyrinth
Holy Fools & Mad Hatters
A Pilgrim's Almanac
Pray All Ways
Secular Sanctity
In Pursuit of the Great White Rabbit
The Ascent of the Mountain of God
Feathers on the Wind

The Magic Lantern
copyright © 1991, by Edward M. Hays

Library of Congress Catalog Card Number: 91-75961
ISBN 0-939516-15-2

published by
Forest of Peace Publishing, Inc.
PO Box 269
Leavenworth, KS 66048-0269   USA
1-800-659-3227

printed by
Hall Commercial Printing
Topeka, KS 66608-0007

cover art and illustrations by
Edward Hays

calligraphy by
Thomas Turkle

1st printing: October 1991
2nd printing: September 1998

DEDICATED

with affection and admiration

to

Henry (Hank) O'Donnell

who walks the razor's edge

seeking the mystical

in the marketplace

PUBLISHER'S PREFACE

The book that you are about to read was a manuscript we mysteriously received one day in the mail. As with the author's first book, **St. George and the Dragon**, the package had neither a return address nor an enclosed letter to indicate the author's full identity.

The manuscript was in the form of a day journal or notebook in which our mysterious spiritual seeker detailed his duties and the strange events during his time at a boarding house in an unnamed city.

The old shoe box in which the manuscript was sent additionally contained some floor plan drawings of the boarding house. Also enclosed was a snapshot of a cat, several old photographic slides from his Magic Lantern machine, including one below of the Sacred Shrine at Mecca, and a recipe for curried duck! All of these have been faithfully included herein with the hope that they may be of assistance in unraveling the strange and mysterious story you are about to begin.

CHAPTER 1

"Just call me Mama," said Mrs. Mahathaman as I introduced myself. She was a plump, elderly black woman, white hair tied in a bun at the back of her head. Her appearance was dignified yet friendly. "Come in, please," she said, her face beaming like a chocolate pie. I stepped inside the entrance way of the turn-of-the-century mansion and set down my suitcase and the tattered, black Magic Lantern box. From my coat pocket I removed a newspaper which was folded open to the Help Wanted section. Halfway down the page was an ad I had circled in pencil, "Position for woman or man. Light household cleaning and preparation of one daily meal. Room, board and salary. Inquire at Mrs. M. Mahathaman's Rooming House, 3535 Woodbine."

"If you haven't already hired someone for this position, I would like to apply. From this description it sounds like the sort of situation that would fit my needs. It should afford me the time to pursue my special interests." As I spoke, I was struck by the image of the black woman framed by the aged, walnut-paneled foyer and the grand winding staircase which led to the second floor.

She smiled her chocolate pie grin, "You're right. What I would expect shouldn't occupy the entire day. The person who was here previously was a writer who spent her free time working on a novel. She left us about two weeks ago, and you're the first person to come and inquire about my advertisement."

"The daily meal preparation mentioned in the ad," I asked, "what does that involve?" Over her right shoulder I could see a pair of open French doors which revealed a walnut-paneled living room. The room had a formal feel with its great stone fireplace, heavy walnut tables and burgundy leather chairs.

"Well, besides myself, there are seven others who are presently living here, six roomers and my son, Lucien. I'm sure you'll find that we're an easy group to live with, and you'll actually only have to prepare dinner for seven. Lucien, my son, doesn't come for dinner. Of course, we would want you to join us at table. So that would make a dinner count of eight."

"I must confess, Mrs. Mahat...—I mean, Mama—that while I enjoy cooking, I've previously only cooked on rare occasions. My wife has handled that department. But I'm willing to give it a try."

"That's all I ask of anyone, George. Excellent, now if we can agree on a salary that's . . . ."

A telephone rang off to the left, and Mama excused herself. She disappeared through a doorway into a large bookcase-lined room just off the entrance foyer. Somewhere in the house, a large clock was ticking like some giant heart. That single sound accentuated the serene yet somehow uneasy silence of the old mansion. As I waited for Mama's return, I studied the patterns in a worn Persian rug at my feet. Soon my eyes came to rest on the old, tattered black case of my newly acquired Magic Lantern.

Talk about impulse buying! On my way here I had gotten lost after getting off the bus. Only about five blocks away, I stopped in at an antique shop to ask for directions. When I opened the door, a small brass bell jingled, and an aged Asian woman bowed and smiled a greeting. I browsed through the small shop, looking at an assortment of old objects, when I came upon a large black box. I lifted the lid. Inside was a turn-of-the-century Magic Lantern slide machine. I looked at it, smiled to myself and closed the lid. I continued to wander around, examining a vase and other old objects. Suddenly, to my surprise, I found myself back again in front of the tarnished oblong box of the Magic Lantern. On the lid was a brass plate inscription, "The Thomas Edison Magic Lantern. Copyright 1908." Next to the machine was an old yellowed box of slides which I picked up and quickly set down again, thinking, "One thing I don't need is an old slide machine." I returned to exploring the shop, only to once again find myself standing in front of the Magic Lantern. On an impulse, I picked it up and carried it to the desk where the old woman was seated reading a book.

8

"I see that the Magic Lantern machine has selected you," she said as she examined me over the top of her eyeglasses. "I believe it has made an excellent choice."

"Excuse me?" I said, taken aback by her suggestion that the Magic Lantern had chosen me. "What price are you asking for this antique?"

Eying me again over the top of her glasses, she answered, "The price is immaterial. In fact, it's not for sale. The Magic Lantern is yours! You may take it home with you. There's no charge here. You see, I run an adoption agency."

Billfold in hand, I stammered, "An adoption agency? The sign over your shop reads **Rare Antique Shop**."

"Yes, I know. There are some antiques in here that are for sale. However, among them are perhaps fifteen or twenty pieces for which I have personal responsibility to find a good home. I know it may sound strange to you, but it is they who choose the persons with whom they want to live. These special and rare objects carefully inspect customers to see if they would like to go home with them. When someone they dislike or distrust comes near, they have the power to emit subtle repelling aromas. When that happens, the customer simply walks away and looks at something else. If one of my precious ones wishes to go home with a customer, it releases a marvelously magnetic aroma. I can tell at once when one of my children has found a... ah...friend, a guardian."

She stood up and bowed slightly, "You are most fortunate, sir. This is an auspicious day for you. My old Magic Lantern, after having been with me for several years, has chosen to go home with you! It's a great honor for you, sir. You are indeed very lucky, very lucky."

"Thank you. I don't understand any of this, but I've learned to accept the unusual in my life." I thought about how Igor, my mentor, had taught me that bit of wisdom.

As I picked up the large black case, the woman removed several small boxes of slides from beneath the desk and put them into a brown paper bag. "Here, sir, are the other boxes of slides that go with the machine. I have kept them safely hidden beneath my desk until it was time for my precious one to leave." She bowed deeply, "Goodbye, and be careful. Take good care of these slides; they may save your life. Be on your guard, for the journey you are on is dangerous. But do not fear — you have a companion who knows the way."

Acknowledging her grave advice, I added, "That reminds me. I need to know the way to 3535 Woodbine Street. Can you direct me?"

"Oh, that's my friend Mrs. Mahathaman's place. Let me draw you a little map."

As I left the shop and began walking toward the Woodbine Street address of the boarding house, I said aloud to myself, "That whole exchange was like a fortune cookie. What did she mean about being careful? How did she know I was on a journey, and what did she mean when she said that I had a companion who knows the way? I've met my share of eccentrics, but she's a classic. She's been around those antiques so long she's begun to look upon them as her children — and upon herself as the operator of an adoption agency! That's a story to tell Martha when I get back home."

"Sorry to keep you waiting. It was a long telephone call." Mama's voice awakened me to the present moment. While heavy set, she moved with the silent grace of a cat. I had not heard her until she spoke. She took my arm, saying, "Let me show you around the house. It was built at the end of the last century by a wealthy factory owner as a family home, but I've converted it into a rooming house. My old legs aren't what they once were, so I live on the first floor — over there to the left. Originally, it was the library and den."

She escorted me through the living room with its rich, old leather chairs and dark walnut tables graced by ornate Chinese vase lamps. At the far end of the living room was another set of French doors that opened onto a foyer. Two stained-glass doors led out to a covered carriage entrance and driveway on the east side of the house. I had noticed when I walked up to the house that the covered entrance had a sun porch built over it. Directly across the foyer was the doorway to an oblong dining room with a long walnut table and matching chairs. As I stood in the dining room doorway, I could see, through the windows at the far end of the room, a two-story carriage house behind the main house. At the peak of its roof was a tall pole topped by a giant gold star!

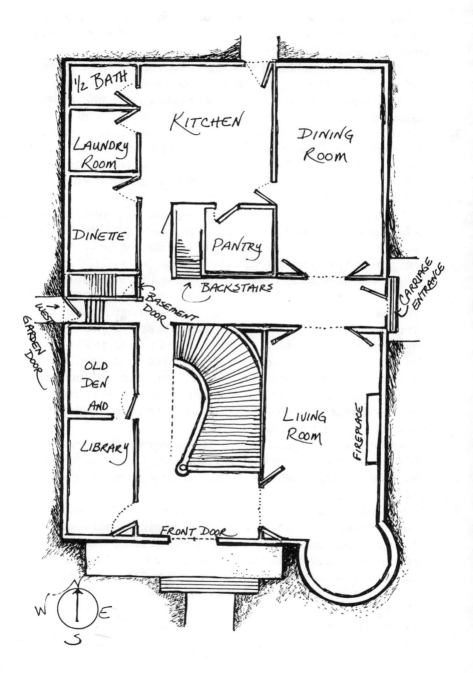

½ BATH

KITCHEN

DINING ROOM

LAUNDRY ROOM

DINETTE

PANTRY

BACKSTAIRS

BASEMENT DOOR

CARRIAGE ENTRANCE

WEST GARDEN DOOR

OLD DEN AND LIBRARY

LIVING ROOM

FIREPLACE

FRONT DOOR

W E
S

In the middle of the wall to the left was a doorway which Mama opened to reveal the kitchen. "And this is the...may I call you 'George'?"

"Certainly, if you like." I wasn't sure why, but I found myself wanting to share with this old black lady something about my spiritual journey that I'd never tell to a stranger. "Actually, Mama, George isn't my full name. Igor, my mentor, gave me a title when he told me that I needed something more to my name if I wanted to go on a quest. Igor said I should call myself 'St.' George – not for 'saint' but as an abbreviation for 'sent' as well as 'servant.' Ah, Igor would be pleased to know that I was about to become a real servant."

"I'm sure he would, George, and I'm glad he gave you such a fitting title for this job. Besides, I like 'George' – sounds like an ideal name for a butler and cook!" She flashed her chocolate pie grin as she made the last comment.

I smiled back at her. I liked the old woman's playfulness.

We stepped into the kitchen which was located at the rear of the house. It contained a large cooking range, a collection of copper pots and pans hanging from racks over the table in the center of the room, a refrigerator and a large double sink. To the left as you entered from the dining room was a doorway leading to a large pantry. The back wall of the kitchen had several tall windows looking out onto the star-capped carriage house. The far side of the kitchen had three doors. The one on the right led to a half bath.

Approaching the middle door, Mama explained, "This room, George – I do like the sound of your name – was once a small bedroom for the cook. Now it's our laundry room. We each do our own laundry here."

I looked inside and saw an automatic washer and dryer. Mama then pointed to the third doorway, "And this is a small dinette. Breakfast and lunch are self-service for all of us. My roomers eat out or, if they wish, can fix something down here. As you can see, it has a lovely view of my garden." On a small stand next to the window was an automatic coffee maker with a half-filled pot.

"Oh, George, excuse me. I'm sorry. Sweet Buddha, where is my old mind? I forgot the first and most important of all the

Gospel sacraments: hospitality! Would you care for a cup of coffee?"

She poured us both a cup. As we sat drinking our coffee together, we settled on my salary. While it wasn't much, it was sufficient – my needs on my sabbatical would be simple.

Although I had many questions, like why there was a gold star atop the carriage house, the conversation turned to the subject of her roomers.

"As I mentioned, there are six boarders. They have rooms upstairs on the second floor. The third floor is the attic, and no one stays there. I would take you upstairs to show you around, but my old legs aren't what they used to be – it's such a long climb! Let me draw you a diagram."

She picked up a pencil that had been used for a crossword puzzle in the newspaper and began to draw a rather professional looking floor plan on the backside of a mail advertisement. "This is the front circular staircase that leads to the second floor. Here at the top to the right is Maria's room. You'll meet her tonight at dinner. She's sleeping now – poor child has to work nights. To the right of her room is the door to the attic on the third floor. It's empty except for some luggage and a few odds and ends."

She drew a hallway to the back of the house. "Here, around the corner from the end of this wall, are the back stairs. They lead down to the first floor. And here, George, next to Maria's, is your room in the northwest corner of the house. Then along the back wall is the bathroom that you'll share with Inspector Bernadone. His room is directly across from yours. From a glance at how little luggage you have, you and he should get along well together. He lives a very simple life. While all the others have rooms with a private bathroom, he has always chosen to share one."

"Inspector?" I had a growing sense of wonder about what kind of people were rooming in Mama's boarding house.

"Yes, Frank is a detective with the police department. I know that 'Inspector' is an old-fashioned term for a detective, but I like the sound of it, don't you? He has lived with me now for almost ten years. I couldn't ask for a better roomer than Inspector Bernardone. He's a quiet man who stays very much to himself. Has a great interest in Islamic mysticism and a special way with animals. He and my cat are the best of friends."

13

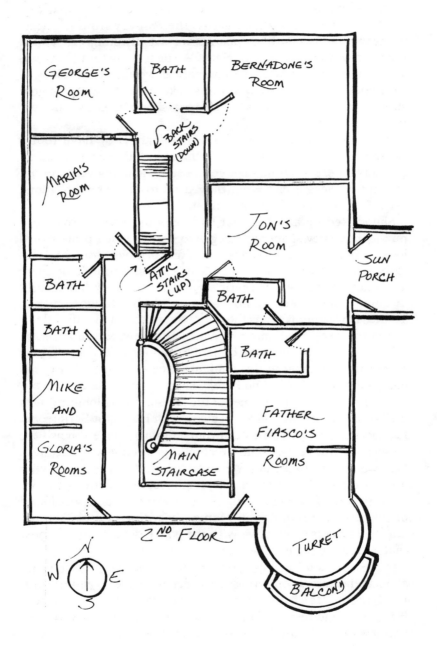

Next, she drew a doorway on the east wall, down the hallway from Bernadone's room and across the hallway from the attic doorway. Pointing with her pencil, she said, "This is Jon Masek's room. I think you'll like Jon. He's very intelligent and independent, a self-made man and rather liberal. Jon's a lovely boy – well he's not exactly a boy. What I mean is, he's young. When you're past seventy as I am, Child, anyone around forty is young, right? He's always slipping his arm around my waist and kidding me about how he wished he'd been around when I was a young woman. Jon has been with me now for about five years. His room opens onto the sun porch above the covered carriage entrance. He keeps all his equipment there – he's into building, you know."

Mama now quickly and skillfully outlined the rooms at the front of the house. "On the southwest corner is a two-room apartment for Mike and Gloria Smith – such a lovely couple. They're in transition and have only been with me for about six months. They're good people, very religious – they read the Bible every day! And I think, from their comments on social issues, that they're also Republicans."

She paused and took a sip of coffee before going on. "Across the hall from Mike and Gloria is Father Fiasco. His church is in the carriage house – perhaps you saw it through the dining room windows?"

She looked up at me from her drawing. "He calls his church 'The Basilica of the New Bethlehem of the Holy Roman Apocalyptic Catholic Church.' " Resuming her sketch, she continued, "Years ago, when he first came to live here, I felt sorry that he didn't have anyplace to hold church. So I told him he could use the old carriage house. It was abandoned and wasn't being used for anything. All by himself, he transformed it into a lovely little church. It's a bit different, I must say, from most churches I've seen. But then again, I'm not of his faith, nor am I much of a believer in churches!"

"Mama, sounds like you agree with St. Paul: 'God made the world and all things therein...and dwells not in temples built with hands'!"

"Yes, George, for me it's more like what Mohammed said in the Koran: 'God is the Master of east and west. Turn whichsoever direction you may, God shall look you in the face, for God pervades in all of space' – or something like that. But regardless of my belief – or lack of belief – in churches, Father Fiasco is a good man. That for me is the acid test of holiness. He's also funny, which may be a more accurate gauge! He's been a roomer here with me now for almost fifteen years. Along with the other five, you'll meet him tonight at dinner. You can judge for yourself."

I had almost forgotten that when I arrived and was walking up the front steps, I spotted a figure on the second story balcony of the turret on the southeast side of the house (Mama was later to explain to me that turrets were most unusual on Victorian mansions but that the original owner liked castles). The man on the balcony was dressed in a black cassock and white Roman collar and was wearing a cowboy hat. "I believe I've already seen Father Fiasco! When I arrived, he blessed me as I walked up your front steps and rang the door bell. It all happened very quickly and was, how shall I say it, a bit unusual, since he was wearing a tan, ten gallon hat."

"Hmm, I thought he only wore that one on Tuesdays! Perhaps today is some holy day – as I said, I'm not of his faith. You know, he also calls his little church 'The Lone Star Cathedral.' With a name like that, I guess a Texan hat would be appropriate on any day!"

Mama handed me the sketch and stood up. Pointing toward the door, she said, "Let me show you some more of the house." Just outside the dinette to the right was another door. I was struck by the fact that besides the usual door lock it also had three dead-bolt locks. She sensed my curiosity. "This door leads to the basement, which isn't used anymore. My child Lucien lives down there. He's...ah...what shall we say...a kind of hermit. And they do guard their solitude, don't they?"

Next to the basement door was a set of a few steps leading down to the outside door at the west entrance of the house. The door led out to the garden. On the other side of the hallway to the left was a doorway with a flight of stairs that ascended sharply to the second floor. Glancing at the drawing, it was clear that these were the back stairs. Across from the stairs was a faded tapestry-covered bench.

Alongside the bench was an old grandfather's clock, which

must have been the clock I heard when I first arrived. Its face was unusual. Encircling the twelve Roman numbers was a large serpent with its tail in its mouth. The head of the snake was turned outward so that its eyes were fixed directly on whomever looked at the clock. The eyes of the serpent were hollow, which gave the sense of gazing into emptiness, into the vast hollow cavern of the clock – perhaps into the mystery of time itself.

"The serpent on the clock is an ancient symbol of time as an endless cycle. Do you like the clock?" asked Mama. "I think it's a wonderful piece of art."

I nodded in agreement but personally found the tail-eating serpent a strange image for decorating a kindly grandfather's clock. Directly ahead was the foyer between the living room and the dining room, as well as the stained-glass doors that led to the covered carriage entrance through which we had passed earlier.

"I'm sure you must be tired after all this," said Mama. "Perhaps you would like to take your bags upstairs and rest a bit. Since you have a map, I will let you find your own way." She led me through a doorway that brought us back to the main-entrance foyer.

Standing beneath the large cut-glass chandelier hanging from the ceiling in the center of the circle created by the curving staircase, Mama concluded our tour. "George, feel free to explore the house, even the attic. Tonight, I'll fix dinner for the household so you can unpack and get your bearings. You might want to come down to the kitchen around 4:30 and watch. That way you can get an idea of where everything is kept. We all gather in the living room at 6:30 for a cocktail before dinner. You know, cocktails are such a civilized custom."

With that, Mama smiled, bowed her head slightly and then regally walked to her room like an African Queen Victoria.

As I climbed the circular staircase to the second floor, I couldn't help but wonder what I had gotten myself into by accepting this job. I had had little experience keeping a house clean, not to mention being a cook. Would I really have the leisure to pursue my inner journey here?

My room in the rear of the house wasn't more than 10' x 12'. It had two large windows; one looked out onto the garden and the other onto the carriage house. In the south wall of my room was a locked door that must have led to the adjoining room, which was Maria's. From the look of the painted door frame, it had not been opened for some time. The two rooms must have once been a suite. My room may have been a sitting room.

My new living quarters were simple. There was a small desk with a straight-back chair, an old easy chair and an old bridge lamp next to it. After I had unpacked my suitcase, I sat down in the easy chair and tried to collect myself.

In the short time since leaving home, so much had happened. Just the departure from home had been draining. Leaving Martha and the kids was difficult. Now I already had a job working at Mama's boarding house. Despite my doubts, it held the promise of being a place where I could do some serious work on my inner journey. I hoped it would allow me both time and space to grow spiritually, even without Igor. God, I missed him. I wished he'd find me, and together we could take up where we left off over a year ago. I liked Mama. She was kind and loving, and it somehow felt like she held a key to this stage of my quest. But there was something unusual about this old mansion. For example, there was that triple-locked basement door. I could understand if...what was his name...oh yes, Lucien, wanted privacy to be a hermit, but three locks? Yes, there was more to this old house than appeared on the surface. I couldn't help but wonder if that priest in the cowboy hat on the balcony knew something. Maybe he figured that if I was planning on moving into this house I *needed* a blessing!

I looked at my empty suitcase and the Magic Lantern and decided that I should find a place to store them up in the attic. I walked down the hallway toward the attic door next to Maria's room. At the end of the hall behind the circular staircase, I saw another tapestry-covered bench. It looked like a companion to the one next to the grandfather's clock in the downstairs hallway.

As I opened the door to the attic, a wave of musty air surged around me. I flicked the light switch and climbed the stairs that led up to the third floor. At the top of the stairs was a large room which appeared to occupy about one-third of the attic space. A single bare light bulb hanging from the ceiling on a long cord cast strange shadows on several suitcases and boxes piled around the edges of the room. Old pieces of furniture and a few odds and ends were stacked around the sides of the room. The back third of the attic was divided by a wall with a doorway. I opened the door and saw what once might have been a servant's room: there was a single bed with a faded yellow spread, a chair and a table. The room appeared not to have been used for years.

At the other end of the attic was another wall and doorway. I walked over, opened the door and turned on the light switch. The room ran the full width of the front of the house. While almost empty, unlike the room at the other end, it apparently had been recently used. Beneath an old ceiling light fixture was a table, chair and wastebasket filled with popcorn balls of paper. This must have been where the writer, who had my job before me, did her creating. Three short arched windows, no more than three feet high, were centered in the front wall that faced the south, or front, of the house. The far left corner of this room opened to the top floor of the round turret on the southeast side of the house. That would put it directly above the rooms of Father Fiasco and the Smiths. From the height of the coat hooks on one wall and a few broken toys, my guess was that original-ly this attic room was a nursery or children's playroom.

On the wall opposite the three arched windows was a single painting. I remembered as a child having seen exactly the same four-track picture in an old book. The painting showed a speeding deluxe passenger train with smoke streaming back across the engine. A four-door touring car was traveling at the same speed on a highway running parallel to the train tracks. Beyond the train, in the background, was a vast body of water and a great ocean liner with smoke rising from its four smokestacks. Far out at sea, above the ocean liner, an early twin-engine airplane flew through sunset-touched clouds.

As I looked with fondness at the old painting, I realized the source of my wanderlust, my desire to travel and go on a quest. Such childhood images surely seed in our souls a lifelong desire for romantic adventures.

"Some romantic quest I'm on!" I thought as I came back to the present moment. "Here I am in an old mansion converted into a boarding house filled with strange people for whom I'll be working as a servant!" Setting my empty suitcase and the tat-tered box with the Magic Lantern on the floor, I turned to leave.

Suddenly I felt very homesick and doubted seriously the wisdom of my decision to leave home on this trip, even if Martha had encouraged me to do so. At that moment, among the musty smells of the attic I sensed another aroma. I looked down at my newly acquired Magic Lantern and felt an uncontrollable urge to open the box.

I lifted the old machine out of the box, studying the felt accordion-like bellows which narrowed to a large, round, brass lens cap. As I did, a time-yellowed piece of folded paper fell to the floor. I picked it up, unfolded it and read it. "The operation of this Magic Lantern machine may be hazardous to your health—your mental health. Caution, excessive viewing can cause insanity."

With a smile, I disregarded the strange warning notice and set it aside, eager to try out the old slide machine. I plugged the electrical cord into an outlet on the wall and set the antique slide projector on the table facing the wall with the painting. While lacking a movie screen, I realized that the plain white wall would serve as well. I removed the old painting, leaning it against the wall. Then I pulled down the faded yellow window shades and took out the box of glass slides from the carrying case. Turning out the light, I sat down in the chair behind the table and turned on the Magic Lantern machine.

As I inserted slides one by one, the wall came alive with turn-of-the-century photographs. Once again I felt the magnetic urge to travel, as old photos of far-off places—Egypt, Europe and the Orient—appeared before me. Then an image of Tibet filled the wall. For some strange reason, it riveted my attention. As I stared at the picture, an unusual thing happened. Without my touching the machine, the image began to move! What once had been a still shot now became a motion picture. A snow-swept mountain appeared on the wall. Near the top of the peak was what looked like a Tibetan Buddhist monastery. As the lamasery drew closer and came into focus, the moving images grew larger and more detailed on the makeshift screen of the attic wall. I became one with the strange images on the wall as they led me inside the lamasery, down a long hallway and into what appeared to be some sort of large shrine. Clouds of incense were rising upward in front of dimly lit statues of various forms of Buddha.

Then the lantern zeroed in on the figure of a Tibetan monk seated in front of a golden altar. The monk was reading from a large, ancient scroll.

There was something strange about the image. I leaned closer to see if I might have been mistaken. No, a large nail was protruding from the monk's left hand! I stared, fascinated by the strange sight. Then I realized that the nail in his hand wasn't part of the slide image. It had to be the nail on which the old painting had hung. Since the pictures had stopped moving, I reached into the box for another slide. Out of the corner of my eye – it happened so quickly I couldn't be sure if I saw it or not – the monk reached over with his right hand and in a flash removed the nail from his left hand! I would have sworn in court that the monk couldn't have moved that fast, yet his hand was now free of the large nail!

I momentarily dismissed the improbable scene and inserted more slides. One by one, photos of Mecca, Rome, the Ganges River, the old city of Jerusalem, as well as other holy places of pilgrimage, appeared on the wall. But nothing unusual happened; none of the images began moving on their own as had the ones of the Tibetan monastery. Only now as I returned to "reality" did it occur to me what a fantastic and frightening thing I had just been a part of. It was one of the strangest things that had ever happened to me. From this side of the magical experience it felt like I had been hallucinating. It really was a *magic* lantern. Glancing at my watch, I realized that I would soon have to be in the kitchen. I had only enough time for a few journal-letter notes. So I switched off the Magic Lantern.

Standing up, I wondered aloud, "Did I really see that Tibetan monk remove the nail from his hand, or did I simply imagine it?" I started to leave the attic room when I noticed the painting leaning against the wall. Being something of a mild perfectionist, I felt a need to leave the room as I had found it. But when I attempted to hang the painting, I discovered that its nail was missing. The nail hole was there in the wall, but the nail wasn't! Then I saw it lying on the floor next to the wall. Did it just fall off the wall? Could it really have been that monk removing it from his hand?

I was beginning to understand the comment by the Asian

woman in the antique shop. This really did feel mysterious — and dangerous! Oh, if only my old mentor Igor hadn't disappeared over a year ago. He would have helped me understand what it all meant. One thing about that afternoon's visit to the attic — I found the perfect place for my new hermitage. My room was too small, and it was quieter up here. What my garage once was back at home, the attic would be for me now.

CHAPTER 2

After my brief letter-journal, I was washing my hands in the bathroom I shared with Inspector Bernadone when I heard the sound of car tires squealing to a stop. Looking down out the bathroom window, I saw a sleek, black sports car, a Beretta, I think. A blond, good-looking, muscular man in his late thirties bounced out of the car and walked rapidly across the driveway toward the kitchen entrance on the north side of the house.

"Hmm, can't be Inspector Bernadone, not with a car like that. I'd guess it must be Jon. He appears to be a very energetic person."

At that moment, I could hear the sound of classical music from Maria's room. "She must be awake now," I thought. Beautiful music. I wasn't sure of the composer, but it sounded like Mozart. The mood was broken by footsteps bounding up the back staircase and down the hallway. Then the door to Jon's room closed. My guess must have been right about the man in the sports car. The door slamming awakened me to the time—my watch showed 4:45. I was late for my meeting with Mama in the kitchen.

Entering the kitchen, I was greeted by Mama in a black dress and a large white apron, busily preparing dinner. "George, I hope you had a chance to rest a bit. You looked tired at the end of our little tour."

"Thank you, Mama, I'm fine, but I didn't rest. I unpacked and then took my suitcase up to the attic. On my way through the upstairs hallway, I saw a sitting bench at the head of the front stairs. It was exactly like the one down here by the grandfather's clock. Are they a pair?"

"Oh, yes, they were built in as part of the original house. But they're not really benches, even though I occasionally use them as such when I'm a bit weary. Way back when this house was built, those benches were the latest time-saving conveniences. They're actually laundry chutes for the maids to drop dirty clothes and sheets straight down to the basement. They're quite large because they were designed to hold big bundles of bed linen. Clever idea, eh?"

"Did they also build in some hidden passageways—sliding panels and all that sort of thing? I always associate them with old mansions."

"Honeychild, I think they only exist in old horror movies!"

Her quip made me think about the "horror story" I'd just witnessed with my Magic Lantern. "I wanted to explain, Mama, why I'm a bit late. On my way here today I purchased an old Magic Lantern machine. I didn't have time for a nap this afternoon because I'm afraid I got caught up in watching it. I had a most unusual experience."

"Only the first of many, I'd wager. And I'm sorry that you didn't have time for a nap. Napping, George, like cocktails, is truly a civilized custom. Napoleon and Thomas Edison swore by naps. There's a very primal, even animal, wisdom about them. I'll bet Fatima, my cat, takes a hundred little naps a day."

"Fatima? Is your cat named after that place of pilgrimage in central Portugal, the shrine of the Blessed Mother?"

"Actually, George, I named her after the daughter of the Prophet Mohammed. And if she took as many naps as my cat Fatima, she must have been as creative as her father. Unfortunately, however, naps are out of style today. People are too busy. They have no time to be kind to the body or to allow the muses to fertilize the imagination. Maybe that's why there's so little real creativity around today. Excuse me though, George, Honey, you mentioned that you had an unusual experience. What happened?"

I told Mama my tale of the Tibetan monk who removed the nail from his hand and asked her what she thought it meant. She responded by saying, "Hand me that large copper pot above your head, will you please, George? Your old lantern slide machine indeed sounds like it's magical—or mystical. Perhaps your experience is a kind of prophetic message, the image of

24

some future event. In my long life I've grown accustomed to accepting things that escape any kind of rational explanation. It seems to me, George, that when it comes to omens, one just has to sit with them."

Sitting patiently with anything was never easy for me, but there didn't seem to be anything else I could do with that strange experience. Remembering my desire to use the attic as a hermitage, I asked her if that would be possible.

"Of course you can. The woman who had your job before you used it as a writing studio. And I like the idea of you using it as a hermitage. That means my old house will have one hermitage in the attic and one in the basement! Besides, who knows what other visions your Magic Lantern will reveal to you up there in the top of the house. Now St.—servant—George, it's time to set the table for dinner. You'll find the china and silverware in the pantry. Please set the table for nine."

"Nine? Are we having a guest?"

"We always set a place for Lucien, even if he can't join us for dinner."

I watched her move about the kitchen with ease. No doubt about it, Mama was a true gourmet cook. As I was taking the glasses and a bucket of ice into the living room for cocktails, she suddenly exclaimed, "Jesus, Mary and Joseph, the wine! I forgot to get a special bottle for tonight. Your arrival, George, means we should have an extra-special vintage. I think I'll go down to the wine cellar and bring up a couple of bottles of good Cabernet Sauvignon." Reaching inside the neck opening of her dress, she removed a small gold chain with three keys. "I'll be back in a moment. Will you please watch the soup for me?"

Moving with amazing grace and speed, she disappeared from the kitchen. I heard the basement door being unlocked, opened—and then locked again behind her.

"Hello, I'm Maria." I turned and saw a beautiful Latin American woman in her late twenties standing at the dining room doorway. She wore a sleek black dress which was accented by a string of white pearls. She was so striking; the texture of her skin was almost luminous. Her dark eyes were large and magnetic. I forgot about the soup. My mind was full only with the graceful beauty of her slim, shapely body and her lovely smile.

"I'm George. I answered the ad in the newspaper, and it looks like I'll be your new next-door neighbor. The music you were playing this afternoon was beautiful. Was it Mozart?"

"Yes, it's one of my favorites,'Cosi fan tutte.' I love the wit and irony of it. Mozart's head was in the heavens, but especially in that piece his feet were firmly planted here on the earth. It's marvelous, so refreshing to listen to."

"Are you a musician?"

"Oh no! But Mama Mahatma taught me as a small child to enjoy Mozart and the other great masters. She said Mozart must have taken frequent naps, or something, since he was so creative – such a genius."

"Mama 'Mahatma'?"

"Mahatma is the name we who live here have given her. It's kind of a pet name. I'm not sure how it began. It's a play on words with her last name, Mahathaman. 'Mahatma,' of course, means 'Great Soul.' Where is she now?"

I smiled, adding another piece called "Maria" to the puzzle of this mysterious house. Before I could answer, however, the sound of the basement door being unlocked, opened and locked again captured our attention. In moments, Mama Mahatma entered the kitchen with three bottles of wine in her arms. Upon seeing Maria she beamed with delight.

"Maria, dear, you look absolutely glorious this evening. I see that you and George have met. George, look what I found in the wine cellar: three bottles of 1982 Chateau le Pas Saint Georges! Appropriate, don't you think? Now, Maria, why don't you take George into the living room and introduce him to the others. I'll be joining you in a moment. I have just a couple of last minute touches on the tenderloin roast."

Maria escorted me through the dining room into the living room where four people had begun visiting. "Friends, I would like to introduce to you the newest member of our house. This is George; he came in answer to Mama Mahatma's advertisement."

"Hi, I'm Jon," said the robust man whom I had seen from the bathroom window. He was dressed casually; the first couple of buttons on his shirt were undone. As I shook his hand, I was aware of a surge of energy emanating from him. His grip was strong and athletic.

"I'm pleased to meet you," I said. "Mama has spoken highly of you."

Standing next to him was a shorter man with close-cropped black hair and a short beard. He had large, dark, piercing eyes that danced with friendliness. Unlike Jon, who was dressed in the latest style, he wore slightly rumpled clothing that appeared to have come from a thrift shop. "I'm Bernadone. My first name is Frank, but most people just call me Bernadone. I live across the hall from you—we'll be sharing the same bathroom."

"'Inspector' Bernadone, I believe," I said. "Mama Mahatma told me about you as well. Thank you for the welcome. I assure you there will be no problem sharing a bathroom."

"And this, George," smiled Maria, "is Mr. and Mrs. Michael Smith. They've been living here with us only a few months."

"Just call me Mike," said the man in a dark suit and tie. Mike appeared to be in his late forties, had dark hair with just the beginning of some graying and a narrow, well-trimmed mustache. He wore horn-rimmed glasses that rested low on the bridge of his nose, and the flesh beneath his eyes was creased over in small folds of skin. The lines of his face were unusual: the right side was strikingly different from the left. He was of medium build but appeared to be strong. His handshake and smile came across like those of a clergyman or used-car salesman. While friendly, there was a kind of twitch about his blue-gray eyes that seemed to say that he was uneasy or nervous about something. I dismissed my perception of his uneasiness as an attempt at overcoming a shy personality.

"And you can call me Gloria," said his wife from her seat on the sofa. She was probably about the same age as Mike, with dyed blond hair. Gloria's face was long and narrow, its age concealed by layers of make-up. When she smiled, as she was during our introduction, her jaws almost seemed to be wired together. Although outwardly friendly, like her husband, Gloria also seemed ill at ease in the otherwise amiable and homey gathering. While the others had alcoholic drinks, both Mike and Gloria were sipping on glasses of fruit juice.

"Can I fix you a drink, George?" asked Jon, setting his drink down on the mantel of the fireplace. "And, Maria, allow me to fix your drink—white wine as usual?"

"Thank you, Jon. That's thoughtful of you," Maria smiled. I thought I caught a warm spark in her glance toward him. It reflected the same kind of magnetic attraction that I had felt toward her when we met in the kitchen.

I nodded to him, "Jon, make mine Scotch on the rocks." At that moment, a whirlwind appeared in the doorway of the living room. No question about who this was! Wearing a black cassock, a Roman collar and a biretta, it was the same man I had seen earlier on the balcony – Father Fiasco. He didn't have his cowboy hat on tonight, but glancing down at the hem of his cassock I saw that he was wearing a pair of weathered white tennis shoes. He struck me as a delightful combination of W.C. Fields and Pope John XXIII. His weatherworn face was oval. Its most prominent feature was the deep-set brown eyes over which arched his dark bushy eyebrows. I would have guessed his age to be in the mid-fifties. The age lines of his face, especially those around his mirth-filled eyes, were strangely attractive. It was as if previous adventures had carved each line as an autograph. The priest rushed across the room and with a broad outstretched hand introduced himself.

"I'm Father Fiasco. Welcome to our home. You must be George. Mama Mahatma told me you had moved in with us. I assure you that while we may look dangerous" – he swung his arm around encompassing the group – "this weird company of characters is really quite harmless. Jon, you happy atheist, pour me a Scotch as long as you're tipping the old bottle." Then turning, he made a slight bow toward Maria. "Ah, Maria, you're as lovely as ever this evening. You make this old priest's heart prance at your glance."

Maria appeared both slightly embarrassed and touched by the old priest's obviously great affection for her as he encircled her slender waist with his arm. Everyone seemed delighted with Father Fiasco's entrance except for Mike and Gloria. They stiffened at his arrival as if someone had spiked their fruit juice drinks with starch. Both sat rigid, but, regardless of what they were thinking, their faces remained fixed in polite, plaster-like smiles. An indication that all wasn't blissful was Gloria's left leg nervously bobbing up and down. Aware of it, she placed her free hand firmly on her knee, and the jerking stopped.

"Bernadone, old friend," Father Fiasco bellowed, "solve any mysteries today down at our local P.D.?" Then, taking a glass from Jon, he smiled. "Thanks, Jon, for the drink. Friends and fellow travelers, may I propose a toast to the newest arrival in Mama Mahatma's family."

"Not until I can join you." There, framed by the doorway, was Mama Mahatma in all her regal glory. The black dress accentuated her beautiful white hair and round smiling face.

Jon handed her a glass, "I've had your favorite chilled and waiting for you: 'A Mama Mahatma Martini.'" As she took her glass from him, you could see in her eyes a great fondness for this vigorous young man. The group stood and, with a variety of beverages, toasted my arrival. A warm feeling came over me. I felt very much at home, even if I was among strangers.

After about twenty minutes of conversation and laughter, during which Father Fiasco invited me to come to his early morning Mass, Mama Mahatma announced that dinner was ready. With drinks in hand, we all moved into the dining room. Mama Mahatma sat at the head of the table as her roomers took their usual places. To the left of Mama Mahatma sat Maria, and next to her was Inspector Bernadone, then Gloria and Mike. On Mama's right were Father Fiasco and Jon, leaving two empty chairs on the far right side of the table and one at the end. I stood for a moment wondering which of the empty chairs I should choose. Mama Mahatma smiled graciously at me. "Your chair, George, will be the one next to Jon's. The chair at the end of the table is Lucien's."

In the middle of the table there were two tall silver candle holders with lighted white candles which helped create a sense of reverence that enveloped us. Then Mama Mahatma rang a small brass bell, and silence surrounded the table. I lowered my head, and glancing through my half-closed eyelids, I noticed six other bowed heads. Only Jon sat with head held high, but his eyes were closed. A few moments later, as if by some silent signal, Father Fiasco poured a little of the red wine into Mama's glass. She sipped it and, beaming a broad grin, nodded to me. I stood up, took the bottle and moved around the table filling everyone's glass. Mike and Gloria took only a token amount. Then Mama Mahatma raised her wine glass: "To Life!" We all joined her in that ancient toast which concluded the silent meal blessing.

There followed a charming dinner of excellent food, wine and conversation. Mama Mahatma presided over the dinner with few words until Mike asked Inspector Bernadone if there had been any progress in his investigation of the serial killer.

"No real breakthroughs, Mike. We still lack a profile of the killer, but we're checking out some new leads." Seeing the question in my eyes, Bernadone turned toward me, "You're new in town, George. I doubt if you've heard about our Woodsdale killer. That's the name of this district – all the streets around here have names of trees or woods. Within a ten block area there have been three murders in the last two months. They all seem to be the work of one person. Each of the victims has been a young woman, each having been brutally murdered."

"And, Inspector," interjected Gloria with a look of disdain, "hasn't each one of them had, shall we say, questionable morals?"

"Yes, I guess you could say that. They've all been single women who lived alone and who were sexually...ah...active. We haven't discounted the possibility that the killer selected the victims because of their lifestyles, but it could be just a coincidence."

"George, Chile, I think we be ready for coffee," said Mama Mahatma, using ethnic humor to change the subject.

I had removed the dinner plates and was about to return from the kitchen with a silver coffee pot when I heard the lively table conversation in the dining room suddenly turn to silence. As I returned it felt like the shadow of a total eclipse had fallen over the once-pleasant table. Everyone sat in dark silence. Glancing toward the opposite doorway, I saw a short, skinny man of Mediterranean descent. He was dressed in expensive clothes and had several gold chains around his neck. The chains were emphasized because the top four buttons of his shirt were undone. As I stared at him, he lifted a hand adorned with several rings to his mustache and smirked, "You must be the new cook – and, it appears, butler. What kind of loser are you to join Mahatma's motley crew?"

"Dio, do come in and join us for some coffee and dessert," smiled Mama Mahatma. "You can sit down next to George."

"I'll stand. I'm afraid we don't have time for coffee this evening, do we Maria?"

The reaction at the table to this most recent arrival was jolting. Mike and Gloria looked down at their plates. Father Fiasco and Inspector Bernadone, their faces full of concern, stared at one another. Jon's eyes, on the other hand, were those of a shark, seeming to challenge the stranger's presence. Only Mama Mahatma seemed to extend any hospitality to the little man in the doorway.

"Oh, Dio, surely you have time for a small cup of coffee. Maria hasn't had her dessert yet. We're having a special dinner tonight to celebrate George's arrival in our home. Come and join us for at least a few minutes."

Walking down to the end of the table where Maria sat, he placed his hand tightly on her shoulder. "Not tonight. Business calls, and I left the Mercedes running." He was squeezing her so tightly that the skin of her shoulder turned white beneath his grip. "Come on, Maria, time to go to work! Excuse us, friends, but fame and fortune await us."

"What kind of work do you and Maria do?" I couldn't believe I had asked such a stupid question. Maybe it was because I had absorbed the tension at the table and had sensed Maria's physical discomfort as Dio clutched her shoulder so tightly.

"No one's told you yet? I wonder why? Maria and I are in the...ah...entertainment profession you might say. I'm her manager. What's it to you, anyway?"

"He's a pimp," snarled Mike with obvious disgust. "And Maria is one of his stable of girls." Gloria nodded her head in agreement.

"Sticks and stones, you bastard! And for your information, jerkhead, Maria's not *one* of my girls! Maria's the prima donna, the flagship of my exclusive escort service!" Dio pulled Maria up out of her chair and led her by the arm out of the dining room.

"Good night, Maria. God go with you," said Mama Mahatma — to which Father Fiasco added, "Amen." Jon jumped to his feet, but Mama Mahatma shook her head with the authority of a pope, and he slowly sank back into his chair.

In moments we heard the sound of a car roaring down the driveway, and a pall fell upon the once enjoyable gathering. Mama Mahatma tried to smooth over the disturbance, but the mood at the table was beyond salvage. The meal had ended, and I told Mama Mahatma that I would clear the table and do the dishes. Inspector Bernadone and Father Fiasco offered to assist me.

As we washed the dishes, I couldn't resist asking, "Is Maria really a prostitute? I find that hard to believe. She's so sensitive and refined, so full of beauty and goodness."

"Yes, George," answered Bernadone, "but she's no ordinary prostitute. Dio's clients are among the most powerful, wealthy and famous. He's not only a pimp; he's also a pusher. He supplies 'recreational' drugs to those whose lifestyle or profession allows them to live outside the law."

"I see. He's an unusual man with an unusual name."

"It's short for Dionysius," added Father Fiasco, "which must be his baptismal name. It's rather appropriate, if you think about it, since Saint Dionysius is the patron saint of syphilis sufferers!"

"Fiasco, you're being naughty again! Your deposit of lost information is unlimited," laughed the Inspector, playfully snapping his dish towel at the priest.

"Careful, Bernadone, or you'll get me to laughing and . . . . "

"What's wrong with laughing, Father?" I asked.

"Grounds for dismissal, the worst kind! I've been told that there was a Second Council of Constance in 1418 which had an ordinance that stated, 'If any cleric or monk speaks jocular words, such as provoke laughter, let him be anathema!' Formal excommunication, friends! No wonder that humorous clergy and nuns are rare, eh?"

"OK, OK, Padre," replied Bernadone. "No more horsing around lest you be anathematized – I guess that's the word."

Wanting to get back to our discussion, I asked, "Why would Maria be involved in prostitution? She's clearly an educated woman with refined tastes – a lover of Mozart. Hasn't she been here with Mama Mahatma since she was a child? Why would Mama Mahatma allow such a thing?"

"You'll find out, George, that Mama Mahatma never judges anyone," answered Father Fiasco, "especially someone she loves as much as Maria. She gives everyone of us here absolute freedom to be who, or what, we are at this moment."

"I can only hazard a guess, George, in response to your question about why Maria would choose that kind of work," said the Inspector. Mama Mahatma sort of adopted Maria when she was but a small child. She had been abandoned by her parents, and Mama took her in and raised her like a daughter."

"My guess," inserted Father Fiasco, "is that Maria finds some sort of sense of worth in being the object of desire to those who are at the top of the ladder of success. I'm sure those men generously reward her for her evenings with them. Even after Dio's cut she must do rather well."

"Then why does she live here in this boarding house?" I asked. "I would expect that a woman with such wealthy clients would be able to live in an expensive penthouse. Why remain here where she must face people like the Smiths who look down on her?"

"It's her great love for Mama Mahatma," Bernadone said as he prepared to hang up his dish towel to dry, "and Mama's love for Maria. I'm sure you must have seen the bond between them. Mama is her mother, regardless of who actually gave her birth. So as long as Mama doesn't reject her, she's willing to endure the opinions of those like Mike and Gloria. We who have lived here a long time try to embrace Mama Mahatma's non-judgmental attitude. While that's easy in Maria's case, it's not so easy with Dio."

"Yes, the moment I saw him standing in the dining room doorway, I felt a real dislike for him. My first impression was only confirmed by his rude remarks and his macho treatment of Maria."

We had finished the dishes. The pots and pans were back on their hooks as the Inspector and I said good night to Father Fiasco and headed for the back stairs while the priest went to his room by the main staircase. Bernadone continued answering my questions as we walked.

"Dio was raised among the vast number of unfortunate ones who were robbed of the experience of being loved and valued. Brought up in the inner city, my guess is that he never finished high school but rather got his education on the streets. In that school, he soon learned that drug dealing and prostitution paved the fast lane to wealth. Then one day he latched on to Maria — who knows how or where. Street-smart, alley-wise, Dio knew that, like James Marshall at Sutter's Mill in the mid-1800's, he had discovered gold! With his newly acquired ability to supply the powerful and famous with what they wanted, he too could have money and power."

"Hasn't Dio been arrested for dealing in drugs and prostitution?"

"Dio is clever, George. He's careful not to be linked to what might be a major crime. Besides, he has friends in high places. With any minor felonies, he'd be back on the street before the ink dried on the police register."

As we parted at the top of the stairs, Bernadone and I exchanged good-nights. I closed my door and looked at my bed. The day had been full and long, and I was ready to get some rest. Then I remembered the Magic Lantern up in the attic. Even though it was late, I couldn't resist the urge to go and turn it on again. I felt great anxiety at the prospect, considering my wild first encounter, but at the same time I couldn't wait.

The house was silent as I switched on the old machine and reached for a box of slides. As soon as I inserted a slide, the attic wall was filled with an image of a drab Eastern European city. The only splash of color came from the flags that flew over the government buildings. I inserted another slide that revealed the huge factories whose belching smokestacks gave the city its grayish halo of smoke. The third slide showed a large sterile-looking building. The sign on top of the building read **The United Democratic Workers Daily**. As I studied the image, I was surprised to see a figure walking from the right side into the otherwise motionless frame. It was a tall old man in his mid-seventies with a bushy crown of white hair. He was wearing a shabby blue imperial uniform with a red royal sash, complete with a gold saber. As with the slides of Tibet, once again the images of the Magic Lantern machine had turned into a motion picture film, and I was drawn into the world of the story it told.

The old man entered the building and walked to the desk of the newspaper's front office, handing the editor a piece of paper. The editor, a short, stocky man with wire-rimmed glasses, smiled wryly and shook his head. However, looking up again at the eccentric but stately looking gentleman, he reconsidered and scribbled across the top of the paper, "print as written."

The next day the citizens of the industrial mining city awoke to the morning proclamation: "By the will of God and the desire of the people, I, Franz Stefan III, Emperor and King of

Pravoslavia and Protector of Bohemia, will take residence among you." Having received this royal introduction, the people of the colorless city of the Democratic Union of the Working People immediately and almost universally embraced the lovable old character. No one even suggested that Franz Stefan was not whom he claimed to be.

When the Emperor walked the streets, followed as he usually was by a collection of small children and stray dogs, people would bow with respect and greet him cheerfully: "Good morning, Your Imperial Majesty." The Emperor, in return, would always nod silently with solemn dignity and warmth. He walked with a military bearing, unusually erect for a man his age. He regarded his role as the peoples' resident emperor with great earnestness. He conscientiously showed concern for the welfare of his subjects. Each week he would inspect the city drains and the freshness of farm produce in the marketplace and would visit every construction site.

It was as if the citizens had embraced the aged eccentric as a lost relic of a former age, an age richer than their present time of assembly-line equality and democratic classlessness. The Emperor was invited to dine free in the best restaurants. Theaters and the ballet reserved special seats for him. When he entered a public place, the patrons would all rise and wait for him to take his seat before sitting again. While the newly elected democratic officials opposed such antiquated antics, they were powerless to stop them because of his great popularity. They rationalized the presence of His Imperial Majesty, Franz Stefan III, by saying that he was a living symbol of the era of the monarchy which predated even the Communist Revolution.

Now, there is one significant detail which I have not yet mentioned: His Imperial Majesty had only one eye! He wore a black patch over his right eye, but his left eye was as clear as an alpine lake. When asked why he was in exile from his kingdom, the Emperor would reply: "It was a revolution. I was deposed by a two-eyed dictator who promised progress." While he had only one good eye, his favorite expressions were, "Did you see that?" and "Look at this!"

One day on his afternoon walk, accompanied as usual by a

band of children and stray dogs, the Emperor exclaimed, "Look at this!"

To that the troop of loyal children who marched behind him responded, "See what, Your Imperial Majesty? We see only pebbles."

"No, no, my children, look again closely. They may appear to be pebbles, but each one of them is really a Wishing Crystal. What a lucky day this is for us," the Emperor added as he gave each child a pebble.

"But they look like they're only dull brown stones, Your Majesty," the children answered.

"Ah, yes, perhaps at first glance, little ones. But, you see, they haven't been polished yet. Keep them as precious stones, polishing them daily, and use them to make your wishes come true," replied the Emperor.

When he would pause on his daily walk to pull a leaf off a bush and slowly chew it, citizens would stop and ask, "Is Your Imperial Majesty hungry?"

"No, We are but sampling the Life-Reviving Herb," was his customary reply. Then he would graciously nod and continue on his stroll.

One sunny day Franz Stefan was conducting his weekly inspection of a construction site. An unusual thing happened as he passed by the side of the concrete beehive of an apartment high-rise that bordered a forest. A construction worker shouted, "Look, Your Majesty, a deer!"

"That's no ordinary deer, sir," replied the Emperor. "That's the Golden Deer! Indeed, this is a most extraordinary day, a very fortunate day for each of us." As he left for the next construction site, the workers all joyfully tipped their hard hats.

Then there was the hot summer afternoon when, taken by the heat, the Emperor had paused under a shade tree to rest. A woman came out of a nearby house with a glass of water which she offered to him with a slight bow. He took a sip, and his head suddenly became erect, his one eye glowing with a child's excitement. "My Lady, what a gift you have given to Us: this is the Nectar Against Age!" The Emperor slowly drained the rest of the glass as if each sip were sacred. He made an unusually low bow to her and said, "Know, my Lady, that you shall always be in Our gratitude for sharing with Us such a rare and precious gift as the Nectar Against Age."

Or there was the occasion when he had taken a walk from the city to the forest, an hour's journey, accompanied by his troop of stray dogs and laughing children. He had promised the children that he would show them the All Giving Tree. Standing under the green canopy of the forest's tall trees, the children asked, "Your Imperial Majesty, which one is the All Giving Tree?"

The Emperor opened his arms wide and proclaimed, "Every tree in the forest is the All Giving Tree." The children and dogs all stood silently, their eyes filled with wonder, as they looked up at the great trees.

His Majesty, concerned about all his subjects, visited all the churches in the city, however empty they were. Religion in Eastern Europe during the Communist regime had been relegated to the obsolete and aged members of society. Religion still was considered as outdated as royalty. People stayed home on Sunday morning to watch *Kojak* re-runs on TV. Yet each morning at sunrise the Emperor would attend Holy Mass together with a small handful of old women.

On his first visit to the cathedral, he requested the use of a prie-dieu, a kneeler, in the sanctuary, saying that it was his custom to be present there by right of a papal apostolic indult. The priest flatly refused, saying, "Only the clergy are allowed inside the communion rail."

Franz Stefan, disturbed by this rejection of a royal privilege, said, "Then I shall visit the Archbishop who will surely affirm my papal privilege."

The priest replied, "I doubt that. His Grace isn't likely to resurrect such a lost relic in this new age of European politics."

"Really!" replied the Emperor. "Pray tell, Reverend Father, how many eyes does the Archbishop have?"

Turning with a swish of his black cassock as he walked away, the priest answered, "Why, two, of course!"

The Emperor's devotions after Mass included at least two hours of prayer. Every day this time was entirely taken up with slowly praying two prayers which he read from a tattered yellow page. The few old women present, praying their beads in the last pews of the great, empty cavern of a church, wondered what was written on that creased yellow paper. They only knew the great care with which he ritually removed and replaced the paper kept in the inside breast pocket of his gold-braided uniform.

The reign of His Imperial Majesty, Franz Stefan III, lasted almost ten years. Without doubt, the old eccentric was the most beloved character in the land. When he died on a cold January day, the entire population was heartbroken. The government newspaper ran a banner headline: "THE KING IS DEAD." The editorial in the paper read, "The Emperor Franz Stefan III harmed nobody, robbed no one and treated all — from stray dogs to the highest officials — with great dignity. He never asked for a single thing and accepted everything offered to him as a precious gift. With his one eye the Emperor saw more than the rest of us with two eyes shall ever see."

Thirty thousand people attended his funeral, the fortunate ones crowded inside the cathedral. The funeral sermon, delivered by the Archbishop, consisted simply of reading the old, yellowed, creased page which Franz Stefan had carried in the inside breast pocket of his uniform. Printed on it was a quotation from the Gospels, "Blessed are the single-hearted, for they shall see God." After the word "single-hearted," a short phrase was inserted in the Emperor's own handwriting: "and the single-eyed." On the other side of the paper, as the Archbishop revealed to the crowd in the cathedral, was a prayer by a Hindu woman, a twelfth century mystic named Mahadeviyakka:

> Every tree in the forest was the All Giving Tree,
> Every bush the Life-Reviving Herb,
> Every stone the Philosopher's Stone,
> All land a Pilgrim's Holy Place,
> All water Nectar Against Age,
> Every beast the Golden Deer,
> Every pebble I stumble on the Wishing Crystal:
> Walking around the Jasmine Lord's favorite hill.

Suddenly the frame froze, filled with the prayer of Mahadeviyakka. I too was frozen, stunned by the amazing experience. Who would believe that the seemingly simple slide projector could have added sound to the images and even told a tale! Finally, after some minutes, I stood up and switched off the Magic Lantern. I had become so engrossed in the story of the single-eyed emperor, that I hadn't paid any attention to the fact that it was almost midnight. I quietly descended the attic stairs and went to my room. All I could hear in the house was the tick-tock of the grandfather's clock. Since it was late, I made my night prayers brief – simply a profound prostration on the floor as I recited my version of the great Islamic prayer. I bowed down, touching my head to the floor and prayed, "There is no God but God." As I got into bed, I surrounded Martha and the kids in a cloud of light and love – and was sound asleep in minutes.

CHAPTER 3

In the turquoise early dawn light, I walked from the mansion toward the carriage house to attend Father Fiasco's morning Mass. The large gold star high atop the pole at the peak of the roof glistened in the first light of the sunrise. Mama Mahatma was up and already working in her garden. She waved to me as I walked by, and I waved back.

The carriage house was two stories high and had three large dormer windows on each side of the slanted roof. There were three large garage doors with glass windows which had been covered with gold painted plywood. To the left of the garage doors was a single doorway flanked by two arched windows. Earlier, as I was shaving, I had glanced out the bathroom window and saw several elderly women entering through that door.

I opened the door and entered a small room about four times the size of a telephone booth. It was empty except that on my right as I entered was a small table. On top of the table was a wooden box with the words **Poor Box** painted on it. Directly behind the box was a full-length mirror on which had been written, "If you have more than you need, leave some. If you're a little short and are in need, take some."

Facing the entrance was another door in a makeshift wall. I passed through it into a small lobby area with a few old chairs placed against the walls. The wall directly in front of me had a partially opened door. Father Fiasco stuck his head out of the door. "Welcome, George, I'm pleased that you took me up on my invitation. Just go in and make yourself at home. I'm vesting now for Mass, but we can visit afterwards." He pointed to the remaining door, flashed a big grin and disappeared from view.

The door was large and painted gold. Above the door frame was a scroll inscribed with the words, "Abandon all despair you who enter here." Taking a deep breath, I opened the door and walked into the Basilica of the New Bethlehem Star. It was breathtaking! The pure pre-dawn light streamed in through the six dormer windows high overhead. The yellow shafts of light crisscrossed one another down the length of the carriage house chapel. They seemed alive, as particles of dust danced in the light beams. The walls were bare red brick; the floor, oil-stained concrete. At the far end on a slightly raised platform was a long cafeteria-style table, apparently the altar. A book, along with a chalice and plate were set on a clean white tablecloth.

To the left of the altar was an old, black steamer trunk that was set on a wooden platform. It could be mounted by climbing a series of stacked suitcases. The battered old trunk, covered with colorful labels and stickers from around the world, stood on one end and was opened in a "V" shape with the insides facing the back wall. Apparently it was the pulpit! A sagging, old white piano, which looked like a castoff from a small-time night club, was positioned on the opposite side of the altar. Hanging on chains from the rafters were countless silver votive lamps which cast dancing shadows on the upper part of the building. Instead of pews, the chapel was furnished with an assortment of old kitchen chairs. They were occupied by old women, a few men and several small children.

The chapel at first appeared devoid of images until I noticed the plywood-covered garage doors. On the center door was painted a figure of Christ crucified – but wearing a circus clown suit, complete with a white painted face. The mask-type face was split down the center: one side smiling, the other in pain. On its right was a painted icon of the Virgin Mother with a crowd of children climbing all over her and sitting in her lap, some children as skinny as skeletons. She also wore a clown's mask with a divided face: half joyful, half sorrowful. She was crushing a two-headed coiled serpent with her right foot. To her left were homeless people huddled in packing crates and large cardboard boxes, but they wore expensive clothing, furs and large diamond rings and jewels. To her right was a scene of some grand event which looked like an opening night at the theater. Spotlights combed the skies, and police held back the crowds as ragged street people emerged from long stretch limousines to enter the theater on a red carpet.

To the left of the crucified clown in the center panel was a prophetic figure with both hands raised high in the air. Behind him was a giant nuclear mushroom cloud. To the right and left of the cloud, respectively, the sun and moon were painted to look like huge hunks of melting cheese. All around the prophet stars fell like snowflakes. On the ground were barren trees, withered plants and dead animals. Lighting bolts flashed forth from both of his eyes, and from his open mouth came one of those cartoon balloons with the message, "Lift up your hearts and rejoice, this is the day of the Lord." The bottom fourth of this third icon was unfinished. There were only penciled lines of the images yet to be painted. On the floor beneath the icon were several paint cans, an old coffee can filled with paint brushes and a pile of paint-splattered rags.

Still standing in the doorway of the chapel, I became aware of a flashing red light to my left. Turning, I saw a neon sign with an arrow pointing downward. The blinking sign read **Holy Water**. Directly below the arrow was a drinking fountain! I leaned over and placed my mouth close to the spout, and when I tapped down on the foot lever, a stream of cool, wondrously delicious water shot into my mouth. As I straightened up, swishing the cleansing water around in my mouth, I noticed on the right side of the doorway a large wicker wastebasket with the sign, **Empty all heart trash here before entering**. Mama Mahatma was right: this was no ordinary church!

I found an empty chair halfway down the small chapel. It was next to a young black man who was sitting with his eyes closed, his back straight against the back of his chair. I sat down and closed my eyes as well, trying to find that quiet place in the center of my heart that Igor, my mentor, had taught me to seek when I wanted to meditate.

I was deep in meditation when a large gong abruptly brought me to attention. Everyone stood up and began singing the opening hymn, accompanied by a woman playing the white piano to the right of the altar. To my amazement, the opening hymn was "Oh, what a beautiful morning, Oh, what a beautiful day; I've got a wonderful feeling everything's going my way" from Rogers and Hart's *Oklahoma*. Down the aisle, in flowing oriental vestments, came Father Fiasco. He had on a black circular hat with a black veil – like those worn by Orthodox priests. He was carrying a tall silver staff on which were two intertwined serpents.

Reaching the altar, he made a profound bow, removed his head gear and began the Mass. Everything seemed rather ordinary until it was time for the Gospel reading. He picked up from the altar a large book that looked as ancient as the moon. He carried it high over his head as he processed to the open steamer-trunk pulpit. After ascending the suitcase stairs, he stood behind the open trunk and began: "In this morning's Mass we recall how, after the death of Jesus, the apostles were fishing on the Sea of Galilee when a stranger, who was the Risen Christ, invited them to come ashore and have something to eat." He paused and cleared his throat, then intoned in a loud voice, "God be with you!"

The small congregation stood and chanted back with glee, "Amen, amen. God *is* with us!"

Then he intoned, "Let all children and the faint of heart depart in the name of the Lord."

At that, the small children present processed out as the people sang a joyful "Alleluia!"

"The Holy Gospel according to the Lost Manuscript of Saint John. The missing section between verses 8 and 9."

"Thanks be God that the lost has been found," was the wholehearted response.

Then Father Fiasco read this Gospel story:

> The disciples pulled their boat ashore and dragged the heavy, loaded fishnets to dry land. Jesus was standing by a campfire, fixing breakfast. Simon Peter stood next to Jesus, shaking his head and muttering to himself. The other disciples came up to the fire and, looking into the frying pan, cried out in horror, "What's that?"
>
> Jesus looked up and smiled. "Breakfast! It's bacon and eggs."
>
> "Bacon!" exclaimed the disciples in unison, their faces white with shock. "Jesus Christ! Bacon? God has

forbidden us to eat pork; it's unclean food. Way back God told Moses it was taboo. Surely, Rabbi, you know that some of our people have died rather than eat pork."

"Yeah, I know," said Jesus, "but it doesn't make any sense. I mean that stuff about God making some foods clean and other foods unclean. Don't you remember what I said before I died about what makes us unclean?"

Simon Peter spoke up, "We tried to forget. We put it out of our minds, those words of yours: 'It is not what goes into your mouth that makes you impure; it is what comes out of your mouth.' And remember what we said to you in response: how the Pharisees were scandalized by that statement. Well, to be honest, so were we! We couldn't believe that you said it."

"I know, little ones," said Jesus, "but it's true. And it's true not only about pork and other foods but also about all those other things that the Law says make you unclean, like a woman having her period or even having a baby. The Law teaches that even 'proper' sexual relations make you unclean for worship. But God has made *all things* good and holy. To determine certain actions or food unclean only imprisons you."

Jesus flipped the eggs over in the frying pan as he continued, "Such religious laws only separate you from those people who eat pork or who don't go through the proper ritual purifications. Such a religion forces you to live in a tiny world, while you believe that it's God's world. But as long as your beliefs limit you, cramp your love and growth, how can you believe that such a world is one which God intended for you?" The disciples, however, only shook their heads and looked sick to their stomachs at the idea of eating bacon.

As the sounds of the waves rose and fell in the background, Jesus went on, "Who knows, friends, why pork was prohibited. Maybe, like a lot of taboos, what is forbidden today was once called holy. In ancient times sex was considered sacred as was childbirth and the passing of blood in a woman's cycle.

"Our neighbors of long ago, the Babylonians and Egyptians, at one time sacrificed pigs and ate their flesh as holy communion." Jesus paused and began dishing up the eggs and bacon on their plates.

"Amen, amen, I say to you," he continued, "the time is coming when my followers will celebrate my resurrection by eating pork. Ham will be the main dish of their Easter dinners. And, my little disciples, children will keep their pennies in piggy banks, a symbol of wealth and good fortune."

Thomas leaned over and whispered in Nathaniel's ear, "Can this really be our Christ? Perhaps it is the Anti-Christ, the devil, trying to get us to sin by breaking God's law."

And so the disciples ate breakfast with the Risen Christ. They ate their scrambled eggs, but each one of them left untouched the strips of bacon. They were unable to escape from their prison of pork, the prison of religion that made them God's special and chosen people because it made them different from others.

One day far in the future they would understand the words of their Risen Rabbi. But on that day, on the shore of the Sea of Galilee, they were unable to be free from the Law.

"This is the Missing Gospel of the Lord."

"Thanks be to God and to those who found it."

"Stand ready for the homily."

"We are standing!"

What followed as the homily was a few minutes of silence, as all stood in rapt attention.

"Let those with ears hear and those with eyes see" were the only words spoken at the conclusion of the silent sermon. Father Fiasco took a drink of water from a glass inside the opened trunk, cleared his throat and chanted, "Let the children return in the peace of God."

A joyful "Alleluia" accompanied the procession of little children as they returned to the gathering.

The rest of the Mass continued as usual. At Communion time I was surprised to see Inspector Bernadone and Maria, who was wearing a white mantilla, approaching the altar to receive Holy Eucharist. After the Communion Rite the Mass ended quickly. Father Fiasco donned the black Orthodox hat and veil, and with silver staff in hand gave the final blessing. He then chanted, "The Mass is ended. 'You are looking for Jesus of Nazareth...he is not here. He is going ahead of you to Galilee, where you will see him just as he told you.' Go in peace to the Poor Box room and do something!" The piano played the introduction to the closing hymn as Father Fiasco began to process out. As he did, the small congregation sang "Give Me That Old-Time Religion."

As the notes of the old revival hymn drifted up with the dust particles in the early morning sunlight, several people went to the walls of the church, bowed their heads and prayed in silence for a moment. Then each of them reverently removed a loose brick, kissed it and carried it to the exit.

Leaving the church after Mass required patience since the departing worshipers had to enter the Poor Box room one at a time, closing the door behind them. A buzzer would sound as the front door opened, and then the next person could enter the Poor Box room. As I stood in line, Father Fiasco opened the door to the back room and beckoned me to come in. The room ran the rest of the length of the carriage house and must have once been part of the workshop. The original workshop was now divided into three rooms: the Poor Box room, the lobby area and this back room. Along one wall was a workbench with old tools still on it. On the opposite side was a closet filled with vestments. Next to the closet were large gold-framed portraits of the Pope, the Patriarch of Constantinople and the Dali Lama. The room also had two swayback chairs and a small table.

"Welcome to my pastoral study and sacristy, George. It was an honor having you con-celebrate with us this morning." Father Fiasco had removed his Mass vestments and was dressed simply in a white T-shirt and workman's pants. Without his cassock on, I was aware for the first time of his powerful chest and muscular arms.

"George, I'm sorry that I've only got a few minutes. I have to be at work soon. I work part-time for a freight depot to support myself. I don't want to burden my people, and because it's heavy work it's a great way to stay in shape. The only time you have to work out to keep in shape is when you don't *work* out." He laughed heartily at his cleverly phrased observation.

"I was impressed with your church and the Mass. They are both beautiful and...ah...different. I'd love to visit with you sometime since I have several questions."

"I'm not surprised that you'd have a few questions. I'd be delighted to visit. How about a quick question or two as I gather up my things?"

"I've never heard of any Lost Gospels. I was wondering where those scriptures come from and how you happen to possess them."

"Ah, George, that's a secret. I can, however, share this much with you. I have an old friend in Jerusalem who is one of the biblical scholars on the research team that's translating the Dead Sea Scrolls. It's been over forty years since they were discovered in a desert cave by a sixteen-year-old Bedouin boy. Yet only a few of the translations have been published – for the general public, that is. Most of those two-thousand-year-old scrolls are from the pre-Christian period, somewhere around 200 B.C. However, some were written as late as 70 A.D. and so are from the early Christian period. My friend has smuggled several Gospel manuscripts to me. They must have originally come from early communities of the disciples of Jesus."

"That's fascinating. And I wouldn't want you to reveal all your trade secrets.

"I was also surprised to see some people removing bricks from the walls of your church and taking them out. What's that ritual all about?"

"Saint Paul said that we are the living stones of the New Temple. People easily forget that and continue to cling to the idea of the church being a sacred building. My people take a brick home to awaken them to the fact that they are living bricks of the real temple of God. And throughout the day, whether someone's brick sits on the kitchen sink or beside a computer, it's a reminder to build Church on top of that stone. When people come back to Mass, they place their bricks back into the wall again for the time they are here to worship. Would you like to take one back to the house?"

"Not this morning, Father, thank you. But let me think about it. Who knows, I may want to begin that spiritual practice."

Father Fiasco pulled a bicycle out of the closet and wheeled it out through the Poor Box room. I felt a bit uneasy about what to do as we passed through the room and so this time did nothing. We said our good-byes for the day, and with a big grin he mounted his bicycle and rode off down the driveway. On the way he gave a robust wave to Mama Mahatma who was tending her garden.

I walked over to her to say good morning. Her hands were covered with dark, rich earth.

"Good morning, George, Honey. Beautiful fresh morning, isn't it? I always enjoy working in my garden in the cool of the day. How was your first visit to the Basilica of the Star of the New Bethlehem?"

"I'm glad you tipped me off yesterday that it would be a bit different. It was indeed. It was also beautiful and thought provoking."

"That sounds like a good description of what every worship place should be, don't you think, George?"

"Yes, I guess so. Only it is rather rare."

"I'm ready for a cup of good strong coffee. Care to join me?"

As we sat drinking our coffee in the room off the kitchen, I was overflowing with questions. I wondered about the one-eyed emperor whom I had seen in the Magic Lantern show the night before, as well as what I had just experienced at Father Fiasco's Mass.

"Mama Mahatma, I had another one of those unexplainable experiences last night with my Magic Lantern. It was a story about a one-eyed man who seemed to see ten times more in life than anyone with two eyes."

"Blessed are the pure of heart, those who can focus on one thing at a time, for they shall see God," she said as she poured us a bit more coffee. "Perhaps the one-eyed emperor was able to see with such singleness of vision and so could see what is really here, right in front of all of us."

"But how does one acquire such vision? I don't think that if I had walked with one eye closed this morning, I would have seen anything more than I see using both eyes."

"George, the trick is not seeing with a single eye, but with a single heart. If you desire that kind of vision, attempt today to do only one thing at a time. Be as fully present as you can to whatever you're doing. That won't be easy. Your mind will want to be occupied with something else, what it considers to be a matter of grave consequence."

"Well, Mama, the tasks around the house will give me plenty of opportunities to practice that kind of presence. As for the challenge of it, I guess that I'll just have to trust in God and hope for . . . . "

"Just a moment, George." She left the room and returned in a few minutes. Handing me a six-foot length of old rope, she said, "Here, George, this is for you."

"I don't understand. What am I supposed to do with it?"

"Hang it in your bedroom—it's a reminder. As the Arabs say, 'Trust in Allah, but tie up your camel!' "

I chuckled, but I also appreciated the wisdom of her "reminder."

Having finished our coffee, there was a full day of work ahead of us, and so we parted for the morning. I took Mama's Trust in God symbol to my room and then began my cleaning tasks for the day. I tried to practice the single-minded presence we had talked about, tried to focus my awareness on the activity of vacuuming the rugs, but my attention sooner or later wandered somewhere else. My mind wanted to play with the memories of last night's Magic Lantern show or what I had witnessed in Father Fiasco's church. As I dusted, I tried to be absorbed, like a sponge, in dusting. Even though I wasn't totally successful, Mama Mahatma was right; I was much more aware of what was happening to me than I normally would have been. I had planned on reading when I finished and so was eager to complete my chores. I found, however, that being a one-eyed servant takes longer than doing my work in the usual way.

The first full day of work passed quickly. Before I knew it, it was dinner time. Mama Mahatma told me to prepare a meal for nine as she had invited Dio to join us. My heart took a nose dive at the news that Dio would be a dinner guest. I had seen the effect of his presence on people last night. As I set the table, I was anxious that my first meal for the boarding house would be eaten like K-rations on a battlefield.

After the usual cocktails, we sat down to dinner. Everyone commented on how delicious was the Beef Wellington and asparagus spears, and I was pleased. Dio was surprisingly charming, the picture of politeness.

"Mama Mahatma, how's Lucien doing these days? Is his health good?"

"Thank you, Dio, it's thoughtful of you to ask. Yes, Lucien, the dear child, is well and happy. He prefers his solitude, of course. He wouldn't know what to do at a grand dinner like this."

"What does he do down there all day, meditate? Study?"

"Lucien's a very private type, Dio. I never ask him about his spiritual exercises or his personal life. Nor do I know what books he reads. I do know, however, that he is very clever. In fact, of all my children, he's the most cunningly intelligent. And that ability very well could indicate that he does meditate."

Dio's question turned the dinner conversation to the subject of meditation. Both Bernadone and I admitted that we practiced it. Father Fiasco discussed its history in various religions. He said that he had attempted to practice it but found it difficult. Mike, echoed by Gloria, spoke of its dangers, saying that emptying the mind of all thoughts only opened one up to the powers of the devil. Dio and Jon listened without entering much into the conversation.

At the end of the meal, over coffee, Mike continued to sermonize. Now he took on pornography, asserting that it was one of the chief causes of sex crimes and social immorality. Gloria, who until that time had stayed in the background, now became animated. "Pornography is disgusting. Those repulsive photos of naked women. What kind of woman would do such a filthy thing?"

"Ah, *Mrs.* Smith, isn't it *sex* and not pornography that you find so disgusting?" smirked Dio, pointing his finger at her as if it were a loaded gun.

Mike came to his wife's defense. "We need stronger laws. Sex crimes, like the Woodsdale murders, wouldn't happen if pornography were outlawed like prostitution."

The mood at the table became tense. Knowing Dio's ability to explode over nothing, everyone expected a thunderstorm to break out over what up to that time had been a delightful meal. Instead, Dio only smiled at Gloria and Mike. Gloria's face froze in anticipation as if she were posing for a photograph. Dio simply turned to me and said, "You look like a man who enjoys stories. Since this is the first meal you've served, I'd like your permission to tell one."

"Yes, Dio, you're right. I do like stories. The telling of stories was once an important part of all feasting. Please do tell one."

"Thanks, George." Nodding to Mama Mahatma, who smiled her approval, and directing a sweet smile toward Maria, Dio began.

> Once upon a time there was a pet parlor located on the lower end of Main Street. From the outside it resembled any other pet shop, but it was far from ordinary. The front window was filled with photographs of beautiful dogs and cats, and inside there was a series of small rooms located on either side of a long corridor. Madame Madeline, the owner, was always in the front lobby to greet her patrons.
>
> The Pet Parlor was a service store. It provided people with an experience of being with a loving pet without having to own one. All kinds of people who were lonely for some animal affection came to the Pet Parlor and paid an hourly fee to spend some time with a loving dog or cat. Madame Madeline had schooled her animals to treat each patron with the same affection they would have shown to a long-time owner. They would cuddle up to some stranger and lavish upon him or her all the affection that pets are known to show to a beloved master or mistress. At the end of an hour (or two for especially love-starved folks) one patron would leave the small room and another lonely person would enter. The dog or cat, thereupon, would leap into the new patron's lap with renewed eagerness.

Now I realize that all this might sound bizarre – I mean that people would come to a pet parlor to have an experience of animal affection. You might ask, "If they want the experience of a pet's love, why not just own one?" That does make sense, but there are many reasons why someone might not be able to have a cat or dog. One might live in an apartment that doesn't allow pets or might live with someone who doesn't like pets. Some have other commitments that don't allow adequate time, energy or finances for a full-time pet relationship. Regardless of the reason, however, what's wrong with someone answering that very human need for animal affection? Madame Madeline's Pet Parlor provided a real alternative for those who couldn't take on the long-term responsibility of caring for a pet.

While it seemed to respond to a legitimate need, the existence of the Pet Parlor on lower Main Street wasn't met with wholehearted approval from the town's elders. At best they tolerated its existence. There were also protests from groups like the CPO (Concerned Pet Owners) and the ARO (Animal Rights Organization). Demonstrators appeared at meetings of the city council, demanding that Madame Madeline's Pet Parlor be closed. They spoke out loudly against the "immorality" of the situation. The poor animals' whole existence was one of constantly showing affection toward persons that they hardly even knew.

In response, Madame Madeline denied that it was their "whole" existence. She said that her pets were free to pursue other interests and that most of them were very well-rounded. Her lawyer also came to the council meetings, providing documentation about her patrons – no names were mentioned, I might add – which showed that they were good citizens in the community. The lawyer added that after a visit to the Pet Parlor they returned to home and work as kinder and gentler people. He dismissed as unfounded the charge that the existence of the Pet Parlor encouraged social evils in the surrounding neighborhood. Madame Madeline, he said, ran a clean parlor; her animals were well cared for and checked frequently by the vet for any diseases.

It seemed that he would win his case until the ARO and CPO were joined by some local church leaders who insisted that such an establishment in their city was sinful. Several ministers quoted from the Bible to prove that "what went on in those little rooms" at Madame Madeline's place was "unnatural." They denounced the Pet Parlor's existence, warning that soon the town's teenagers would be frequenting it. The city council was in a turmoil about how to respond to the attacks from such powerful groups within the community. They met in a closed-door session and reached a resolution which they hoped would quiet the moral outrage – and save their seats on the council in the next election (because of the popularity of the Pet Parlor). The solution was to make Madame Madeline's Pet Parlor an X-rated establishment that would require all who entered it to be at least twenty-one years old. Everyone, of course, lived happily ever after.

Dio leaned his chair back on two legs and roared with satanic laughter. I could see from where I was sitting that Gloria's leg was bobbing up and down nervously as she glared at Dio. Mama Mahatma rang her little brass bell. "It's late, children, and some of us have to get up early tomorrow. Let us conclude this meal with a few moments of silent gratitude."

Both Father Fiasco and Inspector Bernadone offered to help me with the dishes as the others departed from the dining room.

"What do you make of Dio's strange story, Father?" I asked as we cleared the table.

"Clever tale. It left old puritanical sin as naked as Adam without his fig leaf. It's a uniquely American moral code. Most other countries have a more realistic way of dealing with sex than we do. The truth of Dio's tale is that it's not perverts that seek out prostitutes, but lonely and unloved people. Love for hire is an ancient profession, if not the oldest. It wouldn't have endured all these millenniums unless it met a real need. Religion's war on it, I'm sure, is largely because it was once also a sacred vocation. Temple prostitutes, both male and female, were once upon a time a priestly people."

"How true," added the Inspector, "and I think Dio's observation of Gloria's attitude about sex was close to the bull's-eye."

"Ah yes, Inspector, your eye for hidden evidence is sharp. The Smiths do appear to be a loving couple, but my gut tells me it's only a shell."

"Yes, things are sometimes the very opposite of what they appear. We are afraid to look at our dark side. So we hate most in others what's dark and dangerous—yet seductively attractive—in ourselves. There was a sergeant down at headquarters who was on this holy crusade against pornography. His desk drawers were filled with what he called 'evidence,' lurid photos of naked women and men. But I'm convinced that he really lusted after the very thing he said he hated."

The three of us continued with the dishes for a while in silence as I reflected on Dio's tale. I too was lonely, hungry for love. I really missed Martha. "Makes good sense," I said, breaking the silence, "I mean about what happens to those who are lonely, perhaps separated by duty or circumstances from their wives or lovers."

"Is that the case with you, George?" asked Father Fiasco as he wiped a wine glass with his dish towel, holding it up to the light to see if it was perfectly clean.

"Yes, Father. I really miss my wife. Her name is Martha, and she truly loves me. In fact, she was the one who first encouraged me to take this sabbatical. She knew that I wanted to continue my spiritual quest but was stalled—had been for months. It was she who proposed that I leave for six months, a year—or however long it might take."

"George, she sounds like a most unique woman. You're fortunate to be loved by someone who is not possessive or afraid to let you follow your dream," said Bernadone as he put his arm around my shoulder.

"She is that. When I objected that it was silly to take a sabbatical in a marriage, she countered with how the spouses of those in the military or certain businesses simply accepted their loved ones' being away for months on end as a reality. Why, she said, wasn't God as valid a reason for a husband and wife being separated as a military tour of duty? Then she quoted to me from something she had read. It said that if there hadn't been a serpent in the garden, Adam and Eve would have needed to invent one. Too much peace and comfort isn't good for any love. Separation and even conflict make the friction that causes the fire of love. It was only after we had decided on all this that she began a spiritual quest of her own. That delighted me to no end! I do pray it's going well for her."

As we finished the dinner dishes, I related the other details of my departure. I told how I had arranged with my company for a six-month leave, how a wealthy uncle had left us a generous inheritance — in short, how all the obstacles had been resolved. I even mentioned a little about Igor and the title he gave me. Though neither said much, the way they listened was affirming. It was obvious that both Bernadone and Father Fiasco were fascinated by the idea of my quest. And they laughed heartily when I said, "I advise you both, however, to be very careful. Everything you say and do will be recorded in a journal I'm writing for Martha."

As we walked out of the kitchen, Mama Mahatma's black-and-white cat, Fatima, crouched down at the crack of the basement door. I asked, "What's the story with Lucien?"

"Lucien," said the Inspector as he reached down and stroked Fatima, who rolled over and allowed him to pet her stomach, "well, he's the unsolved mystery in this house. In all the years I've lived here, I've never seen him — nor has anyone else for that matter. Father and I have conjectured that he may be Mama Mahatma's autistic son. Unwilling to institutionalize him, she keeps him here at home — but hidden away in the basement."

"Or perhaps he's badly deformed," said Father Fiasco, "and so ugly that he can't stand to be seen. Maybe he's like the phantom of the opera, brilliant but brutally ugly, so horrible to look upon that only a mother could find him acceptable. I'm sure you noticed that all the basement windows are heavily barred. Over the years, the roomers have all been afraid of who, or what, lives down there. What kind of child — who by now must be an adult – would Mama Mahatma keep down there, that she can't even bring him up at Christmas? As the Inspector said, it's the great unsolved mystery. But like a lot of mysteries, it's one that you finally learn to live with and not to question. Who knows, maybe at night when we're all asleep Lucien comes upstairs or even leaves the house? You know, recently at night there have been sounds like someone walking around. The seventh step from the top of the main staircase creaks. I've heard that sound many times of late."

"Really, Father, how long have you been hearing someone moving about here at night?" asked Bernadone. "You've never mentioned that before."

"Hadn't really thought about it until tonight. I'd guess for about the past six months or so. Once you pass fifty, as I have, they say you wake up about five times a night. You usually drop off to sleep again in a few seconds. The creak in the old staircase step isn't loud enough to wake me, but now and again, in those brief waking moments, I've heard it. Yes, friends, someone is out and about in our house in the middle of the night, but who? Could be Lucien – or any of the others."

As we climbed the back stairs together, I felt that sharing the strange story of my quest had created a real bond of friendship among us. We said good night and went to our rooms. I debated about going up to the attic. It was already late, but the magnet of the Magic Lantern was too powerful.

In the silence of the old mansion – except for the tick-tock of the grandfather's clock – I left my room and walked down the hallway. When I reached the door to the attic, I switched on the light and climbed the narrow stairs. As I opened the door to the old nursery, I flipped off the light over the open stairwell. In the darkness I reached around the doorway to turn on the light in the nursery. My hand, however, froze on the way to the light switch. I had a feeling that I was not alone in the attic darkness. It wasn't head knowledge. It was more primal, springing from my gut. I stood very still, my heart pounding, as I tried to decide if it was better to let the darkness hide me or to switch on the light to see if my hunch was right. My mind leaped into overdrive: was it Lucien? If so, what would I see when I turned on the light? Nothing is so fearful as the unknown, and I was afraid.

CHAPTER 4

I suddenly felt more ashamed than afraid. "Hell, I'm acting like a little kid who's afraid of the dark." I switched on the attic light and smiled – at the head of the steps was Mama Mahatma's cat.

"Fatima, how did you get up here?" I looked over the railing and saw that the attic door below was slightly ajar. I must have failed to close it tightly. Fatima probably clawed it open and followed me up into the attic. I switched off the attic light over the steps and turned on the nursery light. Then Fatima and I entered the mystical theater of the Magic Lantern.

Fatima jumped in my lap as I sat behind the Magic Lantern. I switched on the machine, and a square of light filled the darkened wall. Selecting a box of slides from the paper bag, I inserted a slide into the Magic Lantern. The wall was filled with the image of a vast desert with sand dunes. The second slide showed a desert village with a collection of brown mud huts. I was petting the cat's back as I looked at the picture. As before, the image began to move. The sand began blowing in clouds, and I felt Fatima's hair become like bristle. She knew something strange was happening.

Far in the distance, two riders could be seen coming out of the desert toward the village. As they drew closer, a crowd of villagers gathered to greet them. When the two strangers had reached the crowd, they were escorted to the house of the village elder. There they removed their desert cloaks. The poor villagers gaped in wonder at the princely robes underneath the outer wear.

The royal travelers wore desert headgear with flowing scarves which covered all but their sunburned faces. From head to toe their splendid clothing was similar except that one rider's head covering was red and the other's was white.

They told the elders and the fascinated crowd that they were seeking the Fountain of Life which had been spoken of for ages. They unrolled an ancient map which showed a green jungle forest on the edge of the desert. The two travelers asked if anyone in the village knew of the way to the forest and its fountain.

Because all water was precious in the barren desert, the people were spellbound at the travelers' talk of their adventure. The oldest of the elders all nodded in recognition at the riders' question. They said that in their childhood they had heard stories about the Fountain of Endless Flowing Water in a green forest. They explained that they were told that this fabled land lay somewhere far over the horizon. But other than the legends, no one there knew anything about the forest or the fountain.

Hovering at the edge of the crowd was a young man whose job was tending the village pigs. He particularly listened with great attention as the travelers told of many adventures in their quest to find the fountain. As the two riders again wrapped themselves in their desert cloaks and prepared to resume their journey, the youth begged to be allowed to accompany them. The crowd of villagers, however, only laughed. "You're too young and too common for such a quest! Only nobility can seek such fabled treasures! No, boy, go back to your pigs."

As the villagers shook their heads at the lad's foolish request, the two travelers rode off into the hot desert. Unseen by all, however, the youth pursued the royal pair out into the blowing clouds of dust and sand.

The two riders went east for several days; the young pig herder mounted a donkey and followed their tracks in the sand. Finally, a narrow green line appeared on the horizon. As they drew closer, they saw that it was a massive jungle forest. Following the old map, they entered the dense forest and rode on until they descended into a valley. The young man from the village stayed cautiously behind.

In the center of the valley the two riders found a large sunken rock formation, in the heart of which was a great pool of crystal water. The two travelers drank deeply from the pool and were instantly revived by the thirst-quenching water. They removed their desert headgear, splashing water on their faces. As the one with the white silken scarf did so, long golden hair fell gracefully about her shoulders. The youth, hiding near the pool, realized for the first time that the second rider was a woman – a beautiful woman!

The prince with the red scarf carried leather flasks to the pool and filled them with water. Affectionately embracing his companion through the long quest, he rode out of the forest and back into the sun-baked desert. He stopped and poured some of his newly found water into the dry well of each village along the way. Each of those wells soon came alive with pure, clear water. Gradually the villages of the desert became transformed. Green grass, plants and trees appeared as life and hope returned to those who lived around the wells. The desert people began to call the prince the "Water Man." Soon rituals arose around the wells and life-giving water to commemorate and honor the "miracle" of the desert.

The princess was also changed by drinking from the pool. She took water from the pool to village after village and used it to tend to the sick and afflicted. Rather than royal clothing she wore the dress of the poor women in the desert. Soon other women, inspired by the selfless service of the Water Woman, joined her in caring for the poor and needy. Like the Water Man, she would return to the pool in the forest when necessary to replenish her supply of the life-giving water.

Now the youth, after the other two had left the forest, went down to the pool. He drank from the water and marveled at its taste. After sitting for hours beside the pool, he decided to remove all his clothing and dive in. At first he floated on the surface and swam about in the invigorating water. Then he dove deeply into the pool. As if attracted by a magnet, he descended deeper and deeper. At the bottom he found a cool, sweet stream. Following the cool current, the youth came to the entrance of the pool's source, a tunnel carved by the water through solid rock.

The young man swam up to the surface and filled his lungs with air. He again dove downward to the entrance of the underground river. His heart was pounding with fear as he navigated against the powerful current of the water rushing toward him. Then he saw a light sparkling in the water ahead of him. When he came to the light, he rose up into yet another pool. Looking up, he saw a tall, narrow canyon-shaft. The sun was filling the opening at the top of the shaft with a blinding light.

Pouring forth from an opening at the top of the cliff was a cascading crystal waterfall. The youth tilted his head back and drank deeply from the waterfall. The water was wildly intoxicating, richer in taste than the water in the first pool. Drawn by an invisible force, he began to climb up the face of the cliff while the water showered down on him. The rocks were made of crystal and obsidian, their edges razor sharp. They cut his hands and feet and sliced across his body. Ignoring the pain, he climbed ever upward toward the top of the cliff where the crystal water poured from a great opening.

The clear waters from the falls were now mixed with the blood flowing from his many wounds. After great effort, he finally reached the opening in the rocks from which the waters were blasting out as if from some giant hydrant. He thrust his head into the opening and drank deeply. The water tasted like liquid lightning! Blinded by glory and overcome with joy, he fell back off the cliff. Tumbling downward through the mist and spray of the waterfall, he splashed into the small pool. He then let the surging underground river carry him outward to the large, quiet pool in the forest.

Climbing out, the young man put on his clothing and left the forest. Unlike the other two, however, he took along no water from the pool in the forest. The former pig keeper returned to his home village a changed person. While he joined his fellow villagers in the holy rituals of the well when the Water Man came, his presence had a quality of detachment. He frequently helped the Water Woman and her assistants in the surrounding villages as they cared for the poor and ill, but he always moved on again. The desert people gave the pig keeper a new name: the "Drunk One."

All who encountered him – the sick and the poor, the lonely and those without hope, the confused and the weary – said that he was like a spring of fresh water. Just to be in his presence was to be revived and renewed. And legend has it that wherever he walked, even in the desert, water oozed up and filled his footprints.

The image froze with the Drunk One standing alone facing

the desert. It began to move again as he walked out into the wasteland. The image drew in close so that his footprints in the sand filled the scene. Then water began to seep up into his footprints, filling them like small pools! The image once again became static. It was the end. Fatima looked up at me, and I only shook my head.

I sat there for a while, reflecting on how organized religion tends to be a secondhand business. It's usually about other peoples' experiences of God, people who lived a long time ago. Each religious gathering place is like a village well where rabbis, priests, mullahs or gurus share water from the pool that they visit. Sad, I thought, how over the centuries people of various religions have fought about which pool is the "true" one. The young pig keeper, however, didn't drink from any village pool. He went in search of the source pool in the forest. When he found it, he wasn't afraid to plunge deeply into it and so found its source.

"I'm thirsty for that water," I thought. "I've taken this sabbatical to find the Source because I wanted something more than weekly visits to 'the village holy well.' I feel drawn to go in search of the Source, even if, like the pig keeper, people think I should be back home 'tending to business.' " Stroking Fatima's back, I reflected in the darkness of the old attic: "Isn't the real business of life to seek the Source?"

Just as Fatima sat in my lap, a large doubt sat in the center of my heart. It was the recurring question of whether I was really where I should be. I felt all caught up in the lives of the roomers, in their petty quarrels and problems. This place seemed to have too many distractions. I wondered again if I should have chosen some quiet monastery for my quest and not this crazy rooming house. Glancing at my watch, I was again surprised to see that it was almost midnight, well past the time I had wanted to go to bed.

Fatima jumped out of my lap as I stood up and began to put things away. Then I heard angry voices coming from beneath me and to the left. It was Mike and Gloria—their room was directly below the nursery. They were arguing about something, but I couldn't make out much of what they were saying to one another. Then I heard a door slam, and the voices became silent.

I closed the door to the nursery and went downstairs quietly so as not to wake anyone. Fatima ran off into the darkness as I walked to my room at the rear of the house.

I recited a brief night prayer and undressed. Sitting on the side of my bed, I resolved that I would ask Mama Mahatma how one goes about finding even the forest in which is hidden the pool that leads to the Source. I was fearful that I would not be as fortunate as the young pig keeper. Then the thought that Mama is a wise old woman encouraged me. I was willing to wager she'd have an answer for me, even if it was in the form of a riddle. My doubts about living and working here dissolved, and I felt good about having chosen this place for the second leg of my journey. I laid back on my bed and fell asleep, my mind filled with images of crystal pools.

I awoke suddenly around 2 a.m., straining for breath, my body soaked with sweat. I had been having a nightmare that began as a beautiful dream. I was swimming naked in a crystal pool. The water was intoxicatingly refreshing as I dove down into its depths. Then, almost instantly as I surfaced to the top of the pool, the water changed color. In seconds it became scarlet red. I looked down at my body and realized that I was bleeding from a thousand long slit-like cuts. I tried frantically to get out of the pool so I could stop the bleeding, but the more I attempted to escape, the more I felt some great force pulling me downward into its depths. I couldn't breathe and fought wildly just to keep my nose above the bloody red surface. It was at that moment in the dream when I woke up.

I now sat upright in bed, gasping for air. I began to relax when my breathing finally returned to normal. As I collected myself, I reflected on the nightmare – or was it another omen? My God! I realized that I was actually beginning to have trouble separating reality from fantasy. Regardless of whether it was prophetic or just a dream, I fearfully realized that finding the Source might mean risking my life, perhaps even losing it.

For some time I tried to return to sleep but found it impossible. My window was open, and I could hear the late-night sounds of a summer evening. A neighbor's dog was barking somewhere nearby, and there was a police siren a few blocks away. I glanced at my clock and saw that it was 3:20! Soon I heard a car drive into our driveway and a door closing. I wondered who would be coming home at this hour. In a few minutes I heard Maria opening the door to her room. Shortly thereafter, I fell asleep.

CHAPTER 5

The following days passed swiftly as I was busy with my work of cleaning the house and preparing meals. While I was tempted, I did not venture up to the attic to watch the Magic Lantern. I certainly didn't need any new stimulants to keep me going on the work of my quest. While I had taken a sabbatical to deepen my inner life, the question that followed me like a shadow was, "When on a spiritual quest, how does one find that 'deep pool'?"

I tried to be faithful to my daily practice of meditation, and I read scriptures and books on spiritual matters. I also practiced being mindful in my duties. As I went about my daily cleaning and cooking, I tried to be "single hearted" at all times. However, I found myself, again and again, doing two things at the same time, like fixing dinner and thinking about some household drama. I didn't realize how distractions had been a habit until I consciously attempted to focus my attention on what was happening in the present moment.

Whenever I set aside time for prayer, especially in the morning and evening, I tried to invest that time with a true thirst for the Source. Unfortunately it often only felt like a duty — something required of someone seriously seeking God. One morning, while Mama Mahatma and I were having our mid-morning coffee break, she said to me, "George, Honey, ultimately prayer is not how you search for God; it's the language of one who has found God!" Now that I had enough time to pray, I realized that I did not really know how to pray. Instead of a deep pool, those times were more like a barren desert in which I longed for the crystal waters, instead of drinking deeply.

Again and again, I fought with the old nagging thought that I had made a big mistake in taking this job in Mama's rooming house. Surely if I had a good master and was in the right place,

I wouldn't be wasting my precious time as I seemed to be here. Whenever I shared that with Mama Mahatma, she would only smile at me, give me a big hug and say, "Patience, George, patience. Next to passion, patience is the most important virtue for anyone on a trip like yours! If you honor your process, the time will come when you will discover the deep pool. Until then, patience will teach you what you need to know. Whatever it is that you must do at this moment, *do* it. As the old saying goes, 'After all is said and done, more is said than done.'"

One day I was intent on vacuuming the rug in the upstairs hallway. I looked up, surprised to see Dio standing at the top of the stairs. He was smiling and holding one hand behind his back. Over the roar of the vacuum cleaner, he shouted, "I've got something for you, George."

I switched the machine off, and Dio walked over. "Maria tells me, George, that you meditate every day."

"Yes, at least I try to! I mean, I sit daily in meditation, but I'm not sure if I'm really meditating."

"Well, I understand that it's a practice done for a certain period of time each day, so I got you a little gift. Here's a quiet, peaceful way to keep track of time." Dio handed me a brass ship captain's hourglass with fine white sand. "It takes thirty minutes to run out – should be just right for your meditation."

"Thank you, Dio, that's very thoughtful. Yeah, it will be an ideal way to keep track of the time. It won't be a distraction – much better than watching my alarm clock."

"Think nothing of it. I only hope it helps your meditation." He smiled again and went to knock on Maria's door. Without waiting for a response, he walked in and closed the door behind him.

I took the hourglass to my room and placed it on my desk, thinking as I did, "Just proves that there's good in everyone. This hourglass is what I'd call a real *surprise* gift."

The next morning at sunrise, I once again attended Father Fiasco's daily Mass. The carriage house chapel was half-full of people, the usual strange mixture of different races and ages. When it came time for the reading of the Gospel, Father Fiasco intoned, "A reading from the Lost Holy Gospel according to Saint Bartimaeus." Everyone, myself included, chanted back, "Thanks be to God that the lost has been found."

A silent pause followed our response as Father Fiasco eyed the small group of us gathered in front of him. Then with a slight nod of his head, he began:

Rabboni had just healed me as he made his way up to Jerusalem for the feast of the Passover. The great crowd that accompanied him had tried to silence me, but I only cried out the louder: "Son of David, heal me." And he did! I tossed aside my blind beggar's cloak, the coins flying everywhere, and I followed him.

The crowds grew larger the closer we came to the Holy City. Some were pulling branches from palm trees; others gathered reeds from the fields. Rabboni's disciples were excited and kept shouting: "Now is the hour! This is the day the Lord has made!" Then Jesus ordered two of them to go ahead of us to Bethany and get a donkey. When they returned, he mounted it and rode in front of the throng toward the Golden Gate of the walled Holy City. I overheard some in the masses saying, "A donkey? Is that any way for the son of David, our glorious Messiah, to lead us in the great battle against the Romans?"

Jerusalem, the Holy City, was a great labyrinth with a thousand complicated passageways, baffling twists and turns of narrow streets. It was a maze more elaborate than the fabled labyrinths of Egypt or Crete. A hopeless course for the blind, I wondered upon entering if we could ever find our way out again. We surged through the massive gate, pouring like a flooded river down the narrow street. Next to me in the crowd was Rebecca, whom Rabboni had cured of deafness. "Hear, Bartimaeus, the loud Hosannas? Blessed is the kingdom of our father David to come, to come this very day."

"I hear, Rebecca, and I see the Zealots, the revolutionaries, with swords hidden in their cloaks. But look, up there on the rooftops: Roman soldiers everywhere."

Suddenly Jesus turned left down a street that led

to the Fortress of Antonio, Gabbatha, Pilate's head-quarters. The shouts of Hosanna grew louder. The crowd became a mob, filled with hate and violence. At the end of the street in front of the fortress, however, Jesus turned right, down a twisting, narrow street. The rebels among us yelled, "Coward, fool, this is the day of the Lord! Strike now, the people are with us!" The Roman legions on the walls of the fortress only roared with laughter at the Jew on his donkey.

Rabboni, however, rode on in silence. A terrorist grabbed my arm: "He's betrayed us. He's afraid to restore the kingdom of David. Let's go home." But I saw. At each blank wall, Rabboni turned down another street till we came to the great Temple of Herod.

The Temple guards stood shoulder to shoulder across its entrance, the priests and scribes stood on the steps behind them. Rabboni rode up to them and thundered out, "My house is a house of prayer, but you have turned it into a den of thieves."

The Temple clergy shouted back, "Blasphemer! On whose authority do you speak?" The palm-waving crowd stood in awe at the drama unfolding before them and at the spectacle of the splendorous Temple. The golden plates on its side reflected the sun's radiance like mirrors. It shimmered like a star come to earth.

"See this Temple?" Jesus declared to the priests. "Not a stone will be left standing upon a stone. If you have faith, you can say to this mountain, 'Fly into the sea!' and it will plunge out of sight." Swiftly Jesus turned the donkey and headed down another passageway deeper into the maze.

"Where's he going?" cried someone in the crowd. But I saw and Rebecca heard.

"He's following the song," Rebecca shouted in my ear over the echoes of Hosannas. "Do you hear?" My ears, keen from years of blindness, could make out the magnetic music.

As we descended deeper into the lane of the labyrinth, one of Rabboni's disciples pressed next to me, his palm branch broken in half. "What does he mean, 'God's house will be destroyed,' and 'My house shall be a house of prayer'? The Rabbi has no house, no family — he's childless!" I saw. We, this crowd of former beggars, of those once blind and deaf, former prostitutes, sinners and rejects — we who could "hear" — were his "house." Suddenly we exited from a twisted alley into a great square. A towering Gothic cathedral rose before us. Bishops and priests in scarlet vestments were processing into the cathedral to the fanfare of trumpets. The crowd, like ours, held palm branches, and robed choirs sang beautiful Hosannas to the music of Handel's **Messiah**.

Rabboni's donkey stood still as he watched the ritual. Then he turned to us, saying, "Be constantly on the watch! Stay awake!" Cocking his head, he listened for a moment. Then he led us out of the square, down a dark, narrow lane. Rebecca cried out, "Do you hear it?"

"Yes, I hear." *Through many dangers, toils and snares I have already come. 'Tis grace that brought me safe thus far and grace will lead me home.*

As we plunged deeper into the maze of the garbage-littered alleyways, I saw expressions on the faces of Rabboni's apostles written large with disappointment. They had seen the scarlet robes, the awe with which the crowds held the cathedral's clergy, and they muttered to themselves, "Why did we not join them? Why did we have to come this way?" Some of those following the donkey and its silent, sad rider whispered, "He does not know where he's going; we'll never find our way out of this maze."

The singing of Hosannas had grown faint. Palm branches, once waved in jubilation, now hung limp upon the shoulders of those remaining in the crowd. Overhead, a springtime storm was brewing; thunder rumbled as a blinding flash of lightning jabbed downward into the Holy City. Twisting and turning in the dim, smelly lanes, we passed the shacks of the poor. Jesus halted his donkey at the entrance of an open door, then shook his head and rode on. As I went past the doorway, I looked inside. An old woman in a black shawl knelt in the glow of vigil lights in front of statues of saints and the Virgin. She was burning a palm branch, praying, "Protect me from the evil eye and from the evil of this storm."

Suddenly we turned from the narrow lane into another great square filled with people. At one end was another cathedral. It was bedecked with flags, its bells joyfully ringing. From a nearby pen an oxen was driven out. It was frenzied because for days food and water had been placed within its sight but out of reach. Men, women and children with sticks, knives, whips and lances attacked the ox. At each exit it was driven back, as people gleefully struck the wild, bloody beast. Women threw pepper into its eyes as it ran crazed with pain in the midst of the attacking crowd. Rabboni rode straight through the wild crowd to the steps of the cathedral where a priest was sprinkling the people with holy water. "What is this madness?" Rabboni asked.

"This is our three-day festival of Easter, stranger. This is Farra de Boi: the ox represents the Jew Judas who betrayed our blessed Lord. Here in the Brazilian state of Santa Catarina, over thirty villages hold to this blessed tradition. It will end two days from now when the ox is finally killed and butchered for a great feast. You and your friends, stay with us. Celebrate our blessed Lord's victory."

Jesus spurred his donkey forward, "What victory, for God's sake?"

Again we wandered this way and that through the Holy City's maze of narrow lanes till we came upon a wide curving street that led upward. "At last he's found a way out of this labyrinth," cried an apostle. But alas, after ascending the ramp we found ourselves on a four-lane freeway with cars bumper to bumper in the endless rush-hour traffic. Rabboni rode his donkey through the traffic as the crowd – what remained of it – tried to avoid being run down by the cars. Some drivers shook their fists and shouted in anger at our slowing down the flow, while others only smiled silly grins at us. Out of nowhere came sirens and flashing red lights, and two police cars herded us off the freeway. "All right, mister, get off the donkey. Who do you think you are? Didn't you see the sign at the entrance of the interstate? No animals, ridden or driven, slow-moving machinery or pedestrians allowed! Do you have a parade permit?"

"I'm only following the song," said Jesus as the police escorted us down the exit ramp.

Before us was a great complex, larger than the Temple and surrounded by hundreds of parked cars. Rabboni rode his donkey through the parking lot and into the shopping mall. We followed, awe-struck by the green trees and pools of water indoors, by the shops filled with wonders beyond imagination. The mall was jammed with people rushing in all directions. A haggard looking woman with several children in tow stopped Jesus: "Where's Penney's? I've got to get new Easter clothes for the kids." A couple with two small children asked him, "Do you know where in the mall is the big Easter Bunny that's giving away free Easter eggs?" Jesus only shook his head sadly and rode on. Then a security guard strongly suggested: "Get your ass out of the mall!" So Jesus, with what was left of us who followed, rode out of an exit.

Again we were back in the maze of the Holy City, twisting and turning, but also, it seemed, ascending. On every side there were small shops selling religious articles: statues, crucifixes and bibles. Over the door of one store was a sign: **Relics of the True Cross. Holy Week Discount**. Rabboni rode on, his head hung in sorrow. Then he stopped, pointing toward one shop. It belonged to a woodworker. Its sign swayed in the wind: **Crosses for Sale**. Jesus turned to us, now only a ragged handful: "Go inside and choose one."

His shocked disciples replied, "Master, crosses are used only for those guilty of revolution, sedition against the Empire, those guilty of treason or robbery!"

"I know! Don't you see?" They only shook their heads, blind to the meaning of his words, but I saw.

Rabboni slowly turned his head right and left, then spurred his donkey onward.

"Hear it, Bartimaeus?"

"Yes, Rebecca."

Faintly coming from somewhere ahead of us, the song went on: *For God has promised good to me. God's word my hope secures. God will my shield and portion be, as long as life endures.* He rode onward and ever upward till we saw it. There in the center of the Holy City's great labyrinth was a hill scattered with sculls and bones. The apostles fled backward down the narrow lane. Jesus called after them, "No, come back! There's no other way through the maze. This is the only way out!" Dismounting the donkey, as black storm clouds swirled menacingly over the hilltop and sheets of rain lashed down, he turned his face upward full into the rain. The handful of us who were left stood over our broken palm branches dangling at our sides as he began to sing: *Amazing grace has banished fear and given life to me. I once was lost, but now I'm found, was blind, but now I see.*

Regardless of my new discipline of being mindful, I could not keep my mind on the rituals or prayers of the rest of the Mass. Rather, my mind was lost in a maze of dead-end questions around that strange Gospel. I wondered if all grace is a-maze-ing as questions poked at me from every side: "Am I among those who hear, or have I been deaf all these years?" "Is the message of Christ about revolution or becoming God-like?" I knew from the first part of the Gospel story when Jesus turned away from battle against the Romans that it wasn't an armed revolution he was calling for. But at the end he definitely invited his followers to revolution and sedition against the Empire. I had never thought about the cross as punishment for treason, but if that's true then I wondered if I was ready, or even able, to take up the cross. In my confounded state, everything seemed to be turned upside down.

I looked at the icon of the Mother of God and saw it afresh, with new eyes. The poor and homeless appeared to be the rich ones, while the rich and powerful were among the homeless. I couldn't help reflecting on how fitting was the icon of the crucified Christ in a clown's suit. It seemed comical, a farce, to think that one can do battle with the powers-that-be in a non-violent way. The only way that seems to work is to fight fire with fire. And after two thousands years of Christianity, the power structures are just as strong today as they were then. Maybe that's because, like the first disciples, we also have turned our backs on the *true* cross. I hated to think that going further on my quest meant becoming a revolutionary. At that moment there seemed to be a lot more questions than answers.

Like the sound of my snooze alarm waking me from a dream, I heard Father Fiasco chanting the ritual conclusion to the Mass: "Go in Peace. You are looking for Jesus of Nazareth...he is not here. He is going ahead of you to Galilee, where you will see him just as he told you." After a few minutes of silent prayer, I stopped by Father Fiasco's room behind the chapel as he was taking off his vestments. "Good morning, Father. I found this morning's Gospel...ah...interesting."

"I find it disturbing myself, George – but still good news! Those Lost Gospels aren't easy ones for me to read. The usual ones – old Mark, Luke, Matthew and John – are so familiar to us. The effect of those two deadening influences, time and repetition, have made them safer and not so threatening – or as you said, 'interesting.' "

"I understand that, Father, but I always thought that the message of the Gospels was to show us how to live a moral life, how to do good and become holy."

"Yes indeed, George, but what does it mean to live a moral life – keeping the commandments, going to church, being good? Does a moral life not also require standing up against the powers of the State and even the Church? Does one become holy simply by a hot pursuit of spiritual disciplines, prayer and fasting? Doesn't holiness call us to become immersed in the Godly activity of radical revolution?"

As he wheeled his bicycle through the Poor Box room, he added, "Doesn't prayer, as it did for Jesus in the desert, include the struggle to refuse to compromise with either religious or imperial powers? An important part of my daily prayer is following Jesus into the desert to meet the Evil One in myself, finding the strength not to make a deal with the devil....I'd like to stay and talk, George – I find our conversation very interesting – but I have to get to work. Maybe we can continue this tonight?"

I agreed to a visit as he wheeled his bike through the outer door. I was left alone in the Poor Box room. The sign on the mirror held me prisoner, "If you have more than you need, leave some. If you're a little short and are in need, take some." True, I had never felt like I had all the money I could use. On the other hand, I certainly had more than I needed. So I dropped some money in the box and went out the door.

Mama Mahatma was working in her garden with Fatima beside her. She waved a greeting to me and joined me as I walked to the house. As I was opening the kitchen door, Fatima jumped on top of a small concrete platform located on the north side of the house, just to the west of the kitchen door. I had noticed its round, green metal lid before but didn't know what it was. So I asked Mama about it.

"You're too young to know, Child. This house once had a coal furnace, and that's the outside entrance to the old coal bin. Fatima loves to use it as a regal throne. Cats, you know, love to sit up on top of things."

As we shared our morning coffee, I laid some of my concerns on Mama's wise lap – even though I hated to bring up my recurring problem again. "I came here seeking solitude and silence, an opportunity, free of distractions, to deepen my spiritual quest. What I keep finding . . . ."

"More distractions, George?"

"Yes, Mama, so much of what I hear, see and experience here seems to get in the way of my spiritual practice. Like this morning over in the carriage house. Father Fiasco read a Gospel to us about a blind man who saw, but I didn't like what he saw!"

"And what was it that *you* saw, George?"

"A cross that seemed to require revolution."

We sat in silence over our coffee for several moments, long enough for my uneasiness about the morning's questions to settle like sediment to the bottom of the cup. Then Mama began again, "Ah yes, George, a difficult vision to hold your eyes – and mind – open to. We all practice selective seeing. What we allow ourselves to see or not see is determined by our culture, our early childhood and education, as well as by what we fear. If by your coming here to live with us, you are seeing things you never saw before – even if that vision doesn't make you comfortable – isn't that new sight a great gift?"

"Yes, I guess it is. But I wouldn't be honest if I didn't admit that it's a bit frightening. New vision means changing, and change isn't easy – especially if it has a high price tag."

"True, such new insights are more than a bit upsetting. Still, a peaceful life without distractions may not be such a good alternative. At the Treaty of Amiens in 1802, Napoleon Bonaparte lamented, 'What a beautiful fix we are in now; peace has been declared!' If life in this old house were truly peaceful, George, I wonder how much real progress you'd make in this part of your spiritual quest."

Then, turning on her playful smile, Mama concluded our morning conversation, "George, if I was to do it all over again, I would tattoo on the foreheads of all my kids these words, 'eerf si efil ni gnihtoN.' Then every time they looked in a mirror they would see one of life's most important lessons, 'Nothing in life is free'!"

As I went about my household duties that day, I pondered my conversations with Mama Mahatma and Father Fiasco. While maybe being maid and cook to this household didn't provide the solitude I originally had hoped it would, perhaps this was the place to pursue my quest. I felt that I had a new assignment: together with trying to perform all my tasks mindfully, I now had to consider anew the message of the cross. After hearing that Gospel reading this morning, I began to see the cross as more than just a personal issue. I started considering the role of the cross in resolving our common and global problems.

That afternoon, before beginning to prepare dinner, I went

to wash up in the bathroom. I could hear Bernadone singing in his room across the hall. The Inspector was one of the happiest men I'd ever met. His material possessions were few – he must have had some hidden wealth to be so cheerful. As I washed my hands, I wondered why people don't seem to sing much any more. Is it out of politeness, or do people lack a good reason to sing?

Bernadone saw me as I entered the hallway and invited me in. I stepped inside the room and was surprised by how stark and simple it was. Instead of a bed, there was only a sheet-covered mattress on the floor. In one corner of the room was a small desk and a bookcase made from concrete blocks and unfinished boards for shelves. The walls were bare of decoration except for an almost life-size wooden cross. At the foot of the cross was a small prayer rug. Bernadone sat in an old, faded green easy chair, an open book on his lap. "Hi, George, how have things gone for you today?"

Eying the large cross with new insight, I replied, "Fine, how about yourself? You're home early today."

"A little flex time for putting in some extra hours these past nights on the Woodsdale murder case. So I'm enjoying one of my favorite books."

"Looks like it's been read many times, judging from its worn condition. What's it about?"

"It's **The Life and Teachings of Najmuddin Kubra**. He was a Moslem Sufi master who lived around 1100. Better known as whirling dervishes, the Sufis are the mystical branch of Islam, interested in the deeper meaning of the Koran. I'm especially attracted to Najmuddin's teachings about love and respect for all creation. Look at this picture of him surrounded by birds. Once he tamed a wild dog simply by looking at him. As you may know, I love animals. Maybe that's why I find this old mystic so fascinating. I've long dreamed of going to the Near East where Najmuddin founded a religious order of Sufis called 'The Greater Brethren.' I'd love to go over there and see if the order still exists and learn firsthand whatever I can about his spiritual way. Books are helpful as a source of information, but they pale before actual experience."

I nodded in agreement, still looking at the picture of the

Moslem saint in his coarse brown robe. As I did, I couldn't help but recall the Magic Lantern story of the young pig keeper who went in search of a profound experience. "I can understand your desire. In fact, it was just such a longing that brought me here in the first place.

"I see you have a cross." I motioned to the cross on the wall. "Mind if I ask what it means to you?"

"Many things, George – as it does to most of us. I often ponder the Sufi words, 'You may have the cross, but we have the meaning of the cross.' For many Christians it stands for the sacrifice necessary for their personal salvation. The Sufis regard excessive concern for one's personal salvation as a vanity."

Glancing at my watch, I saw that it was past time for me to be down in the kitchen if dinner was going to be on time. I left Bernadone to reading his book and started down the back stairs, smiling to myself, "Funny how things all seem connected – all these different reflections on the cross. Interesting house, filled with messages. If I only had time to sort them all out and piece them together."

As I was fixing the evening meal, baked chicken in a white wine sauce, I happened to glance out the kitchen window and saw Maria and Jon talking together in the yard. I had noticed that recently they were spending more and more time together. I didn't need special vision to see that Jon was becoming very attracted to Maria. Who wouldn't fall in love with such a beautiful young woman? Likewise, it was easy to see why she would be equally drawn to a handsome man like Jon, even if he was some ten years her senior. While I found their budding romance delightful to watch, duty called. After a last minute check of the rice, I set the table for dinner.

The meal conversation was the usual potpourri of daily news, until Gloria introduced her favorite subject: religion!

"I just don't understand how any thinking person can be an atheist or an agnostic. It's a plain fact that should be perfectly obvious: God does exist!" Her voice had all the authority of a papal pronouncement. It made me wonder if Gloria didn't secretly believe the same thing as Richard Nixon, who was once reported to have said, "I would have made a good pope!" Gloria continued, her voice drawing me out of my silly reflections. "The second obvious fact is that if God exists, then he should be worshiped and obeyed." She looked at us as if expecting a round of applause.

"*He?*" replied Father Fiasco. "Isn't that rather a limiting pronoun for God, even if it is traditional?"

"Personally," said Jon, "I find the matter of God's existence rather questionable because of the number of gods that seem to want to be obeyed and worshiped."

"There is only one true God," snapped Mike, "and that's the God of the Bible."

"Children, children, if we are going to discuss religion at the table, let us do so with love and respect," said Mama Mahatma. "God and religion are such ancient concerns, and there are so many perspectives on both. My old mother, God be good to her, always said that religion and politics were two things never to be discussed in polite company! Personally, I've always found that both of them make excellent dinner conversation — challenging and never dull, unless the wine isn't very good."

The look in Gloria's eyes said that Mama's comment about God being good dinner conversation, if the wine were also good, had left a bad taste in her mouth.

"I'm not opposed to religion," said Jon. "As you always say, Mama Mahatma, religion can answer life's great questions. I guess that, like George, I'm also a seeker. I haven't given up hope that one day I'll find what I'm looking for."

"What is there to *look* for?" asked Gloria with mock surprise. "Everything you need to find is already contained in the Apostles Creed. Jon, faith is what you need! If you lack it, all you have to do is pray for it."

Bernadone, who had been silent but absorbed in the conversation, suddenly spoke up. "Strange, Gloria, that you should mention the Apostles Creed. I had a dream about it the other night. Like the rest of you, I learned it as a child. While it's one of those classic prayers that stays with you, I can't imagine why in the world I dreamed about it."

"What was your dream about, Inspector?" asked Father Fiasco.

Well, I know this will sound strange, but I dreamed that I had died and gone to heaven. As I opened my eyes closed by death, I found myself waiting in line outside heaven's pearly gates. Actually, there were several lines of people of all ages, even small children, all wearing their burial clothing. Up ahead I could see people passing through some sort of security checkpoint.

I thought, "What is this: heaven or O'Hare airport? But I guess you have to be cautious everywhere today." My turn came, and before I walked through that metal detector door frame with the little beeper, I asked an angel, "What's this for?"

The angel replied, "No metal allowed. No weapons, gold or silver. And no hard, steely hearts are allowed inside." I passed through the door frame without a beep.

After that, I fell into line for a second security check, another one of those electronic door frames. As my turn came, I asked the angel standing there, "What's this one for?"

The angel answered, "It's a grudge detector. No one carrying a grudge is allowed to enter."

I quickly reflected, "When I died, had I forgiven everyone who ever wronged me?" I couldn't find any still-existing grudges, so I took a deep breath and passed through the electronic door frame. Ah, no beep!

Again, I got into line, thinking to myself, "Glad I'm not in a hurry to catch a plane; this is slow going!" Up ahead, at the end of each line, people were entering a door, one by one. On each door was a sign that read **Dressing Room**. I was relieved: I expected a body search!

When my turn came, I entered a small white room and closed the door behind me. There was a wash bowl, mirror and gold clothing hook on the wall to the left and an exit door on the far wall. On the remaining wall was a sign written in at least fifty different languages which read **Please Remove All Clothing**.

I took off the three piece suit – my best one – in which they buried me. Looking in the mirror, I was shocked, for I was wearing rouge and lipstick! It felt good to wash off all of that mortician's makeup.

I stood there naked and looked around for my white robe, but there wasn't one. I opened the exit door a crack and saw a group of angels visiting with each other. "Psst...psst...excuse me," I said, "there's no white robe in here."

The angels turned my way and smiled, "There aren't any white robes. You come here the same way you left: naked. Remember, on Easter Jesus rose naked, leaving behind his burial clothes."

Well, I was embarrassed, to say the least, and I walked out with my hands in an Adam and Eve position. Throughout my lifetime I had always wanted the body of a movie star or great athlete. But, to my surprise, the angels looked at my body – inadequate as it seemed to me – with eyes of envy. I could hear them saying, "Each one is so *beautiful*, how lucky they are to have bodies!"

My shame vanished as I recovered my early childhood pleasure at being naked, and I looked up and saw the throne of God and the Lamb. The Evangelist was right: flowing from the glorious throne was a great crystal river, as wide as the Mississippi. I started to kneel down to adore God when an angel took my arm and said, "You must cross the River of Heaven and go up to the throne of God."

I walked up to the edge of the crystal river, but I didn't see any boat. "How do I cross the river?" I asked.

The angel only smiled and said, "Walk across! Walk on the water like Jesus and Peter did on the Sea of Galilee."

Now, I remembered what happened to Peter! I mean, he walked a few wet steps and then sank, at which Jesus said to him, "O you of little faith." Now I was worried. I had passed those other tests and was enjoying being naked – but a test of my faith? The degree of my faith in my old life on earth wasn't that outstanding. There had been more than a few times, if you know what I mean, when I doubted the whole works.

Quickly, I recited the Apostles Creed to myself with as much sincerity as possible and started to walk across the Great River of Heaven. My heart was pounding as I actually found myself walking on the water! I must have gone about ten feet – slowly, mind you – when I started sinking into the river. In a matter of seconds I was down to my knees. I cried out for help, and a band of angels came to my rescue, pulled me out and carried me back to the shore. "You're too heavy, friend; you're carrying too much," they said to me.

"Carrying too much? I'm stark naked!" I replied.

"Your problem is that you're carrying too much creed," one of them said. "You have to jettison some of it, or you'll never make it across to the throne of God."

My wrinkled brow spoke of my confused state. One of the angels addressed my bewilderment, "Faith is all one can carry; you're weighted down with too many dogmas."

One by one, I examined my dogmas. "I believe in the Holy, Catholic, Apostolic Church." Now that was one of my heaviest creeds. I tossed it aside and began to walk out on the water but got only a few yards further before again beginning to sink. After being rescued again, I threw away another, then another of my cherished dogmas. But each time, although I made it a bit beyond the previous attempt, eventually I sank.

Finally, all I had left from the creed of my lifetime was one belief. Clutching it closely to my heart, I repeated it with great love and faith as I again started across the river for the throne of God. Though I kept repeating it silently, even the sense of holding on to that creed gracefully subsided. In the instant of a lightning flash I had crossed the river. I found myself at the golden throne of heaven in the vast embrace of God, still repeating my one and only dogma, "I believe in God, I believe in God."

"Bully!" exclaimed Father Fiasco. "Great story, Inspector. I love it!"

Laughing, Mama Mahatma added, "As an old Yugoslavian proverb says with great wisdom: 'Tell the truth and run!' That's a story, Inspector, you should tell and then race to the nearest exit."

Most of us joined her laughter about the Yugoslavian proverb. Bernadone's dream, however, was not appreciated by everyone at the table. "I think that dream—or whatever it was—is disgraceful," said Mike. "How can you believe *only* in God? What about all the other dogmas and truths that Jesus taught us?"

"See what I mean about telling the truth?" asked Mama.

"With your permission, Mama Mahatma," said Father Fiasco as he lit a cigarette. "Mike, I have a question. When Jesus was dying on the cross, what else did he put his faith in, if not simply in God? If that one belief was good enough for him, it's good enough for me!

"Bernadone's dream and this talk about different religious beliefs remind me of another story. Mama Mahatma, with your Ladyship's permission . . . ." Father Fiasco leaned back in his chair, took a long sensual drag from his cigarette and began:

> Once upon a time, a farmer dug a well on his property and up gushed sweet, good water. It was the most delicious water ever discovered. Tasting the water, he knew that it was indeed the best in all the world. His friends and neighbors confirmed this, and soon people from far away were coming to his well to fill jugs and pails with his water.
>
> Now another farmer who lived only two miles away also dug a well and up gushed sweet, good water. He tasted the water from his well and knew that it was the freshest, sweetest water in the whole world. Soon his friends and family as well as great crowds of visitors came with buckets and pails to obtain his wondrously pure water.

Before long the two farmers were engaged in heated arguments over which one's well was the best in the world. The crowds of people coming to their wells passed one another on the road, and as they did they hurled vicious insults at each other. Each farmer condemned the other's well as poisonous, saying that the other's water only appeared to be pure. Eventually the dispute over the two wells led to bloody battles between the two groups of water seekers. All of this was very sad, for if either of the farmers had taken the time to reflect on their gift of water, they would have realized that they both had tapped into the same underground river of crystal clear and pure water.

"Heresy! That's heresy!" scowled Gloria.

"For God's sake, it's only a story, Gloria. Don't have a stroke over it," countered Father Fiasco, blowing a cloud of smoke in the air. "I don't even remember where I read it."

"It's still heretical! The very idea that different religions all flow from the same source. Jesus is the **only** true water that takes away our thirst. And I think . . . ."

Mama Mahatma rang her little brass bell, signaling the end of dinner. Everyone became silent for the thanksgiving and then left the dining room. Jon and Maria went out for a walk together, and Bernadone, Father Fiasco and I did the dishes. We discussed the evening's stories and the Inspector's dream, as well as the budding romance between Jon and Maria. Having finished up the work in the kitchen, we parted and said good night.

I didn't go upstairs to the attic but simply laid back on my bed. I tried to put all the pieces of the day's information into some sort of order. I had planned to do some mental filing and then write a journal-letter to Martha, but I must have fallen asleep. I awoke fully clothed at 2 a.m., roused by voices in the next room. Dio was shouting angrily about Jon to Maria. She protested that she wasn't in love with him but only enjoyed his company. Dio threatened her. Then I could hear her pleading with him not to hurt her. He must have left since I heard a door slamming followed by her sobbing quietly.

It was at that moment that I heard the sound of a truck coming up our driveway and stopping right below my window. I stood up and looked out the window that faced the carriage house. In the light of an almost full moon I could see rather clearly a farmer's old pickup truck parked in the driveway at the corner of the house. As I watched, Mama Mahatma came out of the darkness carrying two wire cages which she handed to the man standing by the truck. The man reached into the back of the pickup truck and removed two similar cages which he handed to Mama. They spoke in such hushed voices that I couldn't hear what was said. I couldn't be sure, because of the shadows, but each of the cages the farmer gave to Mama appeared to hold a rabbit. They must have weighed about five pounds apiece. Mama Mahatma took the cages and disappeared into the darkness around the house as the old pickup truck drove away.

I undressed and climbed into bed, shaking my head and muttering to myself, "Oh, God, what have I gotten myself into by becoming part of this strange household?"

CHAPTER 6

Through the days of the next week, I watched the love between Jon and Maria grow, even if it was more secretly. Maria was afraid of Dio, and whenever he was around she attempted to hide her feelings for Jon. Dio possessed great power over her, but it seemed to be weakening under the influence of her love for Jon. I liked Jon, even though I felt that he couldn't have thought too highly of me. What I mean is, here I was doing "woman's work," cleaning the house and cooking meals, not to mention that I was on some sort of religious pursuit. Traditionally that's three strikes against a man! Knowing his disdain for churches and religion, his feeling that they are the hideouts of the weak and timid, I feared that he viewed me as a wimp. So I was surprised when on Saturday, as I was passing the open door to his room, he called out, "Hey, George, come in! I have a favor to ask of you."

I stepped into his room and saw that he was out on the sun porch. He was working out on a weight lifting machine. Wearing only a pair of gym trunks, he was covered with sweat. So that's what Mama Mahatma meant when she said he was "into building" — of course, body building!

"You look surprised, George, at this equipment. I believe in a healthy body — and a strong one as well."

There was no doubt about him being strong. From the size of his chest and arm muscles, I'd bet he could have wrestled a grizzly and come off the winner.

"As for being surprised, Jon, yes and no. I should have guessed that someone in such good physical shape had to work out. I admire you — and anyone who has the will power for that kind of regimen. But what can I do for you?"

"It's my shower drain, George. It's clogged. Do you think you could find some Drano and unplug it for me? I know that's not part of your duties, but I sure would appreciate it. I keep forgetting to pick some up at the store and thought you might know where that stuff is kept around the house."

"Yes, I do. In fact, I saw a bottle of it in the pantry. I'll be glad to go down and get it and see what I can do. Actually, I guess that unplugging drains would be one of my duties anyway."

I went downstairs and returned with the can of Drano and a plunger I found in the pantry. In a few minutes I had the drain working again and walked back out onto the sun porch.

"Thanks, George, I appreciate that," Jon said, panting as he raised and lowered the weights. "How do you like living here at Mama Mahatma's rooming house?"

"Well, it's not dull, I'll say that. Watching you work out makes me think I should do something like that. I don't do any real heavy work, as you know, so I could use some good exercise."

"Well, you're welcome to use any of my equipment whenever you wish. You can even join me when I'm using it if you'd like. Regardless, I would encourage you to take me up on my offer. Most people today take better care of their machines than their bodies. They eat junk food and spend most of their time sitting. These bodies of ours were designed for action. As I see it, George, *this* is it! I mean this life! So we should make the most of what we've got. All that stuff about waiting till heaven for your reward is nothing more than a pious life insurance policy. It's a policy that nobody yet has proven pays off. Until someone shows me it does, my life insurance will be insuring that I make the most of this life!"

"I know you're right, Jon—I mean about exercise. I've always admired anyone who has the discipline for daily exercise. For me, it's a matter of a lack of time. I'm involved in another form of exercise, and it, together with my work here, fills up most of my day. I wish I could find a way to turn the twenty-four hours of a day into thirty-four. Then I'd have time for more physical activity than cleaning and vacuuming. Which reminds me, I still have to finish this hallway carpet before dinner time. See you then, Jon."

"Thanks again, George. You're a great addition to this household. I like you!"

As I finished my work, his last three words, "I like you," kept circling around in my mind. It felt good to be liked by someone like Jon, even if his philosophy of life was different from mine. It's strange how people who are religious, like Mike and Gloria, are often so unappealing, while the Jons and Marias of life are so attractive. As for Father Fiasco and Bernadone – well, they don't fit into the usual religious category. While spiritual men, they're both enjoyable and challenging.

I finished my pre-dinner meditation and felt good about it. I know that feeling good about a meditation isn't an accurate gauge of its quality, but my time of sitting seemed to be going by more quickly the past week or so. I guess that's a good sign. Because Bernadone's practiced meditation for years, I made a mental note to ask him if that's a sign that I'm making progress. I needed all the signs I could find, 'cause it didn't seem like I was getting anywhere. I've been here almost three months now, and the enlightenment I expected still hasn't happened.

That night I did the dishes alone; both Bernadone and Father Fiasco had commitments after dinner. I didn't mind cleaning up by myself. It gave me a chance to practice my mindfulness. With attention and care, I tried to wash and dry each dish with only that simple action in mind. As I turned out the kitchen light, I decided to go up in the attic and spend some time with my Magic Lantern.

As I set it up, I was curious about where this mysterious old machine would take me tonight. Mama's mansion was as silent as a wren birdhouse in winter. The only sound was the wind outside causing the gutters to rattle. I inserted the slides, one by one, watching images of old amusement parks with roller coasters and Ferris wheels appear on the wall of the nursery. Then the mood shifted when one slide revealed the entrance gate of a park with a sign that read **Lakeside Amusement Park**.

Magically, I could now hear and smell and feel what it was like in the world of the Lakeside Amusement Park. This was no ordinary amusement park. There were no wild rides, no glitter, go-carts or brightly colored lights. Instead, it was illuminated by pale, cool, pleasing moonlight. By all appearances it was an amusement park true to its name. It was a place of old-fashioned peacefulness and easy leisure, as in the old French word *amuser*, "to cause to idle away time." I reflected on how natural it felt being here. After all, I was on a sabbatical, and what is a sabbatical if not an opportunity for genuine leisure. It occurred to me that I needed to inject a greater element of leisure into all my time here at the boarding house, even into my daily tasks, if I were truly to live mindfully.

This park seemed to invite one to come away from a hectic, stop-watch deadline, hustle-and-bustle life and to be amused. There was no blaring band music; the music filtering through the park seemed to be composed of the sounds of waterfalls, mountain brooks, the melody of bird song and the sound of the wind rising and falling in a great, green forest. Nor were there frantic rides meant to raise the hair on the back of your neck. Instead, slow-moving giant turtles carried people leisurely from one old-fashioned, pre-technological form of entertainment to the next.

In the center of the Lakeside Amusement Park was a magnificent merry-go-round. It too was unique. Rather than the usual brightly painted horses, prancing sleek-headed deer and elk and dashing unicorns, the main feature of this unique merry-go-round was a slowly moving circle of trees: it was a forest-go-round! In place of the usual loud steam calliope, the center of this merry-go-round had a great dark lake with islands of green algae growing in it. A great ring of trees slowly circled the green lagoon with its flocks of dragonflies.

At this point my Magic Lantern episode took a different turn than it had in the past. Tonight I was no longer just a spectator. The magic of the machine drew me into the images so that dream-like I began to experience myself being right at the Lakeside Amusement Park. When I first entered through its gates, I spent some time roaming about, soaking up its pleasant sounds and sights. But before long I was magnetically drawn to the merry-go-round in the center of the park. Its friendly attendant took great joy in describing the merry-go-round to me.

"There is a great variety of trees to ride in this peaceful forest-go-round," he began. "You could amuse yourself on the beautiful Apple Tree which is passing by us now. It is fully in bloom, rich with the aromas of springtime romance, young and passionate love, bathed in erotic moonlight. Or perhaps you would like to ride the Survivor Tree, a gnarled old tree that hangs by its tough roots to a tall cliff with jagged rocks. Then there is the Weeping Willow. Its long, slender, delicate branches form a graceful, green umbrella whose ends trail slowly along the ground. Perhaps you'll choose to ride in the huge, gray old Swamp Cypress whose twisting roots and trunk are sunk deep in the dark waters alive with reptiles, water moccasins and alligators.

"As this merry-go-round of trees moves by us, you can see a Toddler Tree, a young shoot no more than five or six feet tall, supported on either side by two strong stakes to keep it upright in the wind. Next comes the tall Evergreen. It has a full green circle of growth at its base and reaches up like a spire to the sky. Finally, you might choose to ride in the massive, ancient Oak Tree, the king of all the trees of the forest-go-round. Which one looks interesting – amusing – to you?"

After some thought I paid the attendant and went up into the lush branches of the Evergreen. The tree sang of life without the bare branches of winter. It sang of one long continuous green life. It was a lovely melody, but after a time I became vaguely uncomfortable. So I asked the Evergreen Tree, "How do you understand the words of Jesus that we are to die to ourselves in order to live?"

The Evergreen replied, "They are not for me. I am a sign of life. I choose life rather than death. Such words are too mystical and threatening for me."

I decided that I wanted to change trees. This time I chose to climb up into the old-but-valiant Survivor Tree. I climbed out onto one of its leather-like branches extending over the jagged cliff. The tree spoke to me of how difficult life is, how one must hang on with all one's strength or . . . . After listening for a time, a question arose which I put to the tree: "Tell me, how do you understand the admonitions of Jesus and Buddha that we must show compassion to all we meet, aid the poor and assist even the stranger?"

The old, gnarled tree gave me a disturbed look and replied, "I would like to help others, to serve the needy. But you can see for yourself that it is all I can do simply to hang on for my life. It takes all my energy merely to cling to this cliff. Where would I find the time or substance to go about helping others? I even find you, sitting on my arm, to be a burden almost too much to bear."

I excused myself apologetically and slipped down, making my way to the Weeping Willow. Pushing aside the curtain of slender branches, I entered the green umbrella and made my way up onto a branch. The Willow was softly sobbing, so I said to it, "Tell me, why are you so sad?" The tree, however, said nothing and only continued to weep. Again, I quietly asked, "Excuse me, please, I know that you are disturbed, but can you speak to me about the words of St. Paul, 'Rejoice always! I say to you, rejoice'?"

The Willow shook its great body and replied, "Perhaps the lucky ones can live that way. For me such words are impossible. My life is full of sorrow. You don't know how much pain I am bearing right now – keeping it here, close to my heart. If I ever let it out, they would call me the Wailing Tree. Those words are not meant for me. I do not know how they could be lived by anyone!" The tree continued to sob quietly to itself.

The attendant signaled that my ride was over. So I paid again and this time selected the beautiful, full-blossomed Apple Tree. I felt the need for a little romance after my rides in the heavily burdened Survivor Tree and the sad Willow. As I ascended the Apple Tree's branches, alive with the sound of birds, I could hear it singing, "God is love. Oh, God is love." Memories of my youth and of being lost in love filled me, and it was truly pleasing. But after a while I could not help but ask, "Tell me, how do you understand the words of Scripture, 'If you wish to be my disciple, you must deny your very self, take up your cross and follow me'?"

The Apple Tree only smiled and said, "Love is fulfillment. Love is an everlasting spring. Love is a heart overflowing with happiness. There is no place here for denial, for ugly crosses that speak of sacrifice and death. Friend, you have chosen the wrong ride. The words you quote are Greek to me."

I left the moon-touched Apple Tree and its songbirds and this time decided to ride in the king of the forest-go-round, the great, ancient Oak Tree. I climbed up and up through its network of branches which held the secrets of countless years. I scaled past carved hearts in its trunk, with initials that pledged eternal love.

More often than not, those carvings in the trunk lasted longer than the promised love. Now here was a tree, I thought, that was ripe with wisdom. So I asked the ancient Oak Tree, "Can you explain to me the meaning of the words, 'Thy kingdom come, thy will be done on earth as it is in heaven'? Doesn't that imply the surrender which both Jesus and Mohammed proposed?"

The Oak stood tall and straight, with an air of regal authority, and replied, "Can't say that I ever gave them a second thought. Who's supposed to think about such words. They may be beautiful and poetic, but holy words are for funerals, weddings and cornerstone dedications. Who, pray tell, really does think about them? For me, the thought of surrendering, having to bend to so-called higher forces or to another's need, abandoning my will or even my plans for the day...well, mister, oaks are hard wood! We don't bend for anyone. They don't call me the king of the forest for nothing!"

As I silently slipped down and away, I thought I would next try a ride on the old, gray Swamp Cypress. As I began creeping up into its branches, I placed my foot on what I thought was a dark, smooth root, only to leap back with a start. What appeared to be a root was actually a huge water snake coiled about the great roots. The cypress laughed and said, "Careful, mister! Taking a ride on me is flirting with danger and darkness."

My heart pounding, I cautiously shinned up its branches heavy with gray-green moss and asked the tree, "What do you think about the words of Jesus that we are to shun all evil and not even allow dark thoughts to dwell in our hearts?"

"If you like a dull life," answered the tree, "I guess that makes sense. I, however, love to live in the part of me immersed in darkness – call it evil if you like. I find it exciting to have reptiles that coil about my roots, and as long as I don't hurt others, who should care what's hidden beneath the surface?" I carefully climbed down, this time watching that what I stepped on was a tree limb and not a serpent.

There was only one tree left. It was still so small that I couldn't climb into its branches. So I leaned up against one of its supportive stakes and asked the Toddler Tree, "Excuse me, I know that you're still very young and inexperienced, but I'm curious. How would you explain these words: 'Whoever does not accept the kingdom of God as a child will not enter into it'?"

The Toddler Tree responded, "Makes good sense to me. I know that I don't have all the answers, but a child is like a young tree which can bend easily with the wind and bend back after the storm. Growing tall involves having to suffer storms and broken branches, but it's all worth it. Nor does it seem as important to become big and tall as to remain supple and responsive. It's a joy simply to be alive. It's the richest of all treasures – I mean, just being alive. And I look forward one day to giving shade to some weary person traveling a long road. Or maybe my wood will someday be used to make a beautiful chair or simply firewood to keep a poor family warm on a cold night. Being young, stranger, is being full of hope, being supple and open in the midst of this or that trial. It's being in love with the game of life, without respect to winning or losing. For in the end we're all winners, right?"

I nodded in agreement and smiled as the Toddler Tree again spoke. "If you don't mind, stranger, I have a question for you: what's a kingdom...and who said those words, anyway?"

The image of the Toddler Tree froze on the wall, and I felt the magic drain from me. I was alone again in the attic of the old house with only my thoughts. "Ah, which tree am I?" I wondered to myself. The words of the Toddler Tree echoed in my head as I turned off the light and walked to the stairs: "It's a joy simply to be alive. It's the richest of all treasures . . . ." I had forgotten that truth in my zeal to get on with my journey. Yeah, I was so busy with my problems, with the swarming host of unanswered questions, that I had choked off the joy of being alive. So what if I was a bit frustrated, if my work was only cleaning and cooking. Despite its mundane element, wasn't I on the kind of adventure that most people only dream about?

Entering my small bedroom, I made a vow that I would seriously attempt to be in love with the game of life, as the little tree had said, for indeed "in the end, we're all winners, right?" I decided to ask Mama tomorrow how she would answer the little tree's question, "What's a kingdom?" As I fell asleep, I realized that I didn't know what that term meant – even though I had heard it since I was a child.

That night I had another nightmare, a flashback to my Magic

Lantern trip to the Lakeside Amusement Park. In my dream I was climbing the old Swamp Cypress, and it whispered in my ear, "Careful, mister, taking a ride on me is flirting with danger and darkness." I laughed, but then I felt something wrapping itself around my legs. Looking down, I saw that it was the large water snake I had seen coiled around the tree's roots. The more I struggled to be free, the tighter the snake coiled around me. I tried to pry the snake loose but without success. The huge serpent coiled its way up to my face and looked at me. I was filled with terror, for its eyes were hollow holes, bottomless, like the eyes of the serpent coiled around the face of the grandfather's clock downstairs. I awoke in a cold sweat, gasping for breath, with the bed sheet twisted in coils around my body.

In the morning the dream was still vivid when I awoke and dressed to attend Mass at Father Fiasco's church. The sky was pink with pre-dawn light as I joined a couple of old black women entering the chapel. My intention was to come early before Mass so that I could do my morning meditation there. As I walked in, I saw Maria kneeling in prayer in front of the icon of the Mother of God. "I know that she's out with her clients till the early hours," I thought, "yet here she is praying." Maria was proof of that old saying, "You can't tell a book by its cover."

When it was time for the reading of the Gospel, Father Fiasco walked to the makeshift trunk-pulpit. I knew we were in for another Lost Gospel. This morning it was a reading from the Lost Gospel of Mark, chapter 10, the missing text between verses 16 and 17. He read the Gospel with the same energy and enthusiasm that one would have expected if he were reading it for the first time:

> One day as Jesus and Peter were walking down the road, they met a young man to whom Jesus said, "Come, follow me."
>
> "Rabbi," he said, "I have heard about you and the good works you are doing. I am honored to be invited to join you, but let me think about it. I need to sit with your invitation awhile and pray over it."
>
> "What? If you need time to think about it, then you are not fit to be my disciple!" Jesus turned and swiftly walked away.

Peter caught up with him. "Master," he said, "that's not an unusual request. Why not let him consider all that it means to follow you?"

Jesus glared at Peter. "You didn't need time to think about it, to ponder all the possibilities. You and your brother immediately joined me when I invited you. No, let him be; I made a mistake. He lacks the 'stuff' of discipleship."

Jesus, feeling a tug at his sleeve, turned and again saw the young man. "Master," he said, "please don't be angry with me. You see, I have commitments. I'm married, and I should go home and talk it over with my wife. I'd also like to see what my parents and friends have to say about it."

"Go home and stay there!" was Jesus' sharp reply. "If you have to talk it over with others, then your heart's not free enough to risk all. If you're not willing to risk everything, then you have no business being one of my friends!" Again, Jesus turned and made a hurried exit.

Catching up with Jesus, Peter said, "I know, Lord, that I didn't ask my wife or family if I should follow you, and I didn't need time to think about it. I knew what I needed to do the moment I saw you and heard your invitation. But this young man is...more prudent...he's not so impetuous. I think . . . ."

At that moment Jesus felt another tug at his sleeve. Turning, he was once more face to face with the would-be disciple. "What is it this time?" inquired Jesus. "I thought you had gone home."

"Please understand, Master, I would like to follow you . . . ."

"Don't call me 'Master,'" returned Jesus. "Your wife, your home, your family and your business are your Master."

The young man begged, "Sir, I believe in what you are teaching, but I need time to think about it. I don't want to make a mistake."

"Make a mistake? What do you mean, 'Make a

mistake'? To follow me is the biggest mistake you, or anyone, could ever make! Don't you realize that I'm the Biggest Mistake in the world? If you can't see that, you're too blind to be my disciple." Like a whirlwind, Jesus turned and stormed down the road. Peter ran after him, confused but committed to following his friend.

A short while later they entered a village and passed a synagogue where a group of men were visiting on the front steps. Jesus stopped and eying a short, stocky man said, "Come, follow me."

The man spat at Jesus and yelled, "You are the last man in the world that I would want to follow! You heretic, you blasphemer!" And he began picking up rocks and throwing them at Jesus. At this, the man's companions joined him in pelting Jesus and Peter.

Jesus, running as fast as he could with the rocks whistling by him, gave Peter a big grin, saying, "I like that man!"

Panting, Peter moaned, "Rabbi, I'm confused. I don't get it. You were so rude to that 'good' man back there. He only wanted time to think over your invitation. Now you invite this man, and he abuses you, calls you names and throws rocks at you. How can you be fond of such a person?"

"Ah, good friend Peter, you don't understand human nature. The young man who needed time to think was afraid of making a mistake. He's wishie-washie, undecided about *all* of life. The man who spat at me, on the other hand—ah, there's real passion! Peter, the flip side of great love is great hate! For the man who spat at me, who hates me, it takes only a split second, a lightning experience, to somersault great hate into great love. By the way, do you know his name?"

"I'm not sure," answered Peter. "I think he is called Saul."

I remained after everyone had left Mass. I wasn't praying so much as prayerfully reflecting, which I guess is also prayer. I was considering the words of Jesus in that Lost Gospel of Mark, the part about making a mistake. Those words sprang from Father Fiasco's mouth like flaming arrows aimed directly at me. Have I not been plagued by the fear that I made a mistake in taking the job of being janitor and cook for Mama Mahatma? If there's one thing I've always feared, it's making mistakes. That thought only surfaced my grade school memories of shame, being the butt of my classmates' laughter when I gave the wrong answer to a teacher's question. I, who hated to make a mistake – and rarely admitted to anyone that I had – looked at the icon of the crucified Christ in that silly clown suit. The icon's impact was greater than ever before.

By the time I came to the back of the chapel, Father Fiasco had already left for work. I walked out of the Lone Star Cathedral feeling very alone – and confused. As I made my way back to the house, a question circled around in the rafters of my mind: "Will I be successful in this quest only if I become a mistake? But who loves a looser?" I was shrouded by the dark power of the fear of failure. No one had actually said it to me, but one of the most powerful lessons of life I ever learned was, "If you want to be loved, don't make mistakes!" Now, however, a flood of questions poured in from the opposite direction: "Ah, but what's a mistake? Isn't living only half-alive a mistake? Isn't going through life half-blind and half-deaf to life's great gifts a mistake? So what if people think I'm the world's greatest success if in the process I miss the whole purpose of life itself?"

That day my cleaning duties included washing windows. While getting a bucket and some clean rags from the pantry, I ran into Mama Mahatma.

"Last night, it was another trip on the mystical roller coaster up in the attic. I could use some of your wisdom."

"Your Magic Lantern truly *is* magical! What's your question, George? If I don't have an answer, I'll trade questions with you. Deal?"

I told her about my "tree rides" at the Magic Lantern's Lakeside Amusement Park, concluding with the Toddler Tree's question about the Kingdom. Then I told her about my fearful dream of the serpent and the equally fearful reflections I had about failure. I related my confusion about the great cost of accepting Jesus' invitation to the Kingdom. Mama listened attentively and lovingly. While none of my inner questions were answered, the quality of Mama's compassionate presence lifted the burden of their weight from my soul. Then I asked her, "When Jesus spoke about the Kingdom, what do you think he meant?"

"George, that can be a scriptural, philosophical or metaphysical question, in which case you should ask Father Fiasco. One thing I am quite certain about is that Jesus didn't mean it as a political reality, like a lot of folks would love it to be – at least not in the narrow sense of 'political.' Historically, there have been plenty of attempts to make religion a ventriloquist and the State a dummy, in perfect accord with the 'Kingdom's' views and doctrines. Of course religion has also too often been a puppet for the State. I have a hunch that when Jesus spoke about the Kingdom he was talking about relationships. It seems to me that Jesus taught about how to cultivate a holy relationship with God, with oneself and with others – not to forget a *right* relationship with the earth and creation." Then, beaming her famous smile, Mama concluded, "Speaking of creation, I've got some weeding to do in my flower garden. I hope that gives you a start for a fresh look at the Kingdom."

"Yes, thanks, Mama. I appreciate your taking time to visit. I'm on my way upstairs. See you later."

I was on the second floor, in Bernadone's room, washing the inside of his east window, thinking about Mama's insight into the meaning of the Kingdom. I found the notion of it having to do with relationships worth expanding. My musings were suddenly interrupted by the sound of Dio's Mercedes roaring up the driveway. Looking down, I saw Fatima sitting in the middle of the driveway like it was her private property, as cats have a way of doing. I gasped with horror as Dio seemed to intentionally steer his car toward her. Fatima instinctively sprung off the drive onto the lawn. Dio instantly changed direction like a radar missile. As his car wheels swerved onto the lawn, Fatima shrieked in pain. She was crushed to death! Dio routinely parked his car on the driveway, emerging with a wicked smile on his face. Ruthlessly, he picked her up by the tail and threw her crushed body into the bushes.

He never looked up as he walked across the driveway and

so did not see me in the upstairs window. I slowly sank to the floor, weak from the sight of such a sadistic killing, unable to have prevented it. At the same time, I felt a rage, like the searing flame of a blowtorch blazing in my heart. Why would Dio want to kill Fatima in such a violent way? Leaning back against the wall, I realized that I hated Dio more than I had hated anyone in a long time – perhaps ever.

I was caught in a double bind, for at the same time I hated the fury that flared inside of me, that intense hate for another person. I felt paralyzed, powerless to escape the vice grip on my heart. I tried to practice my deep breathing to diffuse my anger so I could think and act clearly. At that moment, however, I heard Dio's voice from Maria's room across the hall.

"You dumb bitch. What do you mean, you're 'going to resign?' None of my girls ever quits! I dump 'em after they're worn out or too old. You're no different from any of the others. I knew you were falling in love with that jerk. Falling in love is poison in your profession, Miss Maria. You know that, don't you? You must know too that no decent man would want you as his wife after all those other men have used you. You must be crazy, woman! As much as that jerk's into clean living and all that crap, how could he want *you* for a wife?"

I couldn't hear Maria's reply, but soon there was the sound of a slap, followed by her sobbing. Whatever peace I had rescued by my deep breathing was swept out to sea in another tidal wave of anger. Part of me wanted to rush in and protect Maria from the abuse. Not only would that have been in the pattern of my patron saint, George, the dragon slayer and rescuer of damsels in distress, it's also the kind of dynamic action I envision Jon would have taken. But in that split second of response time, my paralysis prevented such heroics. I just couldn't respond out of the anger and hate that was gripping me.

Above Maria's sobbing came Dio's voice again, "If you ever talk about 'resigning' again – or try something crazy like that – you'll regret it as long as you live. Do you understand that? Remember, no one ever leaves me without paying the price, got that?" Maria cried out loudly in pain again, the door slammed and I heard Dio going down the back stairs. I stood up and watched from the window as he got into his car and drove off down the driveway.

Returning to my room, I could hear Maria crying next door. Then she turned on her tape player to cover her sobbing. All I could hear was the beautiful **Requiem** of Mozart. I wanted to console her but was still in inner turmoil myself. And I felt she would be ashamed if she knew that I had heard what happened. So I decided to reverence Maria's privacy and do the best I could at comforting her from a distance. As I went downstairs to the kitchen, I also mourned Fatima's death. My heart was pounding as I attempted to occupy myself with the task of cleaning the kitchen. Hard as I tried, I couldn't be mindful of anything but the roaring forest fire of my anger.

"George," came a voice that shattered my preoccupation. I jumped, for I hadn't heard Mama Mahatma come into the kitchen. "What are we having for dinner today?"

I wanted to scream at her that Dio had killed her cat, but I couldn't. For some reason, I was afraid to confront the issue. Perhaps I couldn't speak the words that would cause her such pain. Perhaps I was still too overcome by my own response to the incident. All I could get out was, "I'm...ah...not sure yet. I . . . ."

"Is something wrong, George? You look distressed."

"You have good eyes, Mama Mahatma. No, I'm just preoccupied with some stuff I need to work through. It'll pass, I'm sure. Thanks for asking."

"I came to look for a little tuna for Fatima. I know that it's not healthy for her, but I like to give her a little treat now and then."

"There's a half-empty can in the refrigerator. Let me get it for you." She bent over and placed a couple of spoonfuls from the can I had handed to her into Fatima's dish. Just then Inspector Bernadone came in through the back door.

"Hello, Inspector," she said, rising from the cat's dish, "you're home early today. By the way, did you see Fatima outside anywhere? I've got a little treat for her."

Bernadone leaned over to the kitchen window and looked out toward the carriage house. "No, I don't see her. How about you, George. Have you seen her?" His voice had a professional edge to it that left me uneasy. To my chagrin, I found myself lying.

"No, no, I haven't seen her either. Maybe she's out roaming the neighborhood."

"Well, if you hear her at the door, let her in and surprise her with her treat. See you two at dinner tonight." Mama began to leave the kitchen. Pausing at the door, she turned and smiled. "Oh, George, please set an extra place at dinner tonight. Dio called me and said that he would be joining us. Isn't that nice?"

I nodded my head and forced a smile. Bernadone poured himself a glass of water and sat down in a chair at the kitchen table. He was looking at me with x-ray eyes. I felt uneasy as he studied my face. "Sure you haven't seen Fatima? Your denial was rather strong. Your eyes betrayed you, George."

"I saw her earlier this afternoon," I said as I flipped through a cookbook. "Tonight I'm thinking about fixing . . . ."

"How was Fatima killed?"

"Killed?"

"Yes, and I believe you know how it happened. When I walked up the driveway, I saw a small patch of blood in the yard and followed its trail to the bushes. And there she was! Why did you lie to Mama Mahatma?"

"You're right, Inspector. I'm not sure why I couldn't tell her. I couldn't bear to see her hurt, but that's not all of it. I hated to lie. Damn it, I'm becoming full of things I hate. Bernadone, I'm so angry I can hardly control myself. Earlier today, I was cleaning the windows in your room when I saw Dio, the son-of-a-bitch, intentionally run Fatima down with his car and then throw her body in the bushes. The stupid thing is that I'm angry that I'm so angry, even if it is justified anger."

I sat down at the kitchen table with the Inspector and told him all of what happened to Fatima and Maria.

"He's a sick man, George. He gets pleasure from inflicting pain on others, a perverted satisfaction in exercising power over others. His sadistic behavior is a way of gaining self-esteem. Since Fatima's body was hidden in the bushes," Bernadone's eyes watered and he sighed a deep breath before he continued, "I guessed that her death wasn't accidental. Also, since there were bloody tire prints on the driveway, it was clear that she had been run over. Having known him for years, Dio was my prime suspect. I can understand your anger, but it makes you as much a victim of his power as Maria or Fatima."

"What can I do with it? I've tried to banish it from my mind, but it only blazes up more fiercely."

"Own it, George! First of all, acknowledge it to yourself. Don't try to pretend that you're not angry. At the same time, beware. Anger is a poisonous emotion that makes both body and soul sick. Anger is a thief that robs us of the power to act. It leaves us only with reactions. In my profession, I've had to learn how to live with anger. More than anger, I've known great rage at brutal killings, child abuse and some of the most vicious forms of human behavior. I've found that being angry about things which we lack the power to change only makes us frustrated and fuels more anger in our lives. It reappears in strange ways over and over again in different situations. Some people have been able to redirect angry energy into something positive, people like prophets and reformers. Their anger became a secret power-source for working long and hard to change society. But you and I aren't likely to change Dio, so our anger has to be resolved. The very desire for that to happen is a powerful catalyst for change. We need to be patient, however. It takes time."

"Damn it, Inspector, more than ever I feel that I should have found some quiet monastery in which to pursue my spirituality instead of coming to work at this madhouse."

"George, this 'madhouse' is a basic training camp, a prime place to encounter the demons of rage within you. If you want to grow spiritually, you must learn how to live without anger. Giving up being angry is part of basic poverty. What makes you angry is not something external, but the kind of thoughts that say, 'Dio should be kind and loving' or 'Everyone should be honest' or 'Everyone should treat me with respect.' That's not reality. Life is a mixed bag, friend, and the purpose of growing up spiritually is to embrace reality.

"But look at the clock. I think you need to get dinner ready. We can talk about this later tonight. Let's not say anything about Fatima for now. I also won't mention anything about Maria just yet."

CHAPTER 7

Dinner that night was pure purgatory. My anger for Dio boiled inside my heart. As Bernadone had advised, I tried to embrace it as it was and just be present to the company at the table. Dio was obnoxiously pleasant. If you didn't know what had happened that afternoon, you would have thought he was the essence of charm. He praised Maria, complimented Mama Mahatma and even treated Gloria with respect. After dinner, Bernadone, Father Fiasco and I did the dishes. Father Fiasco excused himself when we were finished, saying that he had some work to do preparing for tomorrow's big feast of the Purification. I asked him, "I thought that feast came at the beginning of February?"

"In the traditional liturgical year it does, but at the Lone Star Cathedral we celebrate it at the end of summer. Of course, both of you are invited, if you wish to come to the feast."

After Father Fiasco had left, we brewed up a short pot of coffee and took our cups into the living room to visit.

"How do you feel now, George?"

"I'm still upset, but I'm trying to resolve my anger as you suggested. I can see that you're right — I mean, about not setting up an ideal world inside my head that's in conflict with the real world. Tonight at supper, I saw the other side of Dio, but I must confess that I thought it was all a show."

"George, no one is completely evil. Some of what you saw was the real Dio. Like you and me, regardless of how perverted he may be, he longs for acceptance from others."

After a couple of moments of silent reflection, I said, "I have to say, Inspector, that seeing more of the whole picture does help to diffuse the anger a bit. And Dio did give me that hourglass for my meditation times. Speaking of which, I know that you meditate, Bernadone. I have a question for you. Lately, my times of sitting seem to be going faster than before. Is that a sign that I'm making progress?"

"Could be. I'm no guru, but I guess if you're not fighting distractions and can be absorbed like a sponge in what you're doing, be it meditation or anything else, time seems to disappear at the speed of light. You're using Dio's hourglass?"

"Yes. I know this may sound silly, but can an hourglass, like a watch, gain time?"

"None that I've heard of, but then again there are more mysteries in life than you or I know about. Maybe there are hourglasses whose sands do run fast. Perhaps it can be caused by the weather!"

"Thanks, I'll have to time it with my clock.

"I just thought of another question. I know you and Mama Mahatma love animals. Does she keep rabbits as pets?"

"No, to my knowledge her only pet is—was, that is—Fatima. Why do you ask?"

"One night, near midnight, I heard the sound of a truck driving up to the house. I got up and saw Mama from my bedroom window. She got two wire cages with a rabbit in each one from a man in the old farmer's pickup truck. Then two nights ago when I was awakened by a nightmare, I witnessed the same exchange beneath my window. She handed the farmer two empty cages, and he gave her back two cages with large rabbits inside. But I've never seen rabbits anywhere around the house."

"That's an interesting observation, George. I've never known Mama Mahatma to keep rabbits as pets. If you're curious, you might want to ask her about it."

"I don't know. She very graciously never asks me any personal questions. I want to respect her and do the same. Yet these rabbits have been among the many unanswered questions that plague me about this place."

At that moment we could hear quite a commotion from the main staircase behind the living room. Mike and Gloria were having a heated argument over some issue. After a series of angry words, Mike shouted, "Go to hell!" That was followed by the sound of the front door being slammed.

"Sounds like a little domestic trouble, eh?" Bernadone said with a smile. "Care for another cup of coffee?"

"No, thanks. I think it's time for me to retire. This has been a long day, and I'm ready to turn in."

"That's a good idea," the Inspector said as he stood up. "I'm tired as well, and if we're going to attend Fiasco's Fiesta at sunrise, we should get some sleep. I think I'll stop by Mama Mahatma's room and tell her about Fatima. I won't mention what you saw from the window. Knowing her as I do, she will mourn the loss of her beloved cat but will not pursue the question of who killed her. My guess is that she'll have no trouble knowing who's responsible. Mama has perfected her sixth sense – one that I wish I possessed to the same degree.

"I'll also ask Mama Mahatma to try to talk some sense into Maria. I'm concerned about Maria's well-being, but she would need to press charges for an official police response. At this point, I don't even think Maria would want intervention from her friends. The best you and I can do for now is keep our eyes open and pray."

We said good night and parted. I was glad that Bernadone – and not I – had the unpleasant task of telling Mama about the death of her beloved Fatima.

The next morning before my alarm awakened me, an explosion of fireworks did! Raising my head from the pillow, I could see skyrockets exploding in brilliant showers of stars over the roof of the Lone Star Cathedral. As I was shaving, I heard strings of firecrackers exploding to the rhythm of a mariachi band. I momentarily wondered what the neighbors would be thinking but decided that they probably long ago had given up trying to figure out what went on at Father Fiasco's cathedral or Mama Mahatma's boarding house. As I started down the back steps, I was joined by Bernadone, who said, "Sounds like Father Fiasco is having a real fiesta."

"Sure does. I bet it'll be a feast day to remember."

At the bottom of the stairs we met a beaming Mama Mahatma dressed in a regal black dress. "Good morning to both of you. I see we're all headed for the celebration. A beautiful morning for a festival."

As the three of us walked out the back door of the house, I marveled at how Mama was able to move into the joyfulness of the feast even though just last night she had learned of Fatima's death. We made our way into a crowd of people enjoying the band music and an occasional skyrocket soaring into the early morning sky. There was still a sprinkling of real stars, including the planet Venus, the morning star, which was positioned right next to the gold star on the roof of the carriage house. It was as if the heavens also had decided to be part of the fiesta. The serenity of the stars also reflected Mama's serene countenance.

An old Asian man wearing a long, red coat struck a giant brass gong, a resounding signal for the band to stop playing. Father Fiasco, wearing lavish gold vestments, appeared at the door of the carriage house. In an equally resounding and joyful voice, he announced to the crowd gathered in front of his little chapel, "Welcome one and all, friends and enemies, strangers and neighbors, believers and unbelievers, orthodox and heretics, to the glorious feast of the Purification of the Holy Mother of God. Let us pray."

A silence that was full of the inner activity of all present fused the group together as one. After a period of a few minutes, Father Fiasco intoned, *"Procedamus in pace...*let us process in peace." The Asian man once again sounded his great brass gong, and the band struck up a brisk Latin hymn. Two by two, the crowd processed into the Lone Star Cathedral to the vibrant song of the band.

The chapel was filled with large sprays of flowers in a variety of colors. I wondered if the flowers might have come from some funeral home. The arrangements looked just like the kind you see at wakes and funerals. As if she had read my mind, Mama Mahatma leaned over and whispered in my ear, "Father Fiasco has friends who are morticians. They usually see to it that he has lots of flowers for his big feast day celebrations."

The liturgy was more ornate than usual. Not just puffs but billowing clouds of incense tumbled upward into the chapel rafters. Every hanging votive light was lit, making them appear like flickering stars lost in the clouds. The piano, drums and the mariachi band provided music for the hymns, which the people sang as lustily as if they were at a football rally. The first scriptural reading in the Mass was done by Maria! She was radiant in her white dress accented by a red tropical flower in her black hair. When she finished her reading and sat down, I was surprised to see Jon in the chair next to her.

The Asian man in the brilliant red coat once again struck his large brass gong, and all stood as Father Fiasco processed to the trunk pulpit to read the day's Gospel.

"God be with you!"

"God *is* with us!"

"Sister and brother pilgrims, open your minds and hearts."

"They are open and ready."

"A reading from the Lost Gospel of Luke, the missing text between verses 21 and 22."

"Thanks be to God that the lost has been found."

> Now, as the thirty-third day after the circumcision drew near, Joseph and Mary discussed her need to be purified after the birth of their son, Yeshua. Joseph objected, "I don't see any need for such a ceremony. You're not impure, Mary, just because you gave birth to our son. I don't look upon you as impure or dirty, and I don't believe God does either. Why should we make that long, hard journey up to the Temple in Jerusalem?"
>
> Mary, who was rocking their infant son in her arms, answered, "Because, Joseph, it's the law of Moses! God's law states clearly that for the past forty days I have been impure. I cannot engage in public worship until we perform the ritual purification. If we fail to fulfill this ancient custom of our people, think of the outcry from our relatives and neighbors. And, Joseph, what would our parents say if we didn't present our first-born son to God in the Temple?"
>
> "I know, Mary," said Joseph, "but it's like what the prophets say: the priests of the Temple are a fat, lazy and careless lot, their ceremonies are rushed and performed badly. All they're really concerned about are the offerings! I say we don't go. We can have our own little ceremony of presenting Yeshua to God right here in our home. Or we could go to some beautiful mountain top. Who needs all that gold and silver of the Temple to pray or worship God?"
>
> "I know you're angry, Joseph, and I agree with you.

Still, there's tradition! Yet, while neither you nor I want to hurt our parents, we also must respect the voices of our hearts. Why don't we pray and ask God to show us what to do?"

So Joseph the village carpenter and Mary his wife prayed silently. After an hour or so, the silence of their tiny Palestinian home was broken. A mysterious voice spoke, "Go up to the Temple, but . . . ." The voice faded away, lost in the hot afternoon wind.

As the fortieth day drew closer, Joseph pondered what was left unsaid in the message. What was the condition he was to keep in mind? When the day arrived for their departure to Jerusalem, he saddled their small donkey with the provisions necessary for the journey, along with a small cage with two spotless white pigeons. As he packed, he prayed in his heart that God would finish that sentence. After he had lovingly placed Mary and their infant son on the donkey, Joseph returned one more time to the house and stood still, listening. In the silence of the empty house, as softly as a whisper, came the Voice: "Joseph, go up to the Temple, but...remember that you also are a temple!"

"This is the Lost Gospel of Luke."

"Thanks be to God and to those who found it."

"Brothers and sisters, let us stand ready for the homily."

"We are standing!"

"Friends, this morning we celebrate the fiesta of Mary's purification from the need to be purified. Like all truly great religious feasts, this is a celebration of freedom. This ritual, like all religious rituals, hides more than it reveals. In the Vedic scriptures of India are the words, 'Unveil it, O God of Light, that I who love the true may see.' If we truly seek the face of God and God's Way, we will find it. Regardless of how imperfect the religious ritual, how lacking the church, temple, mosque or its clergy might be, it can lead us as we search for the Light. Let us not be dumb sheep following blindly in this holy way or that. Let us choose the way of Joseph and Mary in this morning's Gospel reading. Then, any religious ritual — or the lack of one–can be a meeting place, a rendezvous between you and the Divine Mystery.

"This ancient feast also calls each of us to another kind of purification. Today, may we be eager to purify our hearts, made unclean by our less than noble motives, our selfish desires, our angry thoughts and our need to be always right–to have *our* way. Remember that each one of you is a temple. Remember that collectively we are the Temple of the Spirit of God. When you have cleansed your heart, when your criticism and judgment of others is removed, when you have given up all forms of manipulative power over others, then you will overflow with love for others. And when you have thus become Light, you will learn how to embrace both the darkness and light and will have found peace."

"Thanks be God, *Deo gratias, muchas gracias,*" thundered the gathering in chapel. As Father Fiasco moved away from the steamer-trunk pulpit, we all sat down for the procession of gifts to the altar. I leaned over to Bernadone and whispered, "Why does he have us stand up instead of sit down for the sermon?"

"He told me once that if you tell people something when they are standing they are 45% more likely to act on what you say. Furthermore, studies show that difficult decisions can be made 20% faster when standing rather than sitting. It has something to do with an increased flow of blood stimulating the brain."

"Standing also helps," whispered Mama Mahatma playfully in my other ear, "to keep the sermons short!"

As the liturgy of the Purification continued, it occurred to me that even though this feast was being celebrated on a date other than its traditional time, it was the perfect day for it in my life. I prayed that I would be purified of my anger toward Dio and the other violence in my heart that I found so difficult to own.

After the Communion of the Mass–even Jon received Holy Communion–there was a purification ritual. One by one, everybody processed up toward the altar to a large washtub held by two women. Upon reaching the front, everyone in turn plunged their hands into the water, as the women prayed, "Be purified of all that eclipses the Light in your heart." After removing their hands from the tub and shaking off the excess water, people moved to their left or right. Standing at each of the far sides of the altar was a man holding an electric hair dryer! I hadn't heard the sound of the hair dryers until I got to the front. They had been drowned out by the band loudly playing the old Beatles' song, "Here Comes the Sun." The sun had fully crested the horizon as I stepped forward to one of the men with a hair dryer. As I extended my arms, he passed the dryer over my wet hands, praying, "May the hot Wind of the Spirit of God send you forth."

The service having concluded, I followed the others outside to the front of the carriage house. There Father Fiasco, wearing a chef's hat and a large white apron, was gleefully serving steaming-hot pancakes to the crowd.

"Hi George! Happy feast day! I'm delighted that you came. I know it was an early Mass, but all these people need to get to work, and so we had to begin our celebration before dawn."

"No one here seemed to mind getting up before the sun, Father. This is the largest crowd I've seen at your...ah...cathedral." I thanked him for my plate of pancakes and, grabbing a cup of coffee, walked over and sat on the lawn next to Bernadone.

"I missed Mama Mahatma after Holy Communion. Did she leave?"

"Yes, look behind you. See, over there at the far side of her garden. She's burying poor Fatima."

I turned and saw Mama at the rear of her garden, near the fence, kneeling by a small mound of dirt she had just patted down, her head bowed. The morning sunlight reflected off her white hair, causing it to glisten like dew-touched diamonds. I sensed an air of acceptance and forgiveness about Mama's momentary mourning over Fatima that gave a spiritual quality to that radiance.

I was surprised at the condition of my heart. Whatever happened at the liturgy had made it easier for me to accept Fatima's death. I felt a release from the anger that had washed over me like tidal waves on the previous day. I was surprised to find that now I actually felt sorry for Dio! Who but someone very sick could kill another living being without any remorse—and even take pleasure in such an act? I could even feel a little of the pain at the heart of that sickness.

The following days quickly passed in parade—too quickly, considering that I had been here now for over four months. Recent

108

thoughts of Martha and the kids enjoying their favorite summertime activities gave me cause to smile – and to feel a little homesick. While I was eager to return home to my family, I also felt there was much I had yet to accomplish! In spite of my intentions, time was slipping away from me as fast as the sands in my hourglass.

Speaking of hourglases, one morning I noticed the last white sands of my hourglass run out at the end of my thirty-minute meditation. I glanced over at my alarm clock which read 7:20, yet I had begun my meditation prayer at 7:00 sharp by the same clock. Strange, was something wrong with my clock or with my hourglass? I went downstairs, and on my way to the kitchen I stopped by the grandfather's clock in the hallway. It read 7:21. Apparently my hourglass was off by ten minutes! I walked into the small dinette off the kitchen where Bernadone was reading the morning newspaper and enjoying a cup of coffee.

"Good morning, Inspector. I have a question for you. You know that hourglass that Dio gave me for my meditation? Remember, I told you I thought it was either running fast or I was becoming an expert at meditation? Well, I checked it this morning, and it's off by ten minutes! What do you make of that, Inspector?"

"Curious, George, very curious. As you know, the curious and mysterious are the bread and butter of my life. Let's go up to your room and take a look at it. Bring your morning cup of coffee along with you."

Entering my room, Bernadone stood still and carefully looked around. After a moment, he walked over to the table, picked up the hourglass and examined it. He unscrewed the round brass plate that covered the top of the hourglass, carefully removing it. Then he stuck his finger inside the hourglass into the sand. Removing his finger, he licked it.

"Just as I thought: cocaine! I could arrest you, George, for possession of an illegal narcotic."

"You're joking!"

"About arresting you, of course – but not about this white substance. It's not sand, it's cocaine."

I sat down on the bed, shaking my head. "Cocaine?"

"Yes, ingenious, absolutely ingenious on Dio's part. What better way to keep his stash hidden right here in the house. No fear of ever being searched by me, yet available whenever he wanted to do a line. I've noticed that several nights at dinner he ate very little and seemed to be high on something. I should have guessed that, before coming to the table, he had come up here and snorted. Cocaine not only gives a high, it's also an appetite suppressant."

"But wasn't it risky, I mean coming in and out of my room which is right across from yours?"

Bernadone walked over to the wall and carefully studied the frame of the door between Maria's room and mine. He ran his finger along the cracked old paint and then smiled at me. "This door has been used recently, George. Notice the tiny broken bits of paint around the edge of the doorframe. This is the way he entered and left your room without being noticed. It was perfect for him. You were busy with supper, and the rest of us were having our drinks in the living room. Slick as glass, he could come in the back door, come up here, do a line or two and then join us downstairs as if nothing had happened."

"I never said anything about it, Inspector, but I've had a feeling that someone has been in my room recently. It's just been small things, like a book moved slightly from where I thought I had placed it on my desk. Once I could have sworn that someone had laid down on my bed the way the bed spread was indented. I dismissed those things as curious but not worth questioning. You may laugh at this, but I even wondered if Lucien had been up here in my room when I was up in my attic hermitage. I never mentioned anything, but now it all makes sense."

"Perhaps, George. We can't rule out the possibility that Lucien has visited your room. We don't know for sure that Dio has. We can be quite certain that this cocaine is Dio's. Not certain enough to arrest him. Again, he's quite masterful at covering his tracks, and there is no solid evidence. After all, George, it is your room! But enough home mysteries for now. I have to get down to the office."

"I wish I had your eyes, Bernadone. I seem to miss so much that's right there in front of me."

Bernadone began to empty the contents of his pockets onto the top of my table. "George, I'll share a trick of the trade with you. Look at these things....OK, now close your eyes and tell me what you saw on the table."

"I saw a billfold, a handkerchief, some money and...ah...a pocket knife."

"Good, George. Now let's test your memory for detail. What color was the billfold? Can you describe its shape? Were there initials on the handkerchief? You say you saw money: what kind of coins – dimes, quarters, pennies?"

"I'm sorry, but I don't remember the particulars."

"OK, open your eyes again. Surprising, isn't it, what you didn't see? Most of us never really see. Instead, we only look at things. If you want to learn how to be a true observer of life, then learn the secret of seeing. You can practice paying attention anywhere at any time. It's an art that not only has sharpened my skills as a detective but also has been a significant spiritual exercise in mindfulness."

"Sounds exciting! Can you suggest how to go about it?"

"Sure. As I said, you can practice anywhere. Whenever you have some time to spare, look around the room you're in carefully. Close your eyes and recount to yourself everything you saw. Then open your eyes and see what you failed to notice. Close your eyes again and repeat what you saw. You can do the same exercise with people. Train yourself to describe the details of someone's face, eyes, hair, body type and clothing."

"I'll begin to experiment today. I can see that the possibilities for different ways to practice are almost unlimited. I would also think, Inspector, that such exercises would do wonders for the memory."

"That's true. I've found that my memory has become much better because of my practice of observation. Well, do some experiments, George, and see for yourself. As I said, I have to get to the office. You know, the Woodsdale Killer has struck again. I'm sorry to say that one more prostitute has been murdered, and we still lack a real suspect. George, I hope the rest of your day goes better than your morning. See you tonight at dinner."

Bernadone left me alone in my room, and while I was excited about the possibilities of my new practice of paying attention, I still had to deal with my feelings of violation. Nothing had been stolen from my room, but the very idea that someone, whether Dio or Lucien, had used my room was worse than having some possession robbed. There's something intimate about one's living quarters. An invasion of it by an uninvited stranger feels like a kind of rape. I didn't like the feeling any more than I liked the resentment boiling up in me at Dio for making a fool of me with his hourglass gift. I felt somehow "unclean" by the violation of my personal space.

I spent part of my day cleaning and then tried to read in the afternoon. I was tempted to go up in the attic but chose not to. I couldn't decide what to do with the hourglass. Maybe I should have sent it along with Bernadone so he could check it for fingerprints. I thought about giving it back to Dio just to let him know that I knew. At least I wouldn't feel like such a fool. Then I reflected on the icon of Christ in Fiasco's church, the one of the crucified figure in the clown's suit. It occurred to me that all this was part of my purification – I mean, letting go of my need to be thought of as bright and clever. All I could think at the moment was, "Embrace it, George, and learn to laugh at yourself. You'll be freer because of it." As I let go of the desire for self-justification and being thought highly of, I did feel freer.

That night at dinner, after we had finished the meal and were visiting over our coffee, Maria asked if she could tell a story. She had heard about the death of Fatima from Mama and perhaps felt a need to share with the rest of us something that might help put her relationship with Dio in perspective. I poured a second cup of coffee around the table, and she began.

> Once upon a time, in an age when all things were possible, a child named Christine was given a wonderful birthday gift, a magnificent three-story mansion. It was not a playhouse, mind you, but a real house! Much of Christine's childhood was spent joyfully in the many rooms of the great house.
>
> As the years passed and Christine grew into a young adult, she continued to enjoy the gift of the magnificent mansion. Then one fateful day, the doorbell rang. When Christine opened the door, she saw a stranger with several large suitcases. "Hi! I'm your Cousin Harry. I don't have a home; could I move in with you?"
>
> Since Cousin Harry looked like a pleasant person, Christine said, "Sure, I would enjoy sharing my home with you."

So Cousin Harry moved into a couple of rooms on the ground floor. Christine, however, was horrified when he unpacked. His suitcases were filled with pornographic magazines, XX-rated videos and erotic posters. Christine was ashamed to have such unsavory material in her house. She was also worried about what her neighbors would think if they knew that there were such things in her lovely house. Nevertheless, too embarrassed to expose the situation, Christine simply moved to the second and third floors of her home.

Now a year later, two other distant cousins, Wilma and Walter, showed up at the front door and asked if they could move in. They were such happy looking people and Christine had such a large house, so she agreed to let them move in on the second floor. However, Cousins Wilma and Walter proved to be most unhappy housemates. They had very set ideas about many things and didn't at all like change. They were also bible-carrying church folk who never tired of trying to convert Christine to their beliefs. Christine found Cousins Wilma and Walter to be overbearing and boorish. So she moved to the third floor and tried to avoid both them and Cousin Harry.

Six months after Walter and Wilma arrived, another cousin showed up at the front door. Her name was Rosie, and she had once worked in a traveling circus. Because Cousin Rosie was dressed flamboyantly and had a carefree spirit, Christine thought she would be fun to live with. So she invited Rosie to live with her on the third floor. Cousin Rosie, unfortunately, was very disorganized. Her rooms looked as if a whirlwind had swept through them. Wherever she went, she left a trail of trash behind her. She also smoked cigarettes constantly. When Christine hinted several times about the bad odors in the house, Rosie flew into a rage. Moreover, she was often prone to such violent outbursts.

Because of Cousin Harry's obsession with lurid sex,

Wilma and Walter's preachiness and the pollution of Rosie's cigarettes and her messy rooms, poor Christine was forced to move to the attic to find some peace. She wished that they had never come to live with her, but they *were* relatives. What else could she do but allow them, however offensive they were, to share her home?

Late one afternoon the doorbell rang again. Christine hated to open her door, but she did. Standing at her front steps was a tall, stately stranger with several suitcases. "Good afternoon, Cousin! I'm your famous Cousin Frederick. Alas, while I have been very gifted by God with numerous talents and intellectual abilities, I'm presently without a proper domicile. Because of the worldwide economic crisis and a temporary cash flow problem, I am being subsidized at the moment by the government, a kind of scholar's grant-in-aid, you might say. I would be honored to be invited to reside in your grand home. Is that a possibility, Cousin?"

Now, while poor Christine wanted in the worst way to say **no**, she just couldn't. After all, he was her cousin. So Frederick moved in and shared space with Rosie on the third floor.

Cousin Frederick's luggage, books and belongings filled several rooms. Cousin Frederick also filled every conversation with stories of his life. He had authoritarian views on everything from politics to plumbing. He and Cousins Wilma and Walter frequently argued about anything and everything, while Cousin Harry interjected frequent four-letter words and lewd comments, usually without lifting his head from one of his sex magazines. Rosie, to round it out, smoked incessantly and would often throw uncontrollable fits of anger.

During all of this, Christine increasingly became a recluse. She isolated herself in the tiny rooms of the attic. She was very angry at her relatives who had forced her to be in exile inside her own home. Finally she decided to do something about it.

She first joined an anti-pornography campaign and donated large sums of money, as well as time, to ridding her city of X-rated movie houses and "adult" bookstores. She even picketed some motion picture theaters that were showing risque films. Secretly she hoped that somehow this would make Cousin Harry move away. But while some stricter laws were passed and a few of the porno shops did close, Cousin Harry remained a fixture in Christine's home.

Christine was known to be moderately religious, but that was before Cousins Wilma and Walter had come to live with her. Now she rarely went to church, and more often than not she found herself at odds with stands taken by Church leaders on the issues of the day. She soon became blatantly anti-religious. Yet despite this position, her two cousins only redoubled their conversion tactics.

Christine also joined the Greenpeace Movement and worked zealously for anti-pollution. She was instrumental in having stringent anti-smoking ordinances passed but failed in her attempt to work for a law that would prohibit smoking in private residential homes. However, even with those efforts and with large **No Littering** signs in all the hallways of her home, Cousin Rosie didn't move.

Next, Christine joined a radical-right political movement. She worked diligently for the candidacy of a Conservative candidate for mayor who promised to do away with all welfare programs. She hoped that if her candidate were elected Cousin Frederick would move to another city where there was still welfare. However, even if the Conservative had been elected, Christine's vain cousin was immovable!

Poor Christine! Her every effort had met with defeat, and she found the idea of living in the same house with her relatives to be repulsive. So she simply denied that they existed. She lived alone, cramped in the narrow space of the attic, almost never venturing out into the rest of her own majestic mansion. She was furious at what fate had sent to her doorstep but buried her anger deep inside. Thus Christine was always sad. So ends the tale of a wonderful gift that began as a delight but ended in disaster.

Having finished her story, Maria sat back in her chair as a discussion of her tale began around the table. We only had time for a few comments, like, "That's my story too!" when Dio appeared in the doorway. Having just listened to Maria's tale, I marveled at how Dio's timing couldn't have been better if he had planned it. "Party's over. Time for us working people to be on our way. Let's go, Maria, it's late. Let's go."

"She's not going tonight. She and I have a previous engagement, Dio!" said Jon standing up and walking toward him. Maria turned white and clutched the arms of her chair. The rest of us likewise felt the electricity of crisis swirling in the room. Jon now stood with his arms at his side, challenging Dio with his physical stance as well as his eyes.

"Careful, boy, don't interfere in this. You may be taller and bigger than I am, but you will regret any move you make," said Dio, his hand slipping into his coat pocket. Jon was poised like a jaguar ready to leap on its victim when Mama Mahatma stood up and walked toward the two men.

"I think it would be well this evening if both of you left us for awhile. I would like to visit privately with Maria. Whatever plans either of you have, you can rearrange them for another evening." Then, with one in each arm, Mama showed her amazing strength as she escorted Dio and Jon to the doorway of the dining room. Then she said, "Why don't each of you take a drive by yourself. Let the evening air cool you down."

Turning to the rest of us, she announced, "Dinner is over. Perhaps we should all go about our evening's activities. Maria, dear one, let's you and I have a visit in my room. Thank you, George, your dinner was most delicious."

At the sink in the kitchen Father Fiasco, the Inspector and I visited about the dramatic conclusion to dinner. I was ashamed to admit it, but I got a thrill out of watching Jon dominate Dio. I wasn't pleased with myself, but I had even hoped he would slug him. Bernadone suspected my feelings. "Violence only breeds violence, right Father?"

"Yes and no. It's an ancient dilemma. When is the use of force proper, not violence but a positive necessity? Or is non-violence – I mean complete non-violence – the only way to resolve evil? It's easy to embrace the way of peace in theory; quite another thing when you meet evil face to face. I've noticed that your police officers don't carry olive branches in their holsters. How can you be such a pacifist and a policeman at the same time?"

"How can you, my friend, be a prophet of freedom and still be a priest of the Church? I say that jokingly, Father, because I know the answer. I can believe in the way of peace and still be part of the police department for the same reason that you can believe in Jesus' doctrine that God is too big for any temple or church and still remain part of the Church. Are we not faithful rebels working from inside those two institutions, giving our lives to change them?"

Raising his dish towel over his face and slowly lowering it, Father Fiasco laughed and said, "Ah, you've unveiled me, you Italian Sherlock Holmes."

The three of us laughed together and, having finished the dishes, pots and pans, said good night. I didn't go to my room but instead went up to the attic. After all that had happened on this day, beginning with the pre-dawn fiesta, which seemed like ages ago, I decided I needed some time alone with my Magic Lantern.

As I climbed the attic stairs to the tick-tock beat of the grandfather's clock, I thought to myself, "Perhaps the Magic Lantern will provide a little direction in this mire of a day. At least I hope it will give some answers, since I don't need any more questions."

I entered the nursery, sat down and turned on the Magic Lantern. I reached deep into the paper sack containing the boxes of slides and found one that felt right. Turning off the ceiling light, I inserted a slide. I was surprised to see a picture of Big Ben. A second slide revealed a street scene and the third a cemetery. The sign over its gate read **London's Highgate Cemetery**. My hand paused before I changed slides as I asked myself out loud, "Someone famous is buried in Highgate, but who?"

The riddle intrigued me, but before I could change slides the image on the wall began moving. The experience changed from a three-dimensional to a four-dimensional kind of movie. Like my last Magic Lantern journey, I was in on the action. I was being taken down a lane past tombstones, the names on which were not familiar to me. Then I came to a large, impressive gravestone with the inscription, **Karl Marx 1818-1883.** Of course, it was Marx who was buried there.

From behind the large tombstone I heard two voices caught up in a lively discussion. Cautiously peeking around the large stone, I spied two men seated on the grass. One had a great, flowing gray beard and a bushy head of hair. The other was a dark Eastern Mediterranean with strikingly clear eyes. A wicker picnic basket lay next to the gray-bearded man, and the remains of a picnic dinner were scattered on the ground around them.

"Explain to me, Jesus," asked the older of the two, "your position on the hungry of the world. You spoke out boldly about feeding the poor, but when did you – I mean *you personally* – ever give a piece of bread to any of the starving masses?"

"Brother Karl," replied Jesus, "you became one of my disciples at the age of six when your parents converted from Judaism to Christianity. You've read the Gospel account of how I fed the five thousand in the wilderness. How can you say that I never gave bread to the poor?"

"Ah ha!" exclaimed Marx, "but were they poor or simply hungry? There's more than a philosophical difference between the hungry and the starving. I'll wager that on that morning before they set out to follow you into the wilderness every one of them had a good, hearty Jewish breakfast. Granted, Jesus, at the end of the day they were hungry, but were they the *poor*? Were they *starving*?"

"That's not the real point of what happened in the wilderness, Karl. The 'miracle' was that the few loaves and fishes spread out to the thousands. People began sharing all that they had with each other. Still, what difference does it make if they were rich or poor, they were hungry!" replied Jesus.

"Spoken like a true bourgeois clergyman," replied Marx. "The

118

difference is class struggle, freedom for the oppressed workers, the enslaved masses who are in chains."

"Yes, Karl," answered Jesus, "I'm aware of your efforts to lift the oppression of the poor, but I'm concerned about another kind of freedom, a greater freedom: *liberation*."

"What kind of hair-splitting logic is that?" returned Marx. "Besides, I've never heard one sermon on liberation from any of your priests! As I once said, 'Religion is the sigh of the oppressed...it is the spirit of unspiritual conditions...it is the opium of the people'! But as you know, Jesus, that last remark has been greatly misunderstood. People have forgotten that I said it in the early 1800's when opium was the major medical drug for relieving pain. I didn't mean that religion was a drug used by the ruling classes to keep the poor in a thoughtless stupor, content with their enslaved condition."

"I know, brother Karl, I also was misunderstood. I didn't say that *only* the poor would enter heaven but that *even* the poor would enter heaven. My call to a poverty of possessions and power was intended for men and women who wish to be free of what *really* enslaves a person."

"Very idealistic," replied Marx, "but what about the poor? Take those five thousand who followed you out into the wilderness — were they really looking for liberation? Weren't most of them after some small measure of relief from the pain of life? Or perhaps some were hoping to get lucky and maybe—just maybe—see a miracle or two.

"I was young when I said that religion was the opium of the people, and I meant it in a good sense. Later, however, I came to see that as long as the bourgeois capitalists controlled it, the Church would piously lend support to slavery, child labor, oppression of workers and countless other evils bred by greedy and exploitative masters.

"Decades later, my beloved disciple Lenin paraphrased my remark about religion to more accurately reflect how I later came to see it. He said . . . ."

At that, Marx reached into the picnic basket and pulled out a bottle of vodka, uncorked it and poured a glass for Jesus and himself. Then, raising his glass, he proposed a toast: "As Lenin said, 'Religion is a kind of spiritual vodka in which the slaves of capitalism drown their human shape – and their claim for any decent human life.' "

"I'll drink to the fact that religion often has limited the human spirit."

Both men drank their vodka and set their glasses down. Marx slowly ran his tongue along the edge of his mustache, licking away the tiny drops of vodka that glistened there.

"Religion," said Marx, "yours and all the others – with its teachings of self-denial – cripples decent human life and fosters ugly self-images." Marx paused and reached for a chicken wing.

"Karl, while I appreciate your insight, you, Lenin and the others never really understood my philosophy and my teachings. They were not intended to create a better world, some new society of perfect equality. I may be a romantic, but I'm a realistic romantic. Even if you and I were to remove all of today's social evils from the world, tomorrow humanity would invent new ones! No, my friend, I did not come to raise up the masses but to bring the *Great Liberation* to all people – even though I knew, sadly, that only a few would choose to embrace it.

"My disciples frequently confused the issue. They also became overly concerned about those who were physically poor. So I had to remind them. Do you remember when I said, 'The poor you will always have with you and you can be generous to them whenever you wish'?

"No, my greater concern was with the *real* hunger, the hunger, Karl, that afflicts rich and poor, the aching hunger that is like a knife in the belly to both bourgeois and proletariat. Brother Lenin, as you pointed out, said that 'religion is spiritual vodka.' What I say is that *true* religion is . . . ." At this point Jesus reached into the picnic basket and removed a bottle of wine. "True religion is like this bottle of German wine. I am sure you are familiar with it, Karl, being a good, if exiled, German. No doubt, when you were a student at the University of Berlin you opened many a bottle of this wine."

"*Liebfraumilch?*" asked Marx with large question marks in his eyes.

Jesus responded to Marx's surprised expression: "At my final Seder-Passover meal, Karl, like the ones your family celebrated before they were baptized, I knew that my disciples were hungry. The hunger that gnawed at them was the *real* hunger of the world. So I fed them.

"I gave bread to those hungry souls and said, 'This is my body. And what kind of bread did I give them? I gave them what my body – and your body, Karl – signify, the full expression of who we are.

"They were thirsty as well. So I gave them something to drink: 'This my blood,' my very essence. Then I passed them the cup of seder wine. Those gifts of food and drink were sacraments.

"You were a Christian, Karl. You know what sacraments are. That's what I wanted every gift to the poor to be, every act of charity. They should be sacraments in which those who give bread, or money, give the real gift: themselves!

"That was, and is, the *heart* of the worship of my community. It was my idea of how to feed the poor. For in the act of caring for those in need – rich or poor – my disciples would discover the equality and unity, the classless society that you, Karl, and so many others have sought. The secret of that fundamental unity is not to be found in violent revolution but inside this bottle of wine."

Uncorking the bottle of wine, Jesus added, "The secret's hidden in this wine's name. Brother Karl, would you translate the German?"

"*Liebfraumilch* means 'young mother's milk,' " said Marx, looking a bit confused.

"The liberation of the world," continued Jesus, "and each personal liberation happen only when we invest ourselves totally in every gift we give. A young mother feeds her hungry child with the milk of her very being. In the same way we need to give as much of ourselves as we can in acts of service to the poor, and the rich, giving freely to friends and strangers."

As the two men slowly sipped their wine, Jesus went on, "Karl, you once said, 'Uprising, like war, is an art.' I agree: to 'rise up' to the fullness of being human is an art. It is an art that we learn from our mothers. As we give away all that we have, a wondrous thing happens. We find that there is always *more* to give. When we give freely, we never run out of self. It's like there is an infinite amount of self to give away. Karl, it's truly divine; it's miraculous!"

Marx and Jesus sat in silence for a long time. Then Marx took the bottle of wine and poured some of its contents into both glasses. Raising his glass with an expression of tenderness in his large German eyes, he offered a toast: *"L'Chiam*, to life!"

As both men emptied their glasses, I had a feeling that they were drinking something more than wine.

The image on the wall faded, and I leaned back in my chair, full to overflowing with the Magic Lantern's images – if not with wine. The message of revolution and liberation contained in the images that had miraculously appeared on that wall added more than just a new wrinkle to my recent thoughts about liberation and the cross. The idea of *young mother's milk* also gave a new dimension to the cost of the cross in the total gift of self. I wasn't sure I could make the kind of investment of myself that Jesus said was necessary. As I replaced the slides in their old box, there was one thing that I was certain about: I knew something about the *real* hunger of which Jesus spoke. It was that very same hunger that, like a relentless jackhammer, had driven me away from my work and my quiet, comfortable family life into this old attic. But I was still hungry!

I was also struck by that interchange about uprising, like war, being an art. "Maybe that's been my mistake," I thought. "I've gone about my quest as if it were a business venture with profit and loss balance sheets. When things haven't fallen neatly into place, I've felt frustrated. What if – yeah – what if I began to approach it as if I were an artist? What if I gave myself more freedom to play and wasn't so bound up by winning and losing. Or, to follow the analogy of Marx, I could launch out tomorrow as if I were a warrior marching into war!"

The warm summer wind seemed to mourn heavily outside, and the old attic rafters creaked loudly. It was as if the old house were telling me that it didn't like the image of the spiritual pursuit as war. The rafters groaned again as I turned off the Magic Lantern. Suddenly, the tomb-like silence of the midnight hour was shattered by a voice somewhere below screaming out in great pain. I jumped up and ran down the attic stairs to see what had happened. At the bottom of the stairs, I opened the door to the second floor and gasped in horror at what I saw. Maria was nailed by her right hand to the doorframe of her room!

CHAPTER 8

Blood was oozing from Maria's right hand which was affixed to her bedroom doorframe by a large nail. She was screaming in agony, "Santa Maria," her beautiful face twisted by pain.

"My God, Maria, what happened? Who did this?"

"Santa Maria," she sobbed uncontrollably, "Santa Maria." Within seconds, the hallway was filled with people in bathrobes and pajamas. Bernadone came running from his room. Gloria and Jon rushed out from theirs. Gloria began screaming at the sight of the blood running down the doorframe. Father Fiasco, in an old, faded cotton bathrobe, came racing from his room at the far end of the house, "O my God, O my God, poor Maria."

"Don't move her. I'll call 911," yelled Bernadone. He quickly retraced his steps to his own room as Mama Mahatma came flying up the circular staircase with the intensity of an Olympic racer. As she flew up the stairs, she was shouting, "Holy Mother of God, Holy Mother...oh, no, poor Maria, my child." Looking down the stairs toward Mama, I saw that the front door stood wide open.

"Damn that Dio. I'll kill him," cried Jon, attired only in his undershorts. "He did this to you, didn't he, Maria? I'll kill him!" His tone calmed as he stroked Maria's face with great gentleness. I was shaking both in anger and shock as I tried to stop the bleeding with my handkerchief.

Bernadone returned, assuring us, "The police and the 911 crew are on their way. Don't try to take that nail out of her hand. The blood loss hasn't been severe thus far, and the medics will know how to remove the nail without doing any more harm to her. Just stay calm."

Gloria had stopped screaming and weeping when she suddenly started to slump backwards.

"George, give me a hand, Gloria's fainting!" said Bernadone. He and I helped her to a seat on the covered bench in the hallway, just a few feet from Maria's doorway. Bernadone took hold of her. "Gloria, are you OK?"

"I just got a little weak; I hate the sight of blood."

"Sit here on the bench and rest for a moment...where's Mike?"

"He's out, he's...not here."

"Out? Out where at midnight?"

"Oh, Maria, my child, I'm so sorry," wailed Mama as she wiped Maria's brow with her handkerchief. "Where are the medics? We have to do something for her!"

"The medics will be here in minutes, Mama," called out Bernadone. "They'll take good care of Maria. George, run downstairs and turn on the porch light so the police will know which house it is. Who else is missing besides Mike?" Bernadone was the only calm one in the worried knot of people at Maria's door.

After Jon's initial unanswered question about Dio, no one asked Maria who had nailed her to the door, but we all knew. I ran downstairs, turned on the light and waited at the front door. Soon, the wail of police sirens could be heard above Maria's sobs. In moments the siren sounds and flashing red lights poured in the driveway.

The medics skillfully removed the seven inch nail and wrapped her hand to stop the bleeding. Maria fainted as the nail was removed, and they placed her on a stretcher. Jon insisted on going with her to the hospital, but the police officer requested that he and everyone else remain for questioning.

"Sergeant," said Inspector Bernadone, "let Mrs. Mahathaman go with the young woman. She's her...ah...mother. Maria will need her when she comes to. I personally will vouch for her."

So Mama Mahatma left with Maria and the ambulance crew. The rest of us were ushered downstairs into the living room where the police wrote up their report. We were each questioned about where we were at the time of the attack. When I explained that I was up in the attic working on a project, the police officer looked strangely at me, then wrote the information down on his report sheet.

"Is this all, is anyone missing?" he asked.

"Just one, officer. Michael Smith also lives here but is not present," replied Bernadone.

"He went out for a walk," said Gloria, "and hasn't returned yet. He left at least an hour before all this happened."

"A walk?" asked Bernadone who had been following the officer's questioning with his usual focused attention.

"Yes, a walk! He frequently does his exercise at night. I don't like your tone, Inspector. Why would Mike even be suspected of doing such a horrible thing?"

"Everyone in this house is a suspect, Gloria, including yourself."

"Don't be silly, Inspector. We all know who did it! It was that pimp of hers."

"Pimp?" asked the officer with raised eyebrows.

"I'll explain later," said Bernadone. "Yes, while everyone here is a possible suspect, I'm sure that no one in this room would do such a ghastly thing. I'm also sure that we've all had enough upheaval for one night. Officer, if you'll remain a moment, I'll explain all this, and you can wrap up your report. With your permission, I'd like to suggest that everyone else can leave. I propose that we all return to our rooms and go back to bed. It's late, and we've done all we can."

"If we're free to go," said Jon, "then I'm going to the hospital." As he left, Gloria said good night and went upstairs. Father Fiasco and I remained as Bernadone spoke with the officer. After the police left, the three of us sat in the living room, reviewing what had happened.

"It's obvious that Maria told Dio she was finally leaving him," said Father Fiasco, "so he nailed her to the door as a lesson, a sign to her that she wasn't going anywhere."

"Yes, I expect that was how it happened," said Bernadone. "And I'll wager that Maria will never tell the police, or us, that it was Dio who did it. Without her statement as to the identity of her attacker, we'll be left empty-handed. Dio will never be charged. I'm sure he felt confident that she wouldn't tell anyone who did it."

"While you were calling 911, Bernadone, I saw that the front door was wide open. Dio must have left that way in a hurry. I was the first to reach Maria. By the time it took me to come down from the attic, he had gone down the main stairs and out the front door.

"My God, what kind of man is he? I knew he was cruel; I mean, the way he ran over Fatima, how he took such pleasure in killing her! Like I told you, Inspector, he threatened Maria several times, saying that if she ever tried to leave him she would regret it. But to nail her to the door?"

"My guess, as a professional policeman, is that he knew precisely what he was doing. This was no act of passion; it was premeditated. Dio knew that if you drive a nail in the middle of the hand, the chances are good that you will not hit a bone. It was a vivid warning for Maria, but it was intended to cause only minor damage to a valuable piece of his property. Yes, just enough violence in a vicious lesson to teach her who was in control."

"Maria visited recently with me as her confessor and part-time spiritual director," said Father Fiasco. Raising his right hand, he added, "Not in confession, mind you, so I can share what happened since it may be important for her protection. Maria had decided to leave Dio and her...ah...profession. I encouraged her to follow her heart, but I warned her that such a conversion would not be free, that her freedom might have a large price tag. And I encouraged her to seek your advice, Bernadone, about how to protect herself."

Father Fiasco wrung his hands. "I didn't want to speak about this to either of you. I respected her confidence, even if I wasn't bound by the seal of the confessional. Oh, my friends, how I feared for her safety, but I never guessed this would happen. Poor girl, she's so lovely, inside and out. We know that she's in love with Jon, and when you're in love you're willing to take great risks, right?"

"I share your concern, Father," said Bernadone. "And quite frankly, I'm not sure what we can do about it." We sat without speaking for some time. The only sound was the tick-tock of the grandfather's clock.

Then Father Fiasco wondered out loud, "What about Mike Smith? What's the story on him, Bernadone? Something is missing in Gloria's answer. What's he up to?"

"I've puzzled over that too, Fiasco. George has told me that he's heard some heated arguments between Mike and Gloria. Could it be that...? But, look at the clock, friends, it's late. Perhaps

126

we should let things rest for tonight and try to get some sleep."

We slowly climbed the stairs together, then parted and went to our rooms. I didn't feel tired, too much fight-or-flight energy was pumping through my system for me to go to sleep. More than mere anger, rage against Dio had turned my heart into an inferno. Strange, but at the same time, in the center of the raging fire was a wide, deep pool, a surprising peacefulness reinforced by a real love for Maria. My right hand ached, as if it had been pierced like her's. I felt as violated as she must at that moment. Reflecting on it, I realized that I was still nailed by my anger and hate. While physically I was laying in bed, I was actually fixed in anger to her bedroom doorframe. Yet that insight enabled me to own my hate for Dio.

I took a few deep breaths, remembering Bernadone's words. Though it wasn't easy, I tried to embrace my anger, feeling where in my body or mind that fire blazed the most. Then I tried to let go of my anger, not judging or condemning it, just letting it be like any other emotion that comes and goes. My mantra became, "Life is a river, everything passes. So will your anger." I repeated it over and over, and must have fallen asleep.

My sleep was restless, and I was easily awakened when I heard Jon and Mama Mahatma returning with Maria. Through the thin walls next door, I heard them putting Maria into bed. My alarm clock showed that it was 4:20 a.m. – dawn would shortly come. Soon all was quiet, and I must have slipped into sleep because the next thing I heard was my alarm clock.

The next morning around 10:15 while I was working in the kitchen, Mama Mahatma came in to prepare some soup and toast for Maria. I helped her fix a tray, and as we worked I asked, "Is she in much pain?"

"Some, but they gave her some medicine to kill the pain. Poor child, this morning she's mostly in shock and fear. She would say nothing about the incident to those at the hospital or the police – or even to me. She only sobs when anyone tries to question her."

"Dio did it, we all know that."

"Yes and no, George. I'm not surprised that people feel sure it was Dio, for who among us would inflict such pain on a lovely girl like Maria? But we don't *know* that it was Dio, and so we shouldn't pass judgment on him without evidence."

"How can you be so generous as to not accuse Dio? You love Maria so much. How can you not feel intense anger and resentment toward him? Mama, you know that Dio also killed Fatima! He killed your gentle little cat for the pure pleasure of it. Doesn't that anger you?"

"Of course I feel those human emotions, George, but I also don't know the whole story. Since I have only limited knowledge of his behavior and the underground rivers that are the sources of it, I can't presume to don the role of judge and jury. Inside us is a dark energy that desires to be more than a judge. There's a serpent power that lusts after being the executioner as well! You would be wise, George, to be cautious with those underground rivers in yourself."

Then, with the affection of a mother, she slipped her arms around me as I stood at the kitchen sink. She squeezed me in a warm, broad embrace and kissed me on the cheek. "George, I so love you when you're this passionate, but do you or any of the others know the whole truth of what has happened?"

I was deeply moved by her embrace. I didn't want her to let me go. In her arms, I felt something I deeply desire. My heart had become like a sieve, and the anger was running out like water. It was a magical and timeless moment which only reentered daily reality when she said, "Seems the soup is ready. Thank you, George, for your concern. I'm touched by your love for Maria. I'll tell her that you send your love along with this toast and soup."

"This may sound strange, Mama, but would you mind if I cut some flowers from your garden and gave them to Maria?"

"George, that's a marvelous idea. As all the florists wisely tell us, 'Say it with flowers.' " She left the kitchen, carrying the tray upstairs, and I was left alone with my thoughts.

I had surprised myself by asking if I could cut some flowers for Maria. I mean, I'm a married man! Clever of Mama to quote the florists. What was the "it" that I was attempting to say with flowers—that I loved Maria? I shouted "recess" at my brain and escaped from the perpetual grand inquisitor of my mind. I simply let it be—my fondness for Maria—and took a knife from the kitchen out to the garden.

A short time later, like some teenager, I carried my homemade bouquet of flowers up to Maria's room. "Come in," she said softly when she heard my knock on the door. Maria was propped up in bed with several large white pillows behind her. She was wearing a soft yellow nightgown; her bandaged right hand lay on the outside of the sheet. The beauty of her dark, glowing skin against the whiteness of the sheets and pillows made her even more radiant.

"George, how thoughtful of you, flowers! They're beautiful. I'm sorry to be the cause of so much distress around here. I'm sure that more than once you've been disturbed by . . . ."

"Please," I raised my finger to my lips, "save your strength to get better. These are...a small token of my...ah...concern for you."

Her room was tastefully decorated. Flowing white lace curtains fluttered from the two windows along the west wall. On the east wall, which ran along the staircase that led up to the attic, was an icon of a saint. Hanging from a silver chain was a small vigil lamp with a lighted candle. After placing the vase of flowers on a table, I walked over to look at the icon. "What a striking icon. Who's the saint? I don't recognize her."

"Oh, Father Fiasco gave me that icon of St. Pelagia years ago. It's very precious to me. Beautiful, isn't it?"

I nodded in agreement and smiled. I so enjoyed being in Maria's company.

"George, would you do me a favor, please? Would you fluff up the pillows behind my back? I fear they've slipped down a bit, and with this bad hand . . . ."

"Sure, I'd be happy to." I reached behind her and pulled the pillows up firm behind her back. Before I straightened up, she leaned over and kissed me softly, with moist lips, on my right cheek.

"Thank you, George, you're really kind."

"You're welcome," I stammered out as I backed out of the room and closed the door. I could still feel the moistness of her kiss on my cheek. As I walked down the hallway, the grand inquisitor voice, composed of countless authoritarian tapes from my childhood, again began to interrogate me.

I was pleased as I went about my daily duties to hear Mozart being played quietly in the background. Jon returned from work earlier than usual and went in to visit her. As he passed me in the hallway, he spoke to me in a friendly way, but he looked very disturbed. Going about my cleaning that day, I pondered Mama's statement, "Do you know the whole story?" She was right about being non-judgmental, but all the evidence pointed to Dio. Still, her words – and her embrace – had helped to lift the burden of my anger. Being kissed in the same day by two women for whom I felt great affection certainly lowered the flame on the burner of my anger – even if it kindled another flame.

I was preparing dinner when Mama Mahatma came into the kitchen and shocked me with her announcement, "George, as you prepare the meal, I want you to know that Maria will join us for dinner this evening. So will Dio."

"Dio?" I whirled around from the sink. "Dio! You mean he has the gall to come to dinner after what happened last night? I can't believe it!"

"George, I know how you feel, but Dio will be a guest at our table. As such, he will be received as one of the family. We will have our usual cocktails before dinner in the living room."

With a smile she left the kitchen. As I put the fresh green beans in the steamer, I could imagine the reaction of everyone in the household to Dio, especially Jon. How could such a gathering be anything but a disaster? I was preparing a good dinner, but who would taste it?

As I set the table, my mind became a crazy three-ring circus. In the first ring were the various members of our household, angry and boiling with violence toward Dio. In the second ring was Dio, like a lion who had escaped and was about to leap into the audience. I found myself in the third ring, snapping my animal trainer's whip at my inner wild beasts, frantically trying to get them to quietly sit still. If I ever needed to meditate before dinner, I surely did tonight. I rushed through the remaining preparations so that I could have at least a few minutes of quiet prayer in my room before cocktails.

When I finished my meditation, I joined Mike, Gloria, Father Fiasco, Bernadone, Jon and Maria in the living room. Maria sat in one of the chairs, her right hand bandaged. She looked pale but as beautiful as ever. Jon sat on the arm of the chair with his arm around Maria's shoulder.

"Welcome, George," smiled Father Fiasco. "I hope that you prayed for all of us. The cook deserves a good drink. What will it be?"

"Scotch, Father, my usual. But tonight, make it a double. Where's Mama Mahatma?"

"She hasn't joined us yet, but I'm sure she'll be along any moment. She never misses cocktails!"

At that moment she appeared through the French doors with an arm around Dio. Everyone in the room froze as if they had been zapped by a ray gun. With all the laughing and visiting going on as I entered the room, I had suspected that I was the only one who knew that Dio was coming to dinner. The only one, that is, except for Maria, whose face showed no sign of shock. Mama must have told her as well. Jon leaped off the arm of the chair as Dio and Mama Mahatma entered the living room.

"Friends, Dio will join us for dinner this evening! Isn't that a pleasure?"

"Pleasure? To eat with a snake!" snarled Jon.

"Jon, please. Dio is my guest – he is *our* guest – and as you well know, all guests in this house are treated with respect and reverence. Dio, would you care for a drink?" Mama Mahatma ushered him to the table with the ice and glasses.

"Yes, thank you. I'll take one of your famous Martinis." Dio smiled in obvious pleasure at the intense discomfort of everyone else in the room. "Maria, I see you've injured your hand. I'm sorry, I hope it isn't serious."

Jon stood beside her chair, his fists clenched and his lips firmly pressed together. The usually jovial Father Fiasco was silent, and Bernadone's eyes, like twin magnifying glasses, swept across all of our faces. Mike and Gloria sat as if they were drowning in a pool of acid, their fruit juice glasses glued to their hands. Dio, drink in hand, wound a serpentine path across the room and stood in front of Maria.

"I propose a toast to our beloved Maria, a lovely and *wise* woman."

Like robots, we raised our glasses in imitation of Mama Mahatma, but the toast was broken off mid-stream by Jon's outburst. "You bastard, if it wasn't for the fact that you're under Mama Mahatma's protection, I'd kill you for what you did to Maria!"

"Maria, dear one, what's your muscle-bound friend talking about? Does he think I'm the naughty one who hurt your hand? Tell these nice people the truth – you're a big girl, did I hurt you?"

Maria remained silent, but her dark eyes were firmly fixed on Dio. The temperature in the room rose at least twenty degrees, and I could feel the sweat running down my back.

"See, Maria hasn't accused me. Perhaps she injured herself. Why all this silent accusation of me? I feel your unspoken judgments of me. Shame, shame, nice Christian people, I always thought that was your hallmark – that you didn't judge others, lest you be judged!" Dio laughed satanically, his eyes were deep dark pockets of intense hate. "I'm innocent, aren't I, Maria?"

"This is a farce. We all know that you were the one who nailed her to that doorframe. Who else would be so demented as to do such a thing?" demanded Jon, stepping forward.

"Hold your ground, unless you're also muscle-bound in the head. If you're looking for a suspect, for someone with a motive for attacking a whore, why not start with someone who hates them, like Mr. Pious, Michael the Pure?"

"How dare you accuse me?" shouted Mike, jumping to his feet. "I wasn't even in the house! That's ridiculous, I would never do such a thing. I'm a respectable businessman. I don't understand why Gloria and I even stay in this house."

"Mike and Gloria Smith," snarled Dio as he whirled around to face them. "Talk about phony names. How phony can you get? I'll wager five thousands dollars with anyone in this room that you're in the federal witness protection program! It's obvious: you're without backgrounds, floaters without a history who are hiding out from someone. Old Bible-quoting Michael, I've seen you late at night out on the streets. What are you doing at those hours, Michael the Pious, when only thieves and prostitutes are abroad?"

"This is insane! Gloria and I are respectable people."

Gloria's leg began bobbing up and down as her eyes darted back and forth from Dio to Mike. Dio gave her a twisted smile and said, "Respectable? Really! Inspector Bernadone, have you ever wondered what I wonder? I mean, the strange coincidence between the arrival of Mike and Gloria to our fair city and the appearance of the Woodsdale Killer? The pious couple moved in here at the same time that the murders of those prostitutes began six months or so ago, right?"

I had to give him credit. Dio was clever. In a matter of minutes he had switched the channels of attention from himself to Mike and Gloria. It was clear from Bernadone's face – without his saying a word – that he also had questioned the connection between Mike's late evening absences from the house and the murders. Mike nervously drained his fruit juice in one swallow, slamming his glass down on a table top.

"Come on, Gloria, we don't have to remain here and be insulted. These charges are absolute trash, groundless accusations. And, Mama, you talk about treating guests with respect. Doesn't this pimp have the same responsibility toward others in this house? Gloria, let's get out of . . . ."

"Bible meetin' tonight?" laughed Dio. "Before you go, Mr. and Mrs. Pious, let me give you a little tip. I would suggest that you go at once to a telephone and call the Feds. Tell 'em to get you a new address and a new identity! Tell 'em to hurry because I'm going to pass on the news of your location to my friends in the mob. Like the Orkin Man, they'll be coming around real soon to check you out." Pointing his skinny finger at both of them, he said, "Zap, zap, creeps, they're gonna' get you."

Mike shook his fist at Dio, "You'll pay for this – I promise you, Dio, you'll pay for it."

Gloria grabbed Mike's arm and began pulling him from the room as Dio whirled around to face Father Fiasco. "And you, *Reverend* Father Fiasco, you're not so innocent either. Who gave you the right to stand there in judgment. I've done a little research on you, and you're not as pure as holy water, are you?"

"What do you mean?"

"I mean, hasn't anyone here ever wondered why this priest has his own church and is not under the authority of the local bishop? I'll tell you why. There was a little incident many years ago in another state, in one of his former parishes. In those days the Church was able to keep a lid on things, keep 'em out of the newspapers. What was it, Fiasco, an affair with a teenage girl in your choir?" Then he laughed as if diabolically possessed, "Or was it one of your altar boys?"

With a smirk, Dio raised his glass and drank. With amazing

speed Fiasco seized a poker from its stand by the fireplace and sprang at Dio. With equal speed and agility Mama Mahatma sprang up between the two men and with surprising power restrained Fiasco.

"Father, please, put back the poker. Let's all of us – and that includes you Dio – stop accusing one another. I will not stand for this in *my* house."

Breathing heavily, his face red with anger, Father Fiasco replaced the poker in its rack. He stood glaring at Dio, who had turned to face Bernadone. "Inspector, good and kindly, peace-loving Inspector Bernadone, patron protector of stray animals. You, yes you with the eyes of a Dominican Inquisitor, you've also got a dirty secret in your past. My sources tell me that as a young police officer you shot and killed an unarmed kid you caught in the midst of a petty robbery. Isn't that the reason you've been living this life of, what shall we call it, religious repent-ance? I know that while the police investigation cleared you – cops have that wondrous ability to always whitewash their own – you were never the same after your little murder, eh?"

"You're correct, Dio. That unfortunate mistake did occur many years ago. I've never denied it. I have never forgotten it either. I dream about it, have nightmares of the boy's face, even to this day. But I have tried, in my own way, to . . . ."

"Just wanted the record to show, Detective Bernadone, that you're not so much a mystic as a murderer!"

"Mama Mahatma," Jon interrupted, "do we have to listen to this bastard without doing anything to stop his dumping this garbage on us? What's he doing here tonight, anyway?"

"Ah, Sir Galahad on his white horse," snarled Dio, whirling on one foot to face Jon. "To the rescue, princely protector of virgins! It is innocent virgins that you defend, isn't it? If anyone here is guilty, it's you, our little Czech muscle builder! You're the one who put those insane ideas into Maria's empty head. You and your idealistic overtures of love – and they're only over-tures, right? How old are you anyway, thirty-eight or is it forty, and not married? Doesn't that say something? What's your prob-lem, muscle-man, are you a perfectionist looking for the 'ideal' woman? If so, you've chosen one from the bottom of the scum barrel. Or, is it, Juan the Lover, that you haven't yet figured out your real sexual preference? Which is it, women or men, or both, that turn you on?"

Jon pounced like a leopard, seizing Dio by the neck with his strong hands. Dio was caught off guard by the swiftness of Jon's attack. He struggled, gasping for air. Mama Mahatma once again, with lightning speed and physical strength, was in the middle of the two, pulling them apart.

"Dio, I demand that you stop these accusations. Jon, please, I know that you're upset, but I will not tolerate any violence in this house. It seems that, unfortunately, we are unable to sit together at the same table. I'm sorry, George, but we will not have dinner together this evening. I had hoped that we all could come together in a peaceful way to deal with the issue without anger or violence. I see, however, that it's not possible. I believe we should all go our separate ways this evening. Dio, please leave our home. I think it's better that you do not return here until I invite you back."

Dio turned toward the doors to leave but pivoted around and hurled a threat like a knife at Maria: "I expect you to be back at work next week. If you're not, I'm coming after you—got that, bitch?"

"If I ever see you in this house again, I'll kill you," yelled Jon, held back by Mama Mahatma's strong grip. Dio spat at Jon and the rest of us and stormed out through the French doors. Mama Mahatma and Jon escorted Maria upstairs. She looked faint after the angry exchanges of the evening. Father Fiasco, Bernadone and I retired to the kitchen to snack on some of the evening's uneaten dinner.

Jon joined us briefly as he fixed a tray of food for himself and Maria. He said that Mama Mahatma had retired to her room, saying she wasn't hungry. We briefly discussed the evening's events as he prepared the tray. When Jon left, the three of us sat around the kitchen table sharing the uneaten dinner.

"Good meal, George. It's a shame we weren't able to enjoy it at the table," said Bernadone, pouring himself a glass of wine.

"Excellent, I must say," added Father Fiasco, "far more tasty than if eaten at the same table with Dio. I know that quotes are Mama Mahatma's speciality, but to quote an old Scottish saying, 'His absence is good company!' "

"I'll drink to that," I said as I raised my glass. "I must confess, however, that I'm amazed at Dio's ability to inflict violence in one way or another on others. Mama Mahatma and I were the only ones that weren't targets for his hate tonight. If she hadn't ended it, I probably would have been next."

"I'm sure you're right, George." said Bernadone as he helped himself to more green beans. "My guess is that he would have tried to make you look ridiculous with his old 'cook and maid' routine. Not to mention the fact that you abandoned your wife and family for some spiritual wild-goose chase – at least that's how he would have pictured your time here."

"One thing we can be sure of: that's the last of Dio for awhile."

"I'm not so certain about that, George. I wouldn't be surprised to see him slinking around the house in the coming days. Dio's on the offensive, and he's not about to forsake such a valuable piece of property and leave Maria to Jon. How about you, Fiasco, don't you think that he'll be back?"

"I do, Bernadone. But I'd be concerned about my hide, if I were Dio. Jon's strong and hates him. I'm not sure that the threat of the law's penalties are sufficient to restrain Jon if he catches Dio sneaking around here. I'm afraid that, in a moment of blind passion, Jon would kill him. Jon is physically able to do it. Nor would he need a weapon – his bare hands are lethal. He's a good man, but he's no saint."

"I fear that you're right, Father." After a pause, I added, "Speaking of saints, who is Saint Pelagia? I saw an icon of her in Maria's room. She said that you had given it to her."

"Ah, yes, Saint Pelagia...but did you notice, Inspector, that our friend here has taken to visiting Maria in *her* room?" They both laughed, and he continued, "She's an early Christian saint, a kind of Desert Mother one might say. More accurately, she was one of the 'Harlots of the Desert'! She's a classic example of a penitent prostitute, like Mary Magdalene. According to an ancient story, a certain Bishop Nonnus saw her ride by one day as he and a group of bishops were on their way to a council meeting. After she had passed by, he asked his fellow bishops, "Did not her great beauty delight you?" The next day, it happened that Pelagia went to a church where Bishop Nonnus was preaching. She was so moved by his love-filled words that she vowed to change her life. Ah, brothers, to have such a gift of speech is to truly have the Pentecostal gift of tongues."

"Not to mention the gift of *eyes*, since Bishop Nonnus seems to have seen outer and inner beauty, eh?" quipped Bernadone as he stood up from the table. "But it's been a long day, and this poor Italian is ready for bed."

I turned out the kitchen light, and as we walked along the hallway leading to the back staircase, my eyes fell upon the triple-locked basement door. "One person, Bernadone, who was never even considered as a suspect is Lucien!"

"He did come to mind, George. I would have seriously considered him if it had not been so obvious that Dio nailed Maria to the doorframe. I didn't even tell the police about Lucien, for Mama Mahatma's sake."

Pausing in front of the grandfather's clock, with its measured tick-tock and its hollow-eyed serpent looking down at us, Father Fiasco asked, "What did you think about Dio's accusation of Mike? We know his views on prostitutes and sex. Then there are his unexplained disappearances at night. Do you think – I know this sounds crazy – that he might be the Woodsdale Killer?"

"I have considered it, I must confess. Mike fits the profile of the kind of persons who murder prostitutes. By all outward indications he's anti-sexual, but beneath the surface may be a fascination – if not obsession! Ever since he and Gloria came here, I've felt that they were not who they claimed to be. I hadn't thought about them being in a federal witness protection program, but it does make sense. After Dio made that accusation, I made a mental note to see if I could check into their identity further. I'll let you know if I find out anything. It's usually difficult, since the Feds keep that sort of information restricted, even from local law enforcement agencies."

As we climbed the steps, the house was still, except for the measured sound of the old clock. At the top of the stairs we said good night and went to our rooms. I lay back on my bed, exhausted. Having so much emotion pumping through me wore me out. Before I fell asleep, I could hear Maria and Jon in the next room visiting softly – her bed being up against my south wall. I could imagine them making love together by the flickering light of the small candle burning in front of the shrine of

St. Pelagia. The beauty of their love for each other reminded me of my love for Martha. I've been missing her a lot lately. "Maybe," I smiled to myself, "I'm getting sick – homesick."

My last conscious thoughts were ghost thoughts – the personal ghosts that haunt the attic of my mind: "What in the hell are you doing here? How could anyone pursue spiritual growth in a madhouse? How can you grow in prayer in a place crowded with conflict, anger and hate?" That night I dreamed of some peaceful monastery in Tibet, only for it to turn into a nightmare. I found myself in the same room with that Tibetan monk whom I had seen in my first Magic Lantern show, the one with the large nail in his right hand. I awoke sweaty and disturbed. It struck me that the Magic Lantern image I saw upon my arrival was prophetic. I couldn't go back to sleep, as my mind frantically filed through other Magic Lantern pictures in my memory. As various images surfaced, I found myself asking, "Were they also previews of coming events?"

CHAPTER 9

The next few days passed quickly and without any significant event. Life in Mama Mahatma's boarding house was almost back to normal. Mike and Gloria did not move out, but they did keep more to themselves since the famous battle of the living room. Jon and Maria spent more and more time together, her hand healing quickly. Inspector Bernadone had been right: no bones were broken when the nail was driven through her hand. My meditation was more peaceful, even if my time here was quickly ending. Soon, I would return to my work and my family. Despite my awareness of some small progress, I continued to feel disappointment at my growth in holiness. Since my time was about over, I tried to make the most of the days remaining.

One morning while attending sunrise Mass, the gift of peace which I had enjoyed the past days was kidnapped by one of Father Fiasco's Lost Gospels. I probably should have been prepared for it, but I was taken by surprise when he read to us from "the Lost Gospel of Saint Matthew, chapter 27, beginning with verse 67." Before the reading Father Fiasco explained to us that Matthew's chapter 27 ends with verse 66, which tells of the entombment of Jesus after his death on the cross. He said we had this Lost Gospel to thank for giving us an insight into what happened inside the tomb after they rolled the stone in front of it.

I found myself caught up in that dark scene inside the tomb as Father Fiasco began to solemnly read:

> Now the Great Shabbat of the Passover was almost
> upon them as they walked away from the tomb. After
> the long delay in obtaining Pilate's permission to have
> Jesus' body, in their hurry to bury him before sun-

down, and too overcome with grief to actually check the tomb again, they asked themselves, "Is Jesus truly dead yet?" The sun was disappearing beneath the horizon as they hurried home without returning to know for sure.

Inside the tomb, his body bruised and pierced, Jesus embraced the cool darkness aware that his consciousness was fading quickly. He easily could have reached out for death, a relief from the pain and torture of that day. As life slowly drained from him, he was aware that he was not alone inside the tomb.

Then he heard it, the same low, sinister chuckle he had heard three years before in the darkness of a desert night. Jesus knew that *he* had come again to tempt him.

Out of the darkness of the tomb a voice spoke: "Hello, Jesus, fancy meeting you here of all places. You who called yourself 'the Way and the Life' are dying! You have but minutes left. You also called yourself the 'Son of God.' You said that God called you his beloved son! Surely, Jesus, today must prove to you that you are not anyone's beloved. Would one who loved you expose you to such shame and ridicule? Die like a man! Curse the powers that cast you into this tomb. Die with at least the satisfaction that you had the courage to denounce the myths that common folk cling to!"

"I do not believe that God loves me," returned Jesus.

"Ah, good," cackled the devil.

Jesus interrupted his brittle laughter: "I don't believe it, I *know* that God loves me!"

"Fool!" snarled the devil. "I once offered you all the kingdoms in the world, and you mocked me. You could have been famous, your name immortalized in history. But look at you now, beaten like a dog, dying alone and anonymous. Do you know *where* you are?"

"In my tomb, I guess," whispered Jesus as he clung tightly to life and consciousness.

"Ha! A tomb, yes. But it isn't even your tomb! Another name, not yours, is carved upon it. You're a forgotten man. Not only will a child not bear your name, neither will the very tomb you're buried in. No one will remember you. Fool, how can you say you *know* God loves you? Denounce such an absent-minded lover and let me be your friend. Even now, it's not too late. I possess great powers. I can give you what you seek most at this very moment: *life!*"

"I am dying, stripped of everything I ever valued. I care not if my name is remembered or if it's recorded in the pages of history. I believe that God loves me, in spite of all that has happened...I...." The voice of Jesus faded away, his strength exhausted by the effort to hold body and soul together.

The devil's laughter echoed off the damp walls of the tomb and was almost tangible in the total blackness of that place of death. "Ah, my little Jew miracle worker, now you only *believe*? Listen, put aside your beliefs. I offer you *life*, a second chance! Think twice before you turn me down this time."

Jesus, aware that only slim strands of life remained, forced his mind to find a center, a point of strength, as he felt his will power eroding. The devil came close and, edging next to Jesus, whispered into his ear, "I have always loved you. Why do you think I came to you in the desert? Did God ever offer you as much as I did? If you are Yahweh's beloved, if God promised that angels would prevent you from stumbling upon a stone, then where were they, Jesus, when you stumbled and fell under the heavy load of your cross? Where were they when you were being nailed to the cross? Where was your beloved God? There is no God, Jesus, only an eternal longing for one!"

Leaning so close that his lips touched Jesus' ear, the devil whispered, "You have only seconds of life left, dear one. Turn to me. Abandon the myth, for I promise you real life. There are only seconds left to say yes. If you don't, you'll become nothing. Do you hear me, Rabbi Jesus? You will become **nothing**!"

"I...I..." gasped Jesus, "I believe...in...." And then there was only silence – and darkness.

The devil rose to his full height, looked down on the lifeless body and said, "Fool! You had your . . . ." But he didn't finish, for he noticed a tiny whirlwind of ultraviolet light on the chest of the dead body. Steadily the luminous eddy grew, as did the sound in the narrow tomb. Soon it was filled with a thunderous roar.

It was the same sound made when a great star, far out in the darkness of space, exhausts its nuclear fuel and collapses under its own weight. It was the blast created when all the matter of a massive star begins to burst inward upon itself from all directions to meet at its center, causing a shock wave to race outward in a tremendous explosion. Its brilliance was that of a billion shining stars.

"There is no time; I must hurry!" screamed the devil, gripped with fear. His hands seized at the huge stone blocking the entrance of the tomb. He pushed with all his might, but the stone would not move. As the iron fist of panic grabbed him by the throat, the devil smelled the life-rich aroma of the ocean and heard the Wind as it was when it blew across the earth on that first day of creation. Madly he dug his fingernails deeply into the great stone, lunging against it with all his might, as behind him the Wind roared like a tornado. Feeling the searing heat, with one last lunge he rolled the great stone away from the entrance to the tomb and fled screaming into the pre-dawn darkness.

That was a powerful Gospel, and I wanted to visit with Father Fiasco about it. After Mass was finished and everyone had left, however, I walked to the area of the chapel where people were removing bricks from the walls. Somehow this morning I felt the need to take something tangible with me as I departed. I went to the wall where the icons were painted on the wood-covered garage doors. I selected a brick from the wall next to the icon of the prophet in the apocalyptic scene. I stood, brick in hand, looking at the section of the icon with the sun and moon which resembled melting cheese and the stars falling like luminous snowflakes. This was the closest that I had been to the icon, and so for the first time I saw the artist's penciled lines in the unfinished bottom section. The designs remaining to be painted showed snowflake stars being transformed darkly into a giant, twisting serpent. I raised my eyes to the cartoon-like balloon caption emerging from the prophet's mouth: "Lift up your hearts and rejoice, this is the day of the Lord." I couldn't imagine why such disaster would cause anyone to rejoice. At that moment I felt the presence of someone behind me.

"Good morning, George. I see you got yourself a brick. Glad you want to be reminded that you too are a living stone!"

"Ah, Father Fiasco! You surprised me. I thought that you might be on your way to work at the freight company."

"Not today, George. I've got some pastoral work to do, and I told them that I wouldn't be in today. Did you enjoy Mass this morning?"

"Enjoy? That's an unusual word for going to church."

"Not really. To enjoy is to be enveloped by joy, and God *is* Joy. So if you enjoy a religious experience like Mass, or for that matter any experience, you're into God, right?"

"I can't argue with your theology, but I was more distressed than overjoyed by this morning's Gospel."

"Good, I'm glad to hear that! As I told you before, those Gospels are intended to wake us up, not make us content. Ah, yes, Matthew's tomb encounter between the dying Jesus and Satan: that Gospel always reminds me that Jesus' gift of the Spirit of the Holy was no cheap gift! If we fully understood how Jesus' gift is the same force that shaped the cosmos, fuels volcanoes and makes the oceans teem with life, then would we not call upon such a gift whenever we needed its primal energy?"

"Are you saying, Father, that we should pray for such a spiritual gift?"

"It's not so much spiritual, George, as it is a *spirit* gift. Calling it spiritual can rob it of eighty per cent of its power. It can make you think of it as pious vapor when actually it's the same power force that belches flaming lava out of the earth's great volcanoes."

"I understand. That is the kind of power I need right now. My inner work suffers from a lack of fire, I fear. Or maybe what I lack is a peaceful environment. I seem to be confused on that point."

"Holiness, George, doesn't require a peaceful environment to grow. It requires fire, passion and the willingness to be gifted by the same Spirit that inspired Moses, Esther, Buddha, Gandhi and the Sioux Indian shamans. It's the Spirit of Folly and Madness that drove Francis of Assisi to strip off his clothes and stand naked before his family and the bishop as he declared his freedom to be who God had called him to be. It's the same Primal Spirit that supported Jesus in the tomb when he clung only by the slimmest of threads to his faith in God, a God who often prefers to work through our failures and defeats."

As Father Fiasco spoke about God having a preference for working through our failures, I recalled the accusations that Dio had made about him. Was Fiasco speaking from his personal experience? Regardless of his past, I found him to be a holy man. Perhaps holiness is not the fruit of a blameless life but rather a willingness to let God work good out of evil. These thoughts raced through my mind in seconds.

Father Fiasco continued, "All of us, at times, feel like Jesus did in the tomb. We're tempted to believe that God has abandoned us whenever we feel the absence in our life of the Presence. Our greatest moments, the ones that call forth greatness from deep within us, usually happen when we feel totally abandoned yet still cling to that thread that's thinner than a hair."

"I've felt stripped by the chaos around here these past weeks," I said. "I came here firmly believing in my ability to achieve enlightenment, only to be frustrated again and again. True, I wanted the Spirit of God in my life, but I guess only as sugar frosting on my controlled, well-ordered existence. Like this icon, I feel that I've been caught in an apocalyptic nightmare. Yet I know full well that I have not surrendered to it."

"Complete surrender – to have reached one's wit's end, to be naked and abandoned by all, even by God – ah, George, only heroes and heroines need apply for such a gift! Like you, I have lusted after holiness, but have always stopped just short of paying the price. I've come close, mind you, but we won't go into that now—perhaps some other time. Few desire to go all the way and not even look for the silver lining in the dark cloud that engulfs them. In the midst of great pain, who can step outside of the cardboard fort of faith and become a naked, living experiment in the test of God's love? No, friend, only heroines and heroes, the mad and insane, go all the way."

As I walked back to the house, brick in hand, I didn't need to reflect—I *knew*—that I've never completely surrendered. Like a good military commander, I've only played for time, asked for negotiations with the other side to gain time to regroup my forces. It was quite an awareness. I previously hadn't thought about surrender as an element of one's inner work. For me the quest mainly involved learning how to pray, how to sit still in my silent prayer to become enlightened. Far from surrendering in the midst of the conflicts I found here, I had struggled against them.

Most of all, even after all this time, I still felt uneasy about working as a servant, about my daily chores of cleaning and fixing meals. At times I've longed to be anywhere but here, wasting time. I've been wishing for some spiritual Disney World where everything is sanitary, polite, middle class, efficient and filled with blissful faces. I now felt a real need to surrender. Yet I wasn't sure I knew how to surrender without it seeming more like a concession than a positive act of faith.

I paused by the back door of the house to be attentive to life around me. Not a breeze stirred, the air hung heavy and still. A giant thunderhead cloud loomed over the treetops to the west; a late-summer thunderstorm was brewing. I went to my room and brought the brick to my bedside table. I placed it next to Dio's hourglass, which I hadn't used since I realized that *I* had been used. Then I went downstairs and began my duties for the day. As the day wore on, the house seemed to absorb the stillness outside and the sense of anticipation at the coming storm.

After the evening meal and dishes were finished, instead of going upstairs to my room, I stopped by Mama Mahatma's room across the foyer from the living room. The door was half opened and I knocked.

"Yes, who is it?"

"George, Mama. May I come in, please?"

"Certainly, George, what can I do for you?"

I entered her personal living area which had originally been the library and den. While the library had strong lines and a masculine feel, it also had been touched by the feminine in a graceful and most delightful way. Small touches like the shape of the lamp shades, a tall vase of flowers and paintings of flowers on the walls all reflected a maternal cast. Mama was seated in a tall Queen Ann wing chair with red and blue flowered fabric. She had one foot resting on a small footstool, next to which was an empty cat basket. My heart sank a notch at the sight of Fatima's vacant place beside Mama's chair.

"George, care to join me for an evening cup of tea? It's one of those civilized customs, you know – and good for you too!"

"Yes, but . . . ."

"Have a seat, and no *buts* are allowed, you know, in the presence of an elderly matron. I have a small hot plate over here..." she paused as she rose from her chair with that amazing grace and agility I had witnessed before, "...right next to Aristotle. It won't take but a minute, as I already had my tea kettle on."

She placed two dainty Victorian teacups and saucers on a tray and removed a can of tea leaves from behind a book on the shelf. While she was preparing the tea, I glanced about the room. The yellow light of the table lamps, the tall rows of books that reached from floor to ceiling and the heavy walnut furniture all added to the old room's charm. On one wall was a framed certificate. I leaned toward it to see the printing better. It was a diploma for a doctor's degree inscribed to "Sophia Mahathaman." So that was her first name: Sophia! To the left of her chair was a globe which must have measured at least four feet across.

"That's a very large globe," I said, wishing to fill the void of silence.

"Yes it is – and rather old. My guess is that it's from the turn of the century. While it lacks many of the recently formed countries and new national borders, it's still the same old planet, eh?" She returned, carrying a tray with teacups filled with hot water and silver teaspoons which held the tea leaves she had selected.

"We'll just let it steep a bit," she said, walking back again to the bookshelf with the works of Aristotle and other world literature. "Let me see, ah yes, right behind the *Tao Te Ching* . . . ." She returned carrying a half-empty bottle of Grand Marnier liqueur. Tilting her head to one side, almost childlike, she smiled: "Does Sent George care for some in his tea? It's a very civilized custom."

"Yes, please. I've never had Grand Marnier with tea."

"Really! The marriage of orange, fine old cognac brandy and hot tea is marvelous. One could call it a Chinese and French intermarriage." She poured a large shot of the liqueur into both cups. Placing the bottle on the floor next to the base of the globe, she sat down. After taking a sip of her tea, she exclaimed, "Ah, as Dom Perignon said at the moment he discovered champagne: 'Come quickly, I am tasting stars.' "

"I agree, Mama, this tea does have star quality. I could even get into the British custom of afternoon tea if it was made like this. Thank you for inviting me into your quarters. I know that it's late and . . . ."

"George, sipping stars is always more fun when it's done with a friend. You and the others are always welcome. I'm delighted that you stopped by. Was there a reason?"

"Yes, I wanted to give you notice – I mean, that I'll be returning to my home in two weeks. I know that when I came here six months ago, I gave you the date of my departure. But so much has happened recently. I thought . . . ."

"Thoughtful, George, very thoughtful. Yes, sadly, I'm aware that you don't have much time left here. We'll miss you, you know."

"And I, you – all of you...except Dio!" I took a sip of my tea, but Mama remained silent after my statement about Dio. Then, holding her teacup and saucer in her right hand, she spun the old leathery looking globe with the index finger of her left hand. "Same old planet, just different names and border lines."

She smiled at me and I smiled back. I wondered if that was her response to my comment about Dio? With the same finger with which she had started the globe spinning, she stopped it. Tapping the place on the globe where she had stopped the spinning, she said, "China, George, China."

"Yes, I see. Any particular reason you stopped it at China?"

"Oh, yes. I stopped it where a lot of it began."

"It?"

"Yes, all of it," her arm swept in a wide half-arc across the tall bookshelves, "all this wondrous knowledge. It's interesting that so many of the magnificent ideas contained in the books on these shelves, not to mention so many great inventions, were born in China. They're an unusually gifted people. Oh yes, George, from painted fingernails as signs of nobility and high station to the stuff that these books are printed on – paper – all from this one place on the planet. Allow me to read you something that may address the real reason you stopped in to visit me this evening."

She rose from her chair, placed her teacup and saucer on a nearby table and walked to the bookshelf from which she had taken the Grand Marnier bottle. Removing a leatherbound copy of the *Tao Te Ching*, she returned to her chair. Seated, she opened the book with loving care.

"This, I know you're aware, is one of the old holy books of China, written long before the birth of Christ. I've opened it to chapter 22. Let me read to you from it." She paused for a moment and closed her eyes, as if attuning herself to the holy text, and then began. I was first struck by the quality of her voice. It reminded me of my childhood bedtimes when my mother used to read to me. True, what Mama read was no bedtime story, but her voice had the same clear characteristic of calm love. It created in me the same profound sense of security I once had known when enfolded in my mother's nighttime stories. Mama Mahatma's reading from the *Tao* gently wrapped around me as if it had been a warm, soft blanket:

If you want to become whole, let yourself be partial.
If you want to become straight, let yourself be crooked.
If you want to become full, let yourself be empty.
If you want to be reborn, let yourself die.
If you want to be given everything, give everything up.

She set the book in her lap and looked at me with great fondness. We both sat in silence as I slowly turned over those words

148

that seemed to crystallize my reason for living here.

"The journey, George, is a long one. There are no shortcuts or instant enlightenments. You've done rather well, if you ask me, with this part of your quest. You've planted good seeds that will, long after you've left here, grow into a wondrous harvest. Believe me, I know."

"Thank you, Mama, for your affirmation. I needed it, I'm afraid. I'm grateful that you're able to see so much with that third eye of yours. I sure will miss you and your wisdom. Thank you for the tea and the...ah...marriage of East and West. I fear it's late. I know that I'm tired, and I would guess that you must be too."

Mama escorted me to her door, and once again, as she had done in the kitchen, wrapped me up in her great embrace. It was wonderful and filled me with peace. Then she kissed me on the cheek. I thanked her and began walking up the circular staircase. I looked back, and she was standing in her doorway. She gave me a large licorice smile.

On the way to my room, even though it was very late, I was tempted to go up into the attic to spend some time with my Magic Lantern. So much had happened in the last couple of days that I had neglected the attic nursery. But then again, who needs magic images when one's life is crowded with real life dramas and conflicts?

When I opened my door, I saw that someone had been in my room! My hourglass was laying on its side. The top had been hastily but crookedly put back on. There were white traces of the hourglass' contents on the table. Then I heard voices from Maria's room next door. Turning toward the wall, I saw that the door between the two rooms was not completely closed. I heard Dio's voice pleading with Maria. It sounded like he was drunk. His words were slurred, yet angry and excited. She was pleading with him to leave.

"Dio, get out of here. When Jon gets back, he'll kill you if he finds you here."

"He hasn't got the guts to kill me. It takes courage to kill someone, and he hasn't got the guts. Maria, come back to me. You know that I'm the only one who really cares for you, don't you? Who made you what you are, who opened doors for you that no one else could have? Me, right? Dio, your Dio...I need another line."

I could hear him fall over something in her room. He really must have been drunk. What a fool he was to sneak back in here to see her. Maria was right, I thought. If Jon found him in her room, he would kill him. Dio's comment about needing another line must have meant more cocaine. He would be headed back to my room! I didn't want to confront him, especially that drunk, so I quickly slipped out of my room and stepped into the bathroom.

Looking in the old square mirror at myself, I was ashamed of what I saw. Again I had run away from conflict instead of standing my ground and facing Dio. The familiar face in the mirror spoke to me: "George, this isn't the first time you've chosen to look away, to retreat, instead of meeting reality head on. Isn't that the kind of peace you've always enjoyed – avoidance peace?"

Again I looked at myself and wasn't proud of what I saw. I was about to answer the questioner in the mirror when I heard Dio stumbling around in my room. With another line of cocaine, he'd be so high he wouldn't know what hit him if Jon returned. Then I could hear him back in Maria's room pleading with her again, his speech even more erratic than before.

At that point I heard a car in the driveway. Looking out the bathroom window, I saw it was Jon's. My safe haven in the bathroom had now become a prison, and fear was my warden. I opened the door a crack and listened. I could hear Maria pleading with Dio to leave. She also had heard Jon's car return. She was begging him to leave before Jon came upstairs. It sounded like she pushed him out of her room into the hallway, as she cried out, "For God's sake, Dio, get out of here!"

I couldn't make out what he said, and I couldn't see anything as I peeked out the bathroom door. He must have been around the corner at the end of the hallway. I closed the door when I heard poor Dio stumbling around. Shortly thereafter I picked up the sound of Maria's door closing, and I opened the door a crack. Looking down the poorly lighted hallway, I saw Dio nodding his head toward my end of the hallway. He was stumbling back and forth and appeared both very angry and afraid.

"Gawd, now what'll I do?" he slurred. "I'll hide in that bathroom."

I closed the door and locked it. He must have decided against the bathroom because the next thing I heard was a strange sound, like creaking wood. Within moments, I heard Jon's footsteps up the back stairway. I waited, my heart pounding. All I heard, however, was Jon knocking on Maria's door and her inviting him to come in. I opened the bathroom door a crack and looked out. Where had Dio hidden himself? He was nowhere to be seen. Cautiously I crept out of the bathroom, looking down the hallway. I still saw nothing. Perhaps he had stumbled down the front stairs. Maybe he was even hiding behind the door that led to the attic steps. Wherever he was, I hoped, for his sake, that he would get out of the house as quietly and quickly as possible.

Standing at my door, I could hear Jon and Maria talking. I felt funny about going into my room since I would be able to hear them talking and making love — if that was what they chose to do. So I decided to go down to the kitchen and fix myself a sandwich.

At the bottom of the back stairs in the hallway by the old grandfather's clock, I came face to face with Mama Mahatma who looked very disturbed. "George, did you hear it?"

"Hear what, Mama Mahatma? Dio was up in Maria's room earlier, but I think he must have come down here and out the front door. Is that what you mean?" I wasn't sure what she was asking me, but whatever she had heard caused the greatest anxiety I'd ever seen on her usually placid face.

"Dio, here, in the house? Jesus, Mary and Joseph!" Then, looking frantically at the clock, she said, "George, I can't visit now, excuse me, please, I'm in a hurry. There's something that I must attend to at once."

She turned and almost ran toward her room at the front of the house. I walked into the kitchen and was looking in the refrigerator when I thought I heard something like the sound of a door. The wind, however, had begun to blow with a vengeance outside. The summer thunderstorm that had been brewing all day was about to sweep down on us. As I spread peanut butter on my bread, I dismissed the sound as the wind rattling the gutters. With the low thunder rumbling off in the distance, I took my sandwich and a beer out on the steps of the entrance under the carport.

I sat down, deciding that this would be a good place to enjoy the storm without getting wet. Looking toward the carriage house, I saw a light still on. "Father Fiasco must be working late," I thought as I enjoyed a taste of beer. "That first sip is always the best," I reflected as I also soaked up the electrical energy that charges the air just before the beginning of a big thunderstorm.

As the storm moved closer, leaves began blowing up the driveway, the wind sweeping them along like small clusters of fleeing refugees. No rain had fallen yet, but the old house creaked as it stood its ground against the strong storm winds. I was half done with my sandwich when I heard a woman screaming.

The screams, an unbroken chain of them, came from directly behind me in the hallway between the living room and the dining room. Dropping my sandwich, I jumped to my feet and ran inside. I saw Gloria standing next to the grandfather's clock, her hands to her face, still screaming. Slumped on the bench next to the clock was a body, its head between its legs. I didn't need to see the face to know that it was Dio!

As I ran to Gloria, she kept shrieking, "He's dead, he's dead!"

Within seconds, Inspector Bernadone appeared at the bottom of the back stairs, "What is...oh no, not Dio! George, try to quiet Gloria while I see if I can get a pulse."

Jon appeared next, buttoning up his shirt as he came down the staircase. When he saw Dio's body, he stopped and grabbed his head with his hand, "O my God, someone *did* kill him!"

"George, he is dead," said Bernadone, letting the lifeless hand fall back beside the body. "Call the police. I'll stay here. Do you know where Mama Mahatma or Father Fiasco are?"

"Fiasco must be out in the carriage house," I yelled back as I ran to the phone in the kitchen. I called the police and told the operator what had happened, then returned to the hallway. By this time, Maria had also appeared and was weeping as Jon supported her in his arms. Gloria had also begun to cry and kept repeating, "Mike didn't do this. Mike didn't do this."

"Gloria, get a hold of yourself," said Bernadone, turning toward her after closing Dio's eyelids. "Where is Mike?"

"Out, damn it, out, like he always is at this time of night!"

"The police are on their way, Inspector. Shall I run and get Father Fiasco?" Before Bernadone could answer me, Mama

Mahatma and Father Fiasco rushed in through the carriage entrance doors.

"Father, I believe you're the only one who can help him now," said Bernadone, "if you're willing."

Father Fiasco bent over Dio's body and gave him absolution, slowly tracing the sign of the cross over him. Maria crossed herself and prayed something in Spanish. Mama Mahatma stood with her hands over her face, weeping, "Poor Dio, poor pathetic Dio."

Thunder rumbled in the distance, and the wind continued to rattle the old house. The lights flickered off and then on again, accompanied by the sirens of approaching police cars. In moments they came racing up the driveway and screeched to a stop.

"Ah, Detective Bernadone! Again, the crime business comes to you, instead of you having to go to it," said the police lieutenant. "Only this time it appears more serious than that minor assault you reported here last week. Is he dead, Bernadone?"

"Yes, very dead. I would guess, however, that he hasn't been dead but a few minutes from the feel of his body." Then he addressed the rest of us, "I ask all of you to please go into the living room and have a seat. We will need to question each of you about where you were in the past hour. George, would you please make a large pot of coffee. I have a feeling that this is going to be a long evening."

Two uniformed officers escorted the others into the living room and took up positions at the two entrances as I went to the kitchen. Another police car, red lights flashing and siren wailing, pulled into the driveway.

As I began to brew the coffee and set cups on a tray for everyone, police officers blanketed the house and yard. I overheard Bernadone talking to some of them in the hallway. "He appears to have been hit on the head. See the deep bruise, Lieutenant – I mean, Jim – and the slight bleeding here? He must have been struck with a blunt, heavy instrument from the marks here on his forehead. He smells of booze, and look at the white substance on the hairs in his nose. I'm sure the lab will show it to be cocaine. Strange...notice all these small cuts and bruises on his hands and face?"

"I take it, Bernadone, that you know his identity. Is he one of your fellow roomers here?"

"No, Jim, but he was a frequent visitor. His name is—was—Dio. He's a driver in the fast lane of drugs and high-class prostitution."

"Notice these, Bernadone. Look at all the small rips and snags in his clothing...interesting! It looks like he was dumped into an empty cement mixer, or attacked by an electric fan, before someone hit him on the head. Is this where they found him, here by this clock?"

"Yes, but see these marks on the rug? My guess is that he was dragged to this bench from wherever he was murdered. Let's get some photographs of him here and then see what the coroner has to say about the cause of death."

"The household is in the living room. Do you want to handle this investigation, Bernadone, or do you want me to do it?"

"If you don't mind, Jim, I think it would be better if we both did. I've lived with all these people; perhaps I should do the questioning. But I will count on you to make sure that I don't get personally involved.

"Before we go in there, take a look at that side entrance door behind you, the one at the bottom of those steps leading out into the garden on the west side of the house. Notice that it isn't completely shut! Someone has either come in or gone out that way in such a hurry that he or she failed to completely close it. Worth noting, eh? Perhaps Dio was killed outside and then dragged in here. Have a couple of your men search the yard and garden area. I know that it's night, but let's see if they can find anything using their flashlights. Now, let's question my friends in the living room."

When I carried in the tray with the coffee pot and cups, Bernadone had just begun ascertaining everyone's whereabouts just before the body had been discovered.

"You say, Gloria, you were on your way to the kitchen when you found him? Isn't it unusual for you to come downstairs after you've gone up for the evening?"

"Yes, but I was hungry. Maybe it was the approaching storm. I hate to be alone when it's storming. I guess I was trying to feed my loneliness. All I know is that I came down the main staircase through the small hallway that leads to the kitchen, and..." she paused and began to cry. Regaining herself, she continued, "I saw him. He was slumped on the bench. I knew he wasn't sick or asleep, and I started screaming. I knew he was dead! That's when George came running in from outside through the driveway door."

"Gloria, how did you know he was dead?" asked the Lieutenant.

"I just knew it! Call it what you want, woman's intuition or maybe the . . . ." She left her sentence unfinished as a police officer ushered Mike into the living room.

"This man just came in the front door. He says he lives here."

"What's going on?" asked Mike anxiously.

"Oh, Mike, Dio's been murdered. I told them, dear, that you didn't do it. Mike, I told them . . . ."

"I need to remind you all, and this includes you, Mike, since you just arrived, that anything you say can be held against you. No one is being charged with Dio's murder. We're only trying to determine where each of you were at the time Dio met his death. Since you were absent, Mike, would you like to tell us where you were, and if anyone can confirm your whereabouts?"

"Why are we being treated like criminals. Whoever killed Dio should be given a medal. He did a service to all of us and to the community," interrupted Gloria.

"Gloria, this is a criminal offense," replied Bernadone. Then, turning back to Mike, he again asked, "Mike, where were you this evening?"

"I was...I was at a bar, having a drink, Inspector."

"The name of the bar and its location?"

"The Hot Banana, downtown on . . . ."

"The strip joint, I know it," said the Lieutenant. "Remember in the Woodsdale case, Bernadone, we questioned some of the hookers there at the time the second prostitute was murdered. Will the bartenders verify that you were there and when you left?"

"Yes, I'm sure they will," said Mike, his eyes fixed on his shoes. Gloria's eyes, so recently full of tears, were now filled with fire, but her face remained rigid and expressionless.

Bernadone took a slow drink of his coffee. Setting the cup carefully down on the ledge of the fireplace, he smiled at Jon, "I'm sorry, Jon, but all of us heard you threaten to kill Dio last night, here in this very room. Where were you this evening?"

"I got home late. I was out with a business partner. When I returned, I went upstairs to Maria's room. I've been with her all the time since."

Bernadone looked at Maria who nodded in agreement, her face a bit flushed. Bernadone nodded back, aware that the two must have been in bed together since Jon had appeared at the bottom of the stairs buttoning his shirt, Maria joining us only later. "And, George, where were you?"

I related all that had happened upstairs before I came down to the kitchen, how I had seen Dio staggering in the hallway and how he disappeared after I closed the bathroom door. I told them that I met Mama and then went out on the steps to eat my sandwich and was there until I heard Gloria's screams.

"Father Fiasco, where were you at the time of Dio's death? You entered from the outside, so you must not have been in your room."

"I was out in my sacristy in the carriage house, working on tomorrow morning's Mass. I'm not a suspect am I? I wasn't even aware that anything had happened until Mama Mahatma came to get me in the carriage house. She only told me that Dio needed a priest at once. I didn't know that he was dead until I entered the house."

"I'm sorry to tell you, Father, that it appears Dio was murdered by a blow to the head. I regret having to remind us what happened here last night, how you attempted to strike Dio with this poker from the fireplace stand.

"Mama Mahatma, I'm sorry to have to question you, but George said he saw you just before all this happened and that you appeared disturbed. Is that correct?"

"Yes, I was in the hallway this evening. I met George at the bottom of the back stairs. I had heard a strange noise and left my room to see what it was. When I heard Gloria screaming, I guessed that she found Dio. George had told me he was wandering around the house. I didn't need to come and see what happened – I knew. So I ran to the carriage house to get Father Fiasco to come as quickly as possible. Dio, you know, was Catholic."

The Lieutenant nodded to Bernadone and said to us, "Thank

you for your cooperation. We ask that all of you stay in town for any further questioning . . . ."

"Just a moment, Lieutenant," interrupted Bernadone. "We haven't questioned all the residents of this house. I was in my room when Gloria's screaming was enough to awaken even a deep sleeper like me. I came downstairs immediately. But I wasn't referring to myself. Mama Mahatma, I'm truly sorry, but we will have to question Lucien."

"Lucien?" asked the officer. "Who's Lucien?"

"He's Mrs. Mahathaman's son. He lives in the basement. He's sort of a recluse."

"Really, Bernadone, why wasn't he sent for before now? I'll send an officer down there and have him brought up," replied the Lieutenant, obviously distressed that Lucien wasn't included in the questioning.

Mama Mahatma's face was drawn and drained of life. Bernadone saw it. "No, Jim, I think we should go down there." He looked toward Mama, as did everyone else in the room. Her disturbed look vanished and was replaced by a serene smile.

"All right, Inspector. I understand that the situation is most unusual, and even poor Lucien must be questioned. Let's get it over with so we all can go to bed."

As Bernadone, Mama Mahatma and the Lieutenant were leaving, Bernadone whispered to me, "George, would you mind stepping outside here in the hall." I followed them through the French doors. The police had already removed Dio's body from the hallway. Bernadone took me aside by the carriage entrance door. "I don't know what we're going to find down there. I'm concerned about Mama Mahatma. It's clear that she's very upset about all this, and, well, I'd like someone with us who can support her. George, will you come to the basement with us?"

I nodded yes, but inside I wished that he had asked someone else. I wasn't eager to come face to face with Lucien, who, for whatever reason, was never able to associate with anyone else in the house. Bernadone returned to the living room doors and said, "I ask that the rest of you remain here until we've returned from the basement. Officers, see that no one leaves this room." He closed the doors and turned to Mama Mahatma. "If you would, Mama, please lead us downstairs."

CHAPTER 10

As we stood at the basement door, we were suddenly plunged into total darkness. It was only the electricity going out, but it felt like a trap door had sprung open and we had dropped into a deep, dark pit. The darkness lasted only a few seconds before the lights came back on.

"It's that approaching thunderstorm," said the Lieutenant. At that moment one of the officers, a police woman, came in the side door. "Give me your flashlight, please, officer, just in case the lights go out again. Did you find anything out there in the yard?"

"No, Lieutenant, nothing. We'll have to wait till daylight to really inspect the area."

"Come this way, gentlemen," said Mama Mahatma opening the door to a narrow descending stairway that was dimly lit by a single light bulb.

"Pay attention, George," said Bernadone as we began to descend, "pay close attention."

We descended the basement stairs which halfway down made a sharp turn to the right. At the bottom of the steps to the left was a short flight of stairs. They led up to an outside door on ground level on the west side of the house. Directly in front of us was a large room that occupied about half of the basement. On the far left was an ancient coal-burning furnace next to the new gas furnace. The latter had been adapted to use the existing heating ducts which followed a serpentine path, intertwining with the water and sewer lines along the low ceiling of the room. On the right of the furnace was a large wooden storage shelf. Reaching from floor to ceiling, it contained a collection of old jars and bottles. Originally it must have been a storage place for preserves and canned food. Just beyond the shelf was a door-

158

way. A single dangling bare light bulb on the far side of the room hung over two large laundry sinks, an old wringer washing machine and a wooden table.

"Come this way, please," Mama said as she led us to the right out of the large room along a darkened hallway. This part of the basement was divided into two sections, one open, the other enclosed. The open section was dimly lighted. From its dusty appearance, no one had been in it for years. It was piled high with a collection of old lawn chairs, furniture, boxes and trunks.

On the wall of the enclosed section to our right were two doors. The first was partially open, revealing a bathroom. Bernadone peeked in and said, "No one in here." We continued down the hallway a few steps to the second door which was closed. Mama Mahatma knocked and waited. My breath was coming in short spurts. I dreaded meeting Lucien. But no answer came to her knock. She knocked again without a response. Then she turned, smiled at us and opened the door.

As she flicked on the light, we saw a small room containing a single bed, a small desk with a lamp on it and a wooden desk chair. No one was in the room. Next to the table was an old, tattered easy chair, partially covered by a purple afghan.

"Lucien must be out," she said with a shrug of her shoulders.

"Out where, Mama?" But Bernadone's question was answered only by another shrug of her shoulders. "Do you mind if we look around his room?" She smiled and shook her head no. "I suppose this was once a servant's room, perhaps the family chauffeur's?"

"Correct, Inspector. At least so I was told when I purchased the house."

"So this is Lucien's hermitage." Bernadone walked to the desk. Next to the lamp on the left side of the desk was a small cup with pencils and felt pens. A few sheets of clean paper lay beside the pencil cup. The room was immaculate, not a trace of dust anywhere. Bernadone sat down on the bed, his eyes slowly circling the walls which were bare except for two framed pictures of flowers. He stood up and walked closer to them. "Pressed flowers, a delightful pastime that one doesn't see much these days. Well, nothing here! Let's search the rest of the basement."

We left Lucien's room and walked back toward the first section of the basement. As we passed the bathroom, Bernadone stopped. "Excuse me, Mama, for taking your time, but I'd like to look at the bathroom again." He stepped inside as the three of us waited in the hallway. "Mama," he called from inside, "it seems that Lucien has forgotten to empty his bath water. This tub is full."

"That child's so forgetful . . . ." She stepped inside and, reaching down, pulled the plug on the bathtub. Bernadone smiled at me as the water gurgled down the drain. As he moved on with Mama and the Lieutenant, I stepped inside and quickly looked around the old bathroom. Everything looked normal. I didn't see anything unusual except that the soap dish at the edge of the tub was empty. Not wanting to miss anything, I quickly rejoined the others.

When I caught up with them, Bernadone was standing at the door to the right of the old shelves. His eyes seemed to be survey- ing everything in the abandoned laundry area. "And this door leads to...?"

"The wine cellar. You may see for yourself, if you wish."

Bernadone opened the door and turned on the light. It was a brick-lined room about eight feet long, with built-in wine racks to hold the bottles. Only a few bottles, some covered with dust, were in the racks. The room was cool yet dry. Bernadone stood in the middle, his head tilted back, examining the curved barrel- vaulted ceiling.

"Ah, they really knew how to build houses then, didn't they? An excellent wine cellar, but your supply looks a bit thin."

"Yes, I must be getting old, Inspector. I'm not as disciplined as I once was in keeping it stocked as I should. Shall we go back upstairs?"

"Of course, it's late, and I don't like putting you through all this. Just a few moments more." Kneeling down, he retied his shoelace. As he did, he ran his finger along a long scratch on the floor that ran parallel to the east wall. He stood up and smiled. "Let's go, friends, we've seen all there is down here. Mama, when do you expect Lucien to return?"

"That's difficult to say. I mean, he's a mature adult and comes and goes on his own. As Cain said, 'I'm not my brother's – my child's – keeper.' "

160

"Yes, yes, of course. You don't happen to have a recent photograph of him, do you?"

"Sorry, Inspector. Hermits are such shy folk. They avoid cameras like orthodox Amish."

"Would you be willing to help a police artist with a sketch of Lucien?"

"Of course, Inspector."

"I'll schedule it for the morning if that's OK, Mama."

"Certainly. Well, if we're finished down here, perhaps . . . ."

"One more moment, please," Inspector Bernadone said as he stood looking over a variety of objects stored by the old furnace in the northwest corner of the basement. Piled next to the short flight of steps that led up to the ground level door were some old, wooden coke bottle cases, a bicycle with only a front wheel, several cardboard boxes and a couple of wire cages. Bernadone pointed toward the collection. "Been years since I've seen wooden coke bottle cases...and these cages?"

"Just cages, why do you ask?"

"Curious, Mama Mahatma, just curious. It's my business, you know, to be curious." He reached up and switched on the hanging light which was not connected to the light switch Mama had turned on. Holding his hand up to it, he smiled. "A heat lamp. Curious. Well, that's all we can do tonight, and it is late. Let's do go back upstairs."

We climbed back up the narrow stairs to the main floor. When we reached the top and stepped into the hallway, Mama Mahatma locked the door and turned to us, saying, "I'm very tired. If it's all right, Inspector, I would like to go to bed. This has been a trying night. Poor Dio, poor unfortunate child. I know he wasn't a saint, but he was...well...."

"Good night, Mama Mahatma. I hope that you're able to sleep. I apologize for putting you through all this tonight, but it has been necessary. I hope you understand; it's my duty. You've been most helpful. Thank you, and I hope that tomorrow we will be able to resolve at least some of this mystery. When Lucien returns, you will inform me, won't you?"

"Inspector, I want to be of assistance. Anything I can do to help you solve this horrible crime, know that I am at your service. Good night to the three of you." She turned and slowly walked to her room. It was the first time since I had come to her boarding house that Mama appeared to be her age. I felt for the poor woman. All this must have been so painful for her.

Bernadone turned toward the Lieutenant and said, "Jim, let's tell the others that they can go to their rooms as well. This has been a long night for all of us. From the sound of the wind outside, I think that the storm is about to hit. You and the others here on the case might as well head home too."

"Right, Bernadone. Do you think this guy Lucien did it? I take it that, since you asked her for his photograph, you've never seen him. Where could he be on a night like this?"

"As of now, Jim, Lucien has been one big mystery."

"While we were searching the basement," the Lieutenant responded, "I had a theory about the identity of the murderer. What if this is another attack by the Woodsdale Killer? I mean, all his victims to date have been prostitutes. Why not a pimp this time?"

Cocking his head slightly to the left, Bernadone smiled. " 'He?' What makes you think the Woodsdale Killer is a he? But your theory might be a good one. We'll have to test it out. For now, let's go to the living room and tell the others that they are free to go to their rooms."

"Inspector, what did you find down in the basement?" asked Father Fiasco as we entered the living room. "You were gone a long time."

"Lucien wasn't there. Apparently he's gone out somewhere. We saw his room and inspected the rest of the basement, but no sign of him."

"Something strange is going on in this house," said Jon, sitting with his arm still around Maria. "I thought he never left the basement."

"Well, we didn't find anyone down there, and I think that it's time we all went to bed. That thunderstorm is almost here, and we're liable to lose our electricity. The Lieutenant here tells me that they're predicting it will be severe. Let's all of us go to bed while we can see our way. You're all free to come and go, but we ask you not to leave town for any reason and to keep yourselves available for questioning."

"Bernadone, while you were in the basement, I talked with

the others here about having a Memorial Mass tomorrow for Dio. I know that no one here had any great love for him, but he deserves our prayers and he needs them."

"Good idea, Father – an excellent idea. What time? I'd like to attend the Mass."

"I'm proposing late afternoon, say around 5 o'clock – so that all those who would like to can be there, including Dio's associates."

"If that's agreeable to the rest of you, I'm sure it will be OK for Mama Mahatma. We sent her off to bed after we came up from the basement. She's very tired – and troubled – by all this. Well, good night to all of you."

Bernadone escorted the Lieutenant and the other police to the covered carriage entrance door and visited briefly with them. I was in the kitchen washing the coffee cups when he walked in. He sighed deeply and sank into one of the kitchen chairs.

"Some night, George. I'm tired, but not sleepy, if you know what I mean. My body's exhausted, but my mind is in four-wheel drive trying to pull all the pieces together."

"Yeah, I feel that way too. What did you think about our search of the basement? You know, when I first came here I asked Mama Mahatma if an old house like this had any secret passages. She simply laughed and told me that sort of thing only existed in horror movies. Do you think that, maybe, there are hiding places here? Maybe Lucien's still somewhere in the house."

"I never thought about the possibility of secret passageways. Might be worth checking out tomorrow. Perhaps Lucien *is* still here, somewhere. But I'm too tired to go looking for him tonight. The police checked every room and closet in the house and found nothing, and our search of the basement left us with nothing tangible to show. Yet it wasn't a waste of time. Did you pay attention down there?"

"I tried to pay attention – as you asked – and not miss anything."

"Good. It's important to not miss anything, even the smallest of details. Often, however, what isn't there is more important than what is. In fact, that's what kept my mind hooked tonight – what was missing."

"Missing? I was so busy trying to pay attention to everything we saw that I didn't think about looking for what wasn't there.

What *was* missing, other than Lucien?"

"Several things! For tonight, though, I'll give you just one: did you notice that when we were about to go down to the basement . . . ."

"And the lights went out?"

"Yes, the power was off for a few seconds, and we were in total darkness. Then it came on again, and the Lieutenant had that exchange with the officer who had come in from the garden . . . ."

"Yes, he borrowed her flashlight. We didn't need it since the lights didn't go off while we were down there. I still don't see what was missing."

"Recall, George, that when the lights came back on, Mama opened the door to the basement for us."

"Yes, but what's unusual about that?"

"George, I didn't hear her use even one of her keys on those three locks. That door was already unlocked! She knew it was and so didn't bother to unlock it."

"In the confusion of the lights going off and on again, I missed that detail completely. What do you think it means?"

"That, my friend, I don't know yet. But we're both tired, and I'm reserving all my judgments until I get the coroner's report tomorrow morning. George, let's turn in. And tonight, before you get in bed . . . ."

"Yes – say my prayers?"

"No, take a peek under your bed! Better make sure that Lucien isn't hiding under there."

Rising from his chair with a hearty laugh, Bernadone put his arm around my shoulders and gave me a hug. We climbed the back stairs to the second floor and went to our rooms. After closing my door, I'm ashamed to say, I looked under my bed!

CHAPTER 11

I was awakened from a deep, almost drug-like sleep by the sound of a telephone ringing. I rolled over and with one half-opened eye peeked at my alarm clock. I was shocked to see that it was 8:30! I had overslept. The sun was shining in my window. But while it was up, I wasn't. The telephone must have been over in Bernadone's room. I slowly swung my feet over the edge of the bed. I sat there, rubbing my eyes, trying to wake up. With a determined effort, I stood up and made my way toward the bathroom. Bernadone's door was open. He waved at me and smiled as he spoke on the telephone.

My shower revived me. As I shaved, my mind explored memories of last night – the scene with Dio in the hallway, the questioning after he was found dead, the visit to the basement and all the unanswered questions that hung, this morning, like bats in my brain. As I finished combing my hair, I could hear Bernadone next door singing some song in French. As I walked out of the bathroom, he stopped singing and called out, "Bon jour, George, have a good sleep? The storm didn't keep you awake, did it?"

"What storm? I didn't hear a thing after I hit the bed. As tired as I was, they could have moved the entire Russian army through my room and I wouldn't have heard it. The storm finally came?"

"Yes, there was a lot of thunder, lightning and heavy rain, but it's all passed us now. It's a beautiful day. After you've dressed, let's have coffee together."

"Great, it's a deal! See you downstairs in a few minutes."

As I dressed, I looked out my west window overlooking the garden. The entire house was encircled in those yellow ribbons that read **Do not cross. Police Department.** I could see several police officers carefully inspecting the yard and garden. As I looked down at them combing the yard, I wondered if, considering the rain, they could find anything that might indicate that Dio had been killed outside the house. I hoped so, because if he wasn't murdered outside, then I was living with a killer! But then again, I probably was anyway, regardless of the location of his death.

I found the Inspector waiting for me as I entered the small dinette. He poured me a cup of coffee, and I asked, "Heard anything from the coroner yet?"

"Yes, that was the telephone call just before you took your shower. A very interesting report: Dio didn't die from a blow to the head. He was suffocated! The coroner also found bruises on his chest and ribs. Poor Dio, it must have been a painful death, having his life slowly squeezed out of him. Perhaps God is merciful, and Dio wasn't aware of what was going on. The coroner said that the blow to the head may or may not have made him unconscious at the time of his death."

"Suffocated! You mean someone literally squeezed him to death? You'd have to be pretty strong to do that."

"You're right. Dio was a small man. He only weighed 130 or so, but that's still large enough to resist being suffocated. The coroner's report makes Jim's theory of the Woodsdale Killer having murdered Dio improbable. It's not the pattern that we've seen in the deaths of those women."

Bernadone stood up, walked to the window and looked out at the search team. "I have a hunch that those officers out there in the yard aren't going to find any evidence that Dio was killed outside. I think it happened right here in the house."

The hot coffee was just the jolt I needed to kick my brain into overdrive. "I hate to say this, but Jon's a very strong man, strong enough to squeeze someone to death. Besides being strong, he hated Dio with a passion."

"Yes, I know. And I hate to say this, but our mutual friend, Father Fiasco, is also very strong! Like Jon, his anger toward Dio was intense that night in the living room. He became livid when Dio accused him of being defrocked for some sexual abuse. Fiasco's such a good friend of mine — has been all these years — that I hate to even consider him as a suspect."

"I agree. They're both good friends. Do you really think either one could have killed Dio?"

"Besides them, we can't rule out Mike – and I really hate to say this, but also Mama Mahatma!"

"What? You can't be serious. Mama Mahatma?"

"Yes, while she's an old woman, I'm sure you've noticed that she's also very strong. All her excuses about her poor legs and how she can't climb stairs were made questionable by some of her recent behavior. I don't know if she's strong enough to squeeze someone to death, but like the others she had good reasons to kill Dio. He killed Fatima and brutally violated Maria. No, we can't discount her as a possibility. Then, of course, there's Lucien!"

"I have problems with Mama Mahatma as the murderer. I can't believe that she could actually kill Dio. If anyone in the house truly cared for him, it was she. No, I can't imagine her killing anyone for that matter. I would have to say, however, that she certainly wasn't very cooperative in the investigation last night. Do you think she was covering up for Lucien when she said she didn't have a photograph of him?"

"Shortly, I'll be taking Mama Mahatma to headquarters so she can help with the police artist's sketch. However, I'm not very confident that it will assist us. After all, we're not sure if Lucien even exists! No one has ever seen him, right? Even Fiasco and I who've lived here for years have never seen him. What if he's a purely fictional character, a colorful creation of Mama Mahatma's imagination?"

"Why would she fabricate someone like that?"

"Who knows? Perhaps just to add a little spice to her roomer's lives. Lucien certainly exists in our minds – and fears. She cleverly could have created a symbolic person for what each one of us dreads. Maybe he's a symbol of the unknown itself, which has to be the mother of all fears. Lucien could just represent whatever is too ugly inside each of us to let come to the table. He may be that *something* that's kept imprisoned, locked up in a small room in the back of the basements of our minds."

"Bernadone, that's brilliant! It fits with what I observed last night in the basement. You told me to pay attention, and I did. That room she implied was Lucien's didn't look like a man's room. Everything was so clean and tidy. The pictures of flowers

167

on the wall – pressed flowers at that – gave the room a woman's touch – not unlike Mama's quarters upstairs. I doubt someone as independent as Lucien sounds would let his mother decorate his room. I also observed that the cup with the pencils and pens was on the left side of the desk. That means whoever used them was left-handed, right? And I have noticed, especially at table and when I've had tea with her, that Mama is left-handed."

"George, you may not feel you're making much progress on your spiritual quest, but you're becoming a damn good detective! You're right about the room. I had the same observations. Even the purple afghan didn't fit. It told me the room was more likely to be used by an older woman than a man."

"You know, when I first asked Mama Mahatma if I could use the attic for my hermitage, she lit up and said something like, 'That would be lovely, George, then we'd have a hermitage in the attic and one in the basement.' It sure appears that it's her room, not Lucien's."

"Yes, that's what I think. The pressed flowers, I'll bet, came from her garden, right outside this window. Unfortunately, that's only one mystery solved, and it doesn't exclude the possibility that Lucien does exist!

"Well, I'm on my way with Mama Mahatma to headquarters. Besides the sketch of Lucien, I have to check on some other matters. This isn't the only case I'm on. I'll have another officer bring Mama back later this morning. Don't stop trying to fit the pieces together, George. Remember to fit in even pieces that were not there. I'll see you at Dio's Memorial Mass this afternoon. Maybe by that time, we'll be closer to solving this mystery."

Before I left the dinette, I found some paper and drew a diagram of the basement as I remembered it. With the drawing as a visual aid, I carefully studied the basement, looking for some clue that we might have overlooked. I kept asking myself, "Is there something that I'm missing?" After three-quarters of an hour and no new insights, I folded up my drawing and washed my coffee cup. After all, I wasn't hired as a detective but as a janitor and cook. So I began my daily tasks. I spent part of the day cleaning the house, but it required real discipline to attend to chores. I wanted to let my mind explore the events of last night, looking for clues to Dio's murder. It was really difficult paying attention to my dusting.

I paused before lunch and took time to meditate, since I hadn't prayed when I got up in the morning. As I sat there in silence, I became aware that not only were Fiasco, Jon, Mama and Lucien suspects, so was I! I mean, I also hated Dio! I also had felt intense anger toward him for killing Fatima and abusing Maria. Didn't Jesus say that anyone who is even angry at another is guilty of murder? If that's true, then I could have been convicted of homicide, for I had been violently angry at Dio. In a real way I shared in the action of his murder by my rage. I also felt guilty that I experienced a sense of great relief that he wouldn't be around the household any longer.

I suddenly remembered that I was seated in meditation – at least that had been my intent. My mind was actually caught up in the maze of mysteries around Dio's death. While my thoughts were enlightening – I mean, about my share in the guilt of his death – they were far from centering. I returned to my mantra, feeling the quieting effect of its power.

Soon, I again lost my center as I began to reflect about a statement Gloria made last night. While I'm hardly one of her biggest fans, part of me had to agree that whoever killed Dio did a service to the rest of us. Yes, I was relieved that Maria was now free.

Ah, Maria! In the midst of all this, I had pretty much forgotten about her. She had to be caught in a revolving door of emotions. I could imagine how her sense of relief would suddenly flip into guilt for wanting Dio out of her life. Then that emotion would swing around into sorrow since she did have some feelings for him. Poor Maria, I hoped she was all right.

A sound of hammering outside at the carriage house, like a blow from a Zen master's stick, reminded me that I wasn't praying. Once again I had allowed my thoughts to take me hostage and kidnap me from my prayer of quiet. I gave myself over to the hammering as it continued, letting it be the mantra-of-the-moment, an ally in keeping me centered and momentarily free from reflecting on Dio's murder.

Even the rhythmic sounds of the hammers, however, weren't powerful enough to keep me focused in my meditation. Soon my mind began playing with the thought that I had only a few days left before I was to go home. Once more, I was cast adrift in the whirlpool of considerations about my time here.

The months had passed so quickly. When I left home, I expected that six months dedicated to quiet and reflection would effect a major change in me. I had idealistically believed that such an intense retreat would deepen my meditation to a point where I could do it anywhere at any time. Yet here I was, almost six months later, and I couldn't sit still in silence without a hundred thoughts elbowing one another aside for prime time in my mind. I wondered if my silent times would ever have any real depth, any real density.

I glanced beyond Dio's hourglass to my alarm clock and saw that my thirty minutes for meditation had passed. I made a profound bow to the floor, said my prayer, "There is no God but God," and added, "and I am your unworthy servant."

The hammering outside continued, so I looked out my north window to see what was going on. Down below, Father Fiasco, in work pants and a T-shirt, and two other men were building the framework for some sort of platform. I watched his powerful arms bring down his hammer with great force, and I recalled Bernadone's sad statement that our strong mutual friend was one of the murder suspects. Watching them working, I thought, "It's kind'a like the old days when they built a gallows for the condemned. Is that what old Fiasco's up to?"

"George, are you in your room?" came Mama Mahatma's voice from downstairs.

"Yes I am, Mama Mahatma. I'll be down in a minute."

When I reached the bottom of the stairs, she was standing by the old grandfather's clock. She looked tired and anxious but was smiling. "I hope I didn't interrupt your prayers, but with all that has happened in the past two days, I would like to have a special dinner this evening for everyone. You know, George, some good wine and something really sumptuous for the main course. Could we visit about the menu?"

The two of us walked into the kitchen where we sat down and settled on a menu for the evening meal. We decided on a special dish, one of Mama Mahatma's old family recipes for curried duck.

When I assured her that I would take good care of the worn

DUCK CURRY

2 ducks (4 to 5 pounds each), cut into 6 pieces each
2 large yellow onions, coarsely chopped
6 ribs celery, coarsely chopped
6 cloves garlic, minced
2 Granny Smith apples, coarsely chopped
3 tablespoons mild curry powder
3 tablespoons hot curry powder *← 4 Tbs for those who like it hot!*
1 teaspoon ground ginger
1 teaspoon ground cardamom
1/2 teaspoon fennel seeds
Pinch cayenne pepper
1/3 cup unbleached flour
4 cups chicken stock
1 cup apricot chutney *← This makes the recipe!*
1/2 cup grated coconut
3/4 cup whipping cream
1 cup chopped dried figs
1 cup toasted cashews
1/2 cup minced crystallized ginger

1. Preheat oven to 375 degrees F.
2. Brown the duck in a large skillet over medium heat. Remove all but 1/2 cup of the fat. Roast, uncovered, for 15 minutes.
3. Remove the duck from the skillet and set aside. Add onions, celery and garlic to the pan and saute over medium heat until softened, about 10 minutes.
4. Add the apples and stir in the curry powder, ginger, cardamom, fennel and cayenne. After 2 minutes stir in the flour, cooking 2 more minutes. Then add the stock, stirring constantly until blended. Stir in chutney and coconut. *Simmer over low heat —*
5. Combine the duck and sauce in a large casserole and cook, uncovered, for 90 minutes
6. Remove the duck from the sauce. Stir in the cream. Return the duck and add the figs, cashews and crystallized ginger. Bake, uncovered, for 15 minutes. Serve immediately with hot cooked rice.

recipe card she handed to me, she responded, "No, George, Honey, you keep it as a momento of your time here." In the course of that conversation she emphasized, to an unusual degree, the importance of the chutney as the critical ingredient. It made me wonder.

She then told me that she was going to attend Dio's Memorial Mass. Large tears streaked down her dark cheeks as she spoke about her feelings over his death. As usual, she was compassionate and gracious in her words about him. "George, what would you and I be like today if we had grown up in the same environment as poor Dio? If no one had loved us, encouraged us to do well in school and helped us find a basis for making good choices, wouldn't we have turned out just like Dio – or perhaps worse?"

I agreed with her, at least in theory. While I didn't say anything, I reflected on how I believe many elements, like DNA code, environment, home life and how we are loved shape us as persons. However, I also feel that each of us has to make a decision to be good or evil, and that we're free to make that significant choice. Then I wondered about Lucien. Old Sophia the Wise must have guessed what I was thinking since she asked, "George, you want to say something?"

"Nothing, Mama, just thinking . . . ." I wanted to ask her directly if Lucien actually exists. Like some of my other thoughts, however, I decided not to mention it. It wasn't my business to investigate the crime; it was Bernadone's and the police department's. Once again the sound of hammering came from the carriage house.

"Mama Mahatma, do you know what Father Fiasco is building? It looks like some sort of platform."

"I imagine it's for the Memorial Mass this afternoon. Some time ago I showed him a short play I had written. It's a morality play, like the miracle plays of the Middle Ages that were performed on the front steps of cathedrals. This morning he asked me if he could use it as part of Dio's service, and I gave it to him. I believe he's been busy ever since with giving out parts to some of his parishioners, practicing and directing the play. He has a little church theater group, you know, which does dramatic sorts of things, usually for big feast days. He's probably decided to build a new and larger stage for tonight's production. I would also guess that when they're finished they'll reassemble it inside the church. Earlier this afternoon he borrowed some of my jewelry for the play – and also some of Maria's."

"Mama, I didn't know you'd written a play? You're a woman of many talents. I've enjoyed working for you and being part of your household, even if I haven't made much headway on my spiritual quest."

"What do you mean, George? I think you're a very spiritual person, and you do such a good job of cleaning and preparing meals. I'm going to hate to see you go. I'd like to tempt you to stay by offering you a raise, but I know you have to return to your wife and family. I hope all this terrible trouble with Dio can be cleared up before it's time for you to leave us."

"I do too, Mama, and I want you to know that while living here hasn't been all I had hoped it would be, it has been very educational and adventuresome. It's been a rich experience, and I've made some good friends, like Inspector Bernadone, Father Fiasco and, of course, yourself – oh, yes, and Maria and Jon as well. But it soon will be time for me to leave. I'll have to be satisfied with whatever small progress I've made. It seems that ever since I came here it's been one aggravation after another. Yet in the midst of it all, I've really grown fond of you and the others."

"Thank you, George, that's a beautiful thing to say. You're very dear to me. You know, as Malcolm Forbes said, 'If you have a job without aggravations, you don't have a job!' But, I am truly sorry about the anguish around Dio's murder and that you had to become involved in this terrible thing."

"I appreciate that, Mama Mahatma, and I understand. I'm with you in your pain, and I too hope that Dio's murder is resolved before I have to leave. I have a feeling that Inspector Bernadone is close to solving it."

She smiled. "Well, that is good news, isn't it?" The smile, however, quickly faded from her face. Her usually serene countenance hinted at some kind of hidden distress, but I couldn't be sure. Non-verbal messages, especially ones unintentionally sent, are never easy to read. Without special insight it's best not to try and decode them. I had read the other day that the muscles of the human face have the possibility of making 250,000 different expressions. It takes a rare, even gifted, translator to read correctly as much as a tenth of so many different messages!

Mama rose from her chair, saying that she needed a nap before the evening's activities. I had to wonder, however, if it was only an excuse to end our conversation. We parted, and I decided that since it was a couple of hours before I had to start preparing dinner I would go up to the attic for a session with the Magic Lantern. I had not been up there in days, what with everything that had happened.

I pulled down the shades and darkened the old nursery. Reaching into my bag of slide boxes, I selected a box. The very first slide I inserted into the machine began to move! The image on the wall was of a street scene in front of a courthouse. From the clothing of the people crowded on its steps and the old cars in the street, it appeared to be sometime in the late 1920's.

A newsboy waving a newspaper filled the image area. Giant banner headlines read **The Custody Trial of the Decade**. A large crowd of reporters and photographers swarmed about the courthouse like night bugs around a porch light, eager to get a photograph of one, or both, of the famous parents.

The images quickly moved inside the courthouse, into a courtroom that was packed wall to wall. The clerk brought the gathering to order, commencing the trial's final summations. To the left of the judge were seated the mother and her attorney. To the right of the bench was the father with his attorney. In the middle, directly in front of the judge's bench, sat a police matron, stiff-spined, staunch-faced, rigid in her navy-blue police uniform. The matron, Miss Marbleton, unmarried, in her late fifties, her graying hair swept back in a bun, had been entrusted with the care of the couple's small child during the time of the trial. Miss Marbleton held the child with a sort of sanitary security, as if holding the key piece of evidence.

The mother's attorney was the first to speak. He stated in passionate pleas how unfair and cruel it was for the court to have taken away the child based on the false allegations of the father, a cruel, uncaring man. As the child's mother, large-breasted and wide-hipped, the very picture of a bountiful, nurturing mother, smiled at the judge, her attorney enumerated the reasons why the father was unfit for custody.

"Your Honor, this man is cruel and demanding. He practices corporal punishment on their child, even though she is very young. While claiming to love his daughter, he is distant and indifferent. He rarely pays attention unless the child does something wrong. Even when she obeys, he remains unapproachable and unaffectionate. He is given to loud shouting, loves to lay down house laws, thundering in anger when he doesn't get his way. Your Honor, my client, the mother, asks the court for total custody of her child and that a restraining order be placed on the father to keep him away from the child."

Next, the father's lawyer stepped forward before the bench. "Your Honor, my client, the father of this child, asks for complete custody so that the child will not be destroyed by her mother's permissive addiction. This woman is not a fit guardian of the child. She refuses to discipline her daughter when she misbehaves. Instead, she only showers her with gifts, affection and treats. This child, your Honor, it is clear, is already spoiled! Unless the court acts at once, the child will end up completely undisciplined, immoral and rotten. May it please the court, based on the evidence of this woman's inability to be a proper parent, we implore that the child's father be given full custody."

The judge closed his eyes and folded his hands together beneath his nose as if in prayer. After a few minutes he asked that the mother step before the bench. "I have listened to the case presented by your attorney, but what do you yourself have to say?"

"Your Honor, what *can* I say? I'm a *mother*! This child is flesh of my flesh; how can I not love her? How can I ever inflict pain or punishment upon such a tiny child. The poor dear has no knowledge that she's doing wrong. She's too young to realize the consequences of her behavior. So whenever she cries, how can I not rush to her aid, not rescue her when she's in danger? Your Honor, I don't believe in having to be shaken to be awakened. A gentle word, a kiss, an embrace also awakens one. I am not lax or permissive. It is simply that my love is unconditional. I ask that you grant me, the mother, complete custody of my child."

"Thank you for your words. I will take them into consideration before I make a judgment. You may be seated. I now call the father before the bench." The child's father, a large man in his late fifties, dressed in a dark suit, his head like a snow-capped, wind-swept mountain, stepped before the judge's bench.

"In your own words, sir, tell this court why you believe that you, and not the mother, should be the sole legal guardian of your child."

"Your Honor, thank you for this opportunity. I love my child deeply. I fear that if she is allowed to remain in the care of her undisciplined, scatter-brained mother, she will be ruined for life. She must begin, yes, even at this early age, to realize the consequences of her behavior. No age is too young to learn that every action bears a harvest; evil bears evil and good bears good. She must learn, as soon as possible, that in this life there are things that are permitted, and those that are not. The failure of her mother to properly correct the child – instead only smothering her with love and affection – will create a monster, a plague upon herself and society. 'Spare the rod and spoil the child,' as Holy Scripture says. Your Honor, I plead with you and the court that for the eternal good of this child I, and I alone, be given custody."

The judge nodded his gratitude, and the father sat down. For many minutes the judge sat with his eyes closed, his hands folded in a prayerful gesture as he pondered the case in silence. Then he called the two attorneys to the bench. "Gentlemen, today I am going to do something that is highly irregular, but I feel it is necessary.

"Miss Marbleton, would you and the child please step forward to the bench. Will you, the child's parents, also come before the bench."

Miss Marbleton stood at military attention with the small child positioned in her grasp as if she were a rifle. On either side stood the child's parents and their attorneys. Slowly moving his glance from face to face, the judge said, "It is the opinion of this court that the final decision in this custody case is...to be made by the child!" Looking down at the child, the judge asked, "Young lady, with which parent do you wish to live?"

Now the child was so young that she didn't understand the logic or legal ramifications of what had been said, but she was aware, very aware. Her "awareness equipment" was brand new, not yet having been dulled. The child was keenly conscious of what had been going on around her as she was held in Miss Marbleton's rigid restraint.

When the judge asked her to choose with which parent she wished to live, she considered her two options. Then, in a flash of intuition, she realized that she had another choice! She could choose neither of her parents! Ah, now that was a fresh possibility. As she began to consider it seriously, she suddenly became acutely aware of the cold, icy grip of the matron, Miss Marbleton.

The final image of the child in the matron's grasp gradually faded from the wall. I sat in stillness as I pondered the implications of the strange story of the custody case. It spoke to the age-old conflict between justice and compassion. As ancient as the issue was, I wanted to carefully consider the meaning of the mysterious tale that ended without resolution – or did it? I knew that it had a lot to say about my whole time here, especially all the inner turmoil I had with regard to Dio. From deep inside me came a desire that the child could have a fourth option: a reconciliation of the parents, an integration of justice and mercy. Two parallel ideas ran through my mind. One was a line from the Psalms that I recently heard at a morning Mass at the Lone Star Cathedral: "Mercy and lawfulness have met, justice and compassion have embraced." The second was a line from the **Tao Te Ching** that Mama Mahatma had shared with me at a morning coffee break: "Know the strength of a man, but keep a woman's care." As much as I wanted to continue with these thoughts, I lacked the time for reflection. I needed to be down in the kitchen if the major part of dinner was to be prepared before Dio's Memorial Mass. I would set aside some space later to reflect on all it meant. For now, I turned off the Magic Lantern and hurried downstairs to the kitchen. As I did, I was reminded of the time by the familiar tick-tock of the great grandfather's clock.

As I prepared dinner, I gave myself a dispensation from having to be mindful about my food preparation. Instead, I gave myself permission to review carefully all that had happened last night with the murder. I placed my drawing of the basement on the windowsill, since I wanted to give special attention to what had happened down there. As I peeled the apples, I asked myself what was missing in the basement. I also tried to remember all that I had seen down there.

I almost cut myself when I suddenly recalled the wire cages! Bernadone had pointed them out among the boxes by the old furnace. How could I have forgotten? They were exactly like the ones I had seen Mama Mahatma exchanging with the farmer on those nights when he came to the house. I'd swear that when I saw them there were large rabbits in those cages. Last night, however, they were empty. Now, that's one thing that was missing! I was as excited with my discovery as if I had won the lottery.

While it was a clue, it was one that didn't mean anything. I had nothing with which to connect it. I was so engrossed in my thinking that, even though I had looked out the kitchen window at the area in front of the carriage house, I failed to realize that it was now empty. Earlier they had been building a stage out there. They must have finished their work and moved it inside the chapel.

Dio's Memorial Mass was to begin at 5 o'clock, so I hurried to fix as much of the dinner in advance as possible. I could leave the final touches for my return from Mass. When I was setting the table and came to Lucien's place, I couldn't help but wonder, "What if he appears tonight? Maybe that's why Mama wanted this to be an extra special dinner." While it was quite likely that Lucien was only a creature of Mama's fertile imagination, it was obvious that Bernadone had not completely discounted the possibility of his being very real. I shuddered at the thought of who – or what – might be filling his chair tonight.

Having prepared all that I could, I rushed upstairs and changed clothes for Mass. As I came out of my room, I met the Inspector hurrying down the hallway.

"Hi, George, I'm late. It's been a busy day at headquarters. I did have a chance to see the police artist's sketch of Lucien. He said that Mama was gracious and cooperative but very vague in her description. While it may not be very helpful, it is an interesting sketch. It's hard to imagine the character in the sketch could have hurt anyone. He looks downright angelic. Did you have any new ideas on our murder case?"

"Yes, I couldn't wait to see you. Remember those wire cages you pointed out last night? Do you recall how I told you that on a couple of nights I saw Mama Mahatma exchanging cages with a farmer in an old pickup truck? Well, those cages looked exactly like the ones we saw last night by the steps next to the furnace!"

"Good work, George! I'm delighted to see you're putting the pieces together. The curious fact of those empty cages also crossed my mind last night. Well, what do you think your new-found evidence means?"

"Sorry, I don't have an answer to that question. I've been brainstorming for the past hour or so, but no connection comes. I'm a blank. How about you?"

"Same for me, at least for now. But we're short of time, so we'll have to talk about it later. Don't give up, George. I think we're on to something. I need to clean up and change for Mass — I'll see you later." Bernadone rushed into his room, and as I started downstairs I was surprised to hear him singing cheerfully in French.

When I entered the kitchen, I found Jon and Maria. She was stunningly attired in a sleek black dress with a single strand of pearls, but it was clear that she had been crying. Her eyes were swollen and red. Jon had his arm gently around her shoulders. He smiled as I entered. "Hi, George, want to go to Mass with Maria and me?"

"Thanks, I would enjoy that." Because of all that had happened, I couldn't help but notice again how powerfully he was built — his muscular arms and strong hands. I again wondered, "Is it possible that Jon could have...?"

"George, I know you're aware of how much I detested Dio for the way that he treated Maria. You know how he refused to let her go so she could marry me, but I didn't hit him, even in anger."

"Poor Dio," said Maria, tears filling her eyes, "to have been so brutally beaten. I feel so sorry for him. I know he wasn't very lovable, but in spite of all his violence toward me, I think he really did care for me. In his own strange way, as much as Dio could care for anyone other than himself, he did love me."

I realized from their words that neither Jon nor Maria had

heard the coroner's report about Dio being murdered by suffocation and not by a blow to the head. Of course, Jon could be telling the truth that he had not killed him by a blow to the head and at the same time still have crushed him to death in the strong vice of his powerful arms. At that moment, Mike and Gloria entered the kitchen.

"On your way to Dio's service?" asked Mike. "I wonder if the police have arrested anyone yet for his murder? This whole thing is a mess, and all of us are caught up in the damn thing. How I wish that Gloria and I had never come here to live."

Gloria smiled her usual plastic Barbie Doll smile. One glance at them made it apparent that going to a service at Father Fiasco's church wasn't something they really wanted to do. It sure seemed they were attending Dio's memorial out of a sense of obligation. A small voice inside me whispered, "George, that's a judgment based only on surface evidence." Another little voice said, "That's a reasonable observation, George, since it's based on past information." The first voice challenged the second, "You lack sufficient evidence to make such a judgment even if you call it an observation." I felt guilty and tried to wipe away my negative judgment, even if the second voice did make good sense. It felt like there was too much negative emotion involved for it to be just an observation. It was best to get rid of it as soon as possible.

Returning from my mini inner dialogue to Mike's question, I said, "Yes, we are going to the Memorial Mass. Care to join us?"

The five of us walked across the yard to the carriage house. As we entered the chapel, what first caught my attention was the stage that had been constructed in the afternoon. It was placed just to the left of the altar, in the place where the open trunk-pulpit usually stood. We took our seats in the midst of a congregation composed of street people, prostitutes, barmaids and an assortment of underworld-type characters. Apparently Father Fiasco had invited all of Dio's former associates and friends. Mama Mahatma was seated in the first row and had saved a seat for Bernadone. A variety of floral sprays were placed around the altar. They looked fresh, unlike the second-hand bouquets I had seen before on the feast of the Purification.

The stage itself was hidden by a purple stage curtain composed of various shades and types of purple cloth. From its construction the curtain appeared to have been hastily sewn together with whatever cloth was at hand. The overhead hanging vigil lights cast a yellowish glow to the bluish shadow light of the late afternoon. I looked at my watch, and it was 5 o'clock. Shortly thereafter Bernadone walked down the aisle and took his seat next to Mama Mahatma.

A Black Gospel choir stood around the piano. At the sound of the large oriental gong, they began to sing, "Swing Low, Sweet Chariot." Father Fiasco, attired in purple vestments, solemnly entered from the rear of the chapel. He was accompanied by a woman dressed in red who carried an ornamented, jewel-encrusted Gospel book high above her head. Next in the procession was a young boy, not more than eight or nine, dressed in white and carrying a large wooden-framed mirror. Each time the Black choir reached the line, "Comin' for to carry me home," they more wailed than sang the words.

When the opening hymn was finished, Father Fiasco opened wide his arms in the traditional gesture of prayer. "Let us pray, friends, for Dio, our brother in Christ." We prayed in silence, but my mind was far from silent. I reflected on how those outspread arms of Fiasco, while hidden by his vestments, were extremely strong and powerful. He kept them that way with his part-time job at the freight company. Those arms were strong enough to squeeze the life out of a man!

"O Gracious God," he began to pray, "sweep up into the basket of your heart all our prayers this day as we remember your departed son, Dionysius. May he be at peace, resting in your bosom, and may each of us be at peace with him." He paused and nodded to the young boy dressed in white. The boy stepped forward to the front center of the altar and held up the large mirror so that it faced us.

Father Fiasco continued, "We ask your pardon, O God, for our failures to be kind, loving people. As we look into this mirror, a symbol of your Son, the perfect reflection of your love in human flesh, we ask you to forgive us for failing to mirror your love." Then he paused as we all looked into the mirror. While few people could see themselves individually, the image was more than just a crowd of faces. The effect was powerful. I realized that my image was not so crystal clear as to give me the right to stand in judgment of Dio. Then Father Fiasco went on, "May the ever-green pardon of God, the love of Jesus Christ, the compassion of the Lord Buddha and the mercy of Allah be with us all."

"Amen, amen," chanted all present, and we sat down for the readings of the Mass.

Father Fiasco, instead of being seated, stood in front of the altar. "Brothers and sisters, friends, for this Memorial Mass we will not have the usual scriptural readings. Instead, we will have a Miracle Play which was written some years ago by our own Mama Mahatma." He smiled toward her with affection. "Scripture is the voice of God, but God can speak in ten thousand different ways: in historic events, in newspapers, stories, popular songs, in every form of human expression and in the dramatic voices of nature. May this liturgical drama speak to each of us and touch us in those hidden places of our hearts which have sadly grown deaf to the liberating words of the Gospel." He then stepped down from the altar area to a chair in the front row to the left of Mama Mahatma.

From the rear of the chapel came the old Asian man whom I had seen before, the one with the large brass gong. This afternoon he wore a Mandarin robe, brilliant red with a large golden dragon on the back. He processed solemnly down to the altar with the gong in one hand and a stick with a leather ball on the end in the other. Standing to one side of the curtained stage, he paused in silence for a moment, then struck the gong with a mighty blow.

The purple curtain swept aside revealing a bedroom stage set. In the center was an old-fashioned high-backed wooden bed. There were tall lighted candles in brass candle holders on both bedside tables. To the left of the bed was a straight-back chair and a Japanese-style folding screen. On the left rear wall was a large window. To the right of the bed was a vanity dressing table with a bench. On the right back wall was a door.

A gray-haired woman in a long, flowing white nightgown was brushing her hair before the large, oval glass mirror on the vanity table. She stood up and walked to the bed, smoothed out the satin sheets and fluffed up the lace-edged pillows. Then she walked to the window and stood for a few moments looking out. An ornate gold clock on one of the bed stands struck the hour, and the woman turned and began to pace the floor. Finally, she heaved a great sigh and climbed into bed.

As she laid there, she occupied herself with adjusting the gold necklaces she was wearing. Then footsteps could be heard approaching from offstage right. The door opened and a white-haired man entered. He looked very weary as he sat with slumped shoulders on the edge of the bed.

"I've been waiting for you! Where have you been?" asked the woman in bed.

"I'm sorry, dear. Please forgive me. I had some work to do, and the time just slipped by." He stood up, went to a chair by one of the small end tables, sat down and took off his shoes. He then removed his shirt and pants and climbed into bed.

"You're coming to bed in your underwear? Put on your silk pajamas. Really!"

"Yes, dear, I forgot that you like to have things done properly. I'm sorry." Slowly he climbed out of bed and disappeared behind the folding Japanese screen. He returned wearing a pair of white silk pajamas and got back into bed.

"Ah, that's so much better. You know, dear, that I love you, even if I insist on all these little rituals. It's just so our life – and love – can be better – more civilized."

"Yes, dear, I know that, but you also know how I long for the old days. Remember when you and I would make love in the middle of the afternoon in the vineyard...or under the full moon on the hilltop. In the old days, it was so spontaneous, so vibrant that I . . . ."

"We were young then, very young, and we didn't have a family. A family changes all that. You *have* to have customs, rituals and appointed times. You just can't up and do whatever you feel like. Really, dear! I'm surprised that you can't see that."

"Shhh, quiet, dear. I think I hear something." He eagerly jumped out of bed and ran to the window. Leaning out, he looked both to the left and right. The woman sat up in bed and folded her arms in an angry pose. Slowly he walked back to the bed.

"You thought *he* might be out there, didn't you? That's where you were tonight. That's why you were late, isn't it? You were out on the highway looking for him again. I don't understand you, even after all these years. You look so intelligent, and folks around here call you the Wise One, but you're really so foolish."

She got out of bed, walked to his side of the bed and stood with her hands on her hips, "He's no good! We both know that. He's no good, and he will never make anything of himself. He took his full share of the inheritance, and off he went, whoring and gambling away his life. Oh, how he played both of us for fools! Yet you keep looking for him to return. I say that if he ever comes home, he should come crawling on his knees, begging pardon from both of us for all the disgrace he's caused us. You know as well as I what the neighbors say about us as parents, don't you?"

"I love him, and I'm sure he's been busy. That's why he . . . ."

"Hasn't written? Hasn't called you? Oh, I forgot, he did call you once, didn't he? A year ago wasn't it? He wanted you to send him some money by Western Union so that the Mafia wouldn't send him home in a box." She blew out the candle on his night table, walked around the bed, blew out the other candle and climbed into bed. In the darkness of the room she continued, "Why couldn't he have been like Ralph? Ralph is so obedient. He always does what he's supposed to. He never fails to be here when he's needed. Sometimes, I can't believe they're both our sons. Ralph is such a dear, so thoughtful and dependable...are you listening to me, or are you asleep? Sometimes when I speak to you I feel like I'm talking to myself." With that the curtain slowly closed on Act One.

I could hear the sounds of a scene change behind the curtain as we waited. In a few minutes the stage curtain opened, revealing the design of a high hilltop. Standing on top of the hill, with his back to us, was the white-haired man.

"Where are you, my son, and with whom are you sleeping this night? Are you well, or are you in great need? Oh, how my heart longs for you. How I wish that you would come back to me." He turned, looking left and right. "How my heart yearns to see you again, to hear your voice. Please don't let your youthful mistakes keep us apart. Who cares about the money you wasted? Who cares that you've thrown it away on carousing and drugs? It's you that counts, not the money." Slowly he sank to the ground with his head buried in his hands.

184

"If only I could go to Tijuana. I would walk the streets, climb the stairs to those little rooms where you pay for love and third-rate thrills. I would search the alleys for you. But if I did do that, it would only embarrass you. No, it is *you* who must come when you're ready, come home in perfect freedom, of your own free will. You must come home without even the persuasion of my love to turn you homeward. Your mother, good as she is, says that my lavish love for you only makes it cheap. She says that unless I punish you, cause you to lose face by making you come back crawling, begging for pardon, that my forgiveness will be without substance. Your mother says that I've spoiled you with my many gifts, that I've given you too much freedom. She says that you've used me, mocked my love by twisting me around your little finger. At times, I must confess, I've wondered if she's right. But then my heart is flooded with love for you. Oh, my son, if only you could hear the song that constantly rings in my heart: 'With all your heart, come back to me. With all your heart, come home to me.' "

The Black Gospel choir echoed back those lyrics, the song's haunting melody softly filling the little chapel. From the top of the stage set, a flock of papier-mache birds dropped down, swinging to and fro from strings.

Suddenly the white-haired man jumped to his feet. "Look, a flock of birds headed south! Little friends, come closer. Pause a moment on your journey and listen to the song of my heart. Make my song your song. Sing it to everyone you meet as you travel. Sing it to every stranger on the road, in every city, town and village. Perhaps my lost son will hear it. Little birds, fly south to Tijuana and sing my song to everyone you see."

As the curtain slowly closed, the man and the choir, accompanied by the chirping of the birds, sang, "With all your heart, come back to me."

Again the sounds of a scene change could be heard behind the curtain. The play, I reflected, was clearly a variation on the parable of the Prodigal Son. I was curious as to what would happen in the final act. The twist in the play was the presence of the prodigal son's mother. I had never given a thought to the mother before, since the original story had only three characters: the father, the prodigal son and his disgruntled brother. I wondered if the mother was . . . . My thoughts were broken off by the curtain opening on the third act.

The scene was the back of a large farmhouse. Outside the back door was a barbecue grill with a cloud of smoke rising from it. From inside the house came the music of a rock band and shouts of joy. Above these sounds, a tractor engine could be heard from off stage. From stage right appeared a young man in farmer's clothing. He stopped and looked in a window. Then he turned in rage and began to stomp away. At that moment, the mother rushed out the back door, "Ralph, poor Ralph, I know how you must feel. Your no-good brother has come home from Tijuana, and your father has thrown this big barbecue for him and his worthless friends. The house is full of them."

"Why, Mother? Why all this for someone who not only squandered his share of the farm, but even sponged more money off Dad after that was gone? He never wrote home, never called. Why all this?"

"Yes, Ralph, I know. It's nonsense. Your father wouldn't listen to me. He wouldn't even let him apologize for his ways of lust and drunkenness, for how we've all been shamed by his life. Your father didn't even ask him to explain why he hadn't written or called. Ralph, he gave your no-good brother the family ring! The gold ring that your father was given by his father. Ralph, I'm so . . . ."

The back door swung open, and the father appeared. "Ralph, my son, come in and join the party. Your brother whom we thought was dead has returned. Isn't that good news? Quick, shower, then come and join us."

"No, Father. I will not go in there and be a part of this madness. For all these years, I've stayed home, worked the farm and been faithful to you and Mother. I've never disobeyed Mother or you. I've done everything I was supposed to do, and you've never thrown a party for me or my friends."

"But, Ralph, *everything* I have is yours: the farm, the machinery, stocks and bonds. And I love you. I love your dependability and your faithfulness. But your brother has come home! Come in and . . . ."

"No! I don't want anything to do with you or your cheap love."

"Cheap? No, Son, my love isn't cheap! If you only knew how

costly is my love. Come, Mother, we are the hosts. We must return to our guests."

Ralph turned his back and stood there with arms folded as his father and mother disappeared into the house. In moments, his brother, a good-looking and exuberant young man, appeared.

"Ralph, it's good to see you again. You look great and so does the farm. You've done so much . . . ."

"What are you doing back here? Back for more money, or are you hiding from the police? Father says I should rejoice because you're alive and well. I wish to hell that you were dead! In fact, if I could, I'd kill you myself with my own two hands."

"I don't blame you, Ralph. You and I have never gotten along together. We're different, but I . . . ."

Ralph suddenly swung around and struck his brother with his fist. "Get out of here before I kill you. I hate you!" The two stood facing one another with their fists doubled. The younger brother was clearly angered by being struck, but he slowly lowered his arms to his sides. He walked to Ralph, embraced him and kissed him on the cheek. Then he turned and walked back into the house. Ralph stood with his fists clenched, looking skyward. "God, what am I to do? What?" He sunk to his knees in despair.

The flock of papier-mache birds again slowly descended on strings from above the stage as the choir softly sang, "With all your heart, come back to me. With all your heart, come home to me." As the lights dimmed, the curtain slowly closed.

Gradually all of us began to join in the chant of the choir. A cantor sang verses about the love of God, the ever-green compassionate pardon that is ours the moment we fail in our loving. To each verse we responded, "With all your heart, come home to me."

The woman in the red dress who had carried in the Gospel book walked to the center and proclaimed, "This is the Gospel, the Good News of the Lord."

We all chanted back, "Thanks be to God." Immediately, several women from the congregation, obviously hookers, came to the altar. They prepared the table with a white cloth, the bread and wine and the altar vessels. When all was ready, Father Fiasco walked to the altar. The women assisted him as he changed from his purple vestments to white ones. Then they returned to their seats.

"Friends, this afternoon we celebrate a Memorial Mass for our brother who is now one in the peace of God. We have mourned his death; now we rejoice that he lives in the promise of God's unconditional love. We who have looked into the mirror of the love of Christ know that we cannot judge Dio's life. Instead, like Ralph in the Miracle Play, it is we who must come home, we who must now come to God's feast, where saint and sinner both are table guests. With joy we celebrate not only the good news of the resurrection of the dead but also God's perpetual love for each one of us."

The Memorial Mass went on as I—like Ralph in the play—struggled to truly "come in and join the party." It wasn't easy. Indeed, such love is costly! I found to my surprise, however, that I was willing to pay the price. It wasn't as difficult as it first had seemed, especially when I remembered what was in my heart when that little boy in white held up the large mirror at the beginning of the liturgy. At Communion time, Father Fiasco prayed, "Let all the children of God come forward and share in this feast at God's holy table."

As the choir sang "Amazing Grace," everyone in the chapel came forward—everyone! I couldn't help but wonder about the enormous power there must be in such an inclusive communion, especially with so many of Dio's associates present: hookers, gamblers, bartenders and pimps. The sight of all the "sinners" going to Communion was truly an Amazing Grace. I could guess what Mike and Gloria must have been thinking, since the thought quickly came to my mind: "Why are these people being *allowed* to go to Communion?" I again remembered the ritual of the mirror and just as quickly another thought came to mind: "Who am I to determine who should, or should not, be allowed to feast at God's table? If this is truly the Meal of Christ, then it only makes sense that it should be a table with the same kind of guests that surrounded Jesus when he ate: the good and the bad, saints and sinners. All should be present; indeed, no one should be excluded!"

During the silent reflection after Holy Communion, it also occurred to me that since everyone who lived at Mama Mahatma's boarding house was here, even Dio's murderer must have gone to Communion! I scanned all the people in the congregation, many of whom I had never seen before. I wondered if Lucien was also here. My wandering mind was suddenly returned to the present moment as Father Fiasco stood up to conclude the Mass: "Let us stand and pray."

We stood in silent prayer for several minutes. My prayer was vacant of thought till I remembered Dio. I found myself, in those silent moments, asking him to forgive me for my anger toward him. I asked God to give me the Amazing Grace of being able to love in such a non-judgmental way.

Then, holding up a large wicker basket, Father Fiasco continued, "Into this basket, we place all our prayers to you, O God, as we join them to the prayers of all the peoples of this earth. Grant to your son, Dionysius, his inheritance as your child, that he might dine forever at your table with all the saints and holy ones. We do not ask you to forgive his faults. You already have. Rather, we ask you to help us forgive his sins and failings that have caused us pain. As we forgive him, so may you forgive us. We ask this in the name of your son, Jesus Christ, the holy mirror of your love."

We all responded, "Amen." Then Father Fiasco blessed us, and the choir began the closing hymn, "When the Saints Come Marching In." The congregation followed in procession behind Father Fiasco and marched out of the chapel. As my turn came to join the procession, I noticed that Bernadone was standing by the three icons. Rather than processing out, I went across the chapel to the spot where Bernadone was looking at the unfinished painting of the prophet with the nuclear mushroom cloud. When I reached him, he suddenly turned around toward me and exclaimed, "That's *it*, George! I know who killed Dio!"

"Really? Who was it?"

"Not now, George. It's not a closed case yet. I still have two or three loose ends, but now I have something solid to which I can tie all of them. Let me stay here in church, George. I need to be alone and to pray. I need a quiet place to make sure that all the pieces do fit together. You have dinner to prepare. I'll join you shortly, and *Inshallah* as my Moslem friends say, 'God willing,' I'll have something to share with you at dinner."

Reluctantly, I left him alone kneeling in the chapel. I was excited that he had a lead on Dio's murderer, but I wished he would have told me about his dramatic insight while standing there in front of that unfinished icon. As I left the carriage house, small groups of Dio's old associates stood in small circles visiting. I nodded to them as I crossed the driveway for the house. The sun was low in the west, and an atmosphere of evening calm surrounded the old house. The ritualized memorial service had, like all rituals, healed in a way that words and rational thinking cannot. While I was experiencing a sunset peace with Dio, I was also restless to know the identity of his killer. As I opened the kitchen door, my heart was pounding. This was not going to be just another evening meal!

CHAPTER 12

As we were sitting down to the table, Bernadone arrived. Mama Mahatma had asked me before dinner to set a place for Dio and to place a lighted candle at his plate. She said it was an old tradition to reserve a space for the deceased at the family table. As usual, I had also set a place for Lucien, and in a way had expected that he'd come. He hadn't appeared, however, at least not yet. As Mama Mahatma began the meal blessing, Bernadone nodded to me and smiled. After the ritual of Father Fiasco pouring a sip of the wine for Mama to taste, I filled all the glasses at the table.

Mama Mahatma raised her glass. "To Dio, may he rest in peace." We all nodded in agreement and drank to him. "May this dinner be a continuation of the beautiful Memorial Mass that our friend here, Father Fiasco, just celebrated for Dio."

The dinner conversation at first limped, but slowly the mood at the table became more lively. I hardly tasted my food; I couldn't wait for the Inspector to tell us who had killed Dio. As the meal progressed, it became clear that he wasn't going to do it during dinner.

Mama Mahatma again commented on the memorial service for Dio, thanking Father Fiasco for all his efforts to make it so beautiful. The conversation then focused on the Miracle Play that had replaced the scriptural readings of the Mass. Father Fiasco praised Mama's play, saying, "I've long wanted to use it in a liturgy, but the time never seemed right – that is, until Dio's death." We all agreed that it had touched us, but various opinions were voiced about what it meant. Mike found the father's kind of unconditional forgiveness to be unreal, saying it makes God's grace cheap. An animated discussion about forgiveness followed.

191

As the merits of pardoning one another were weighed, Mama Mahatma said, "It's like what Ingrid Bergman once said, 'Happiness is good health and a bad memory.' "

"Here's a toast to both those qualities," said Fiasco, raising his glass. We all drank, but I could tell that Gloria wasn't pleased. From where I sat, I could see that her left leg was nervously bobbing up and down. She soon became aware of it, stopped it and said, "I thought that the prodigal's mother in the play made women look vindictive. I'm surprised, Father Fiasco, that you of all people would allow that kind of representation."

"Gloria, you're taking the play too literally. Mama Mahatma's play is a parable, like all morality plays. In a parable one must look beyond the obvious to what is being signified. If the father in the play is a symbol of God, what then does the mother symbolize?"

"Easy, Father, she was the Church!" said Jon. "I loved that first act where she wanted to ritualize making love."

"Yes, Jon, the Church does tend to do that. Yet since the Church isn't just an institution, the mother is also us. In fact, as I see it, we can identify with both the mother and older brother in the play. The Germans have a saying that fits each of us: 'We always forgive our enemies, especially after they've been hung!' "

We finished the meal, and I cleared the dishes from the table. I was preparing to serve coffee when Bernadone said, "This evening, shall we have our coffee and dessert in the living room? I have something important to tell all of you."

"Excellent idea, Inspector," said Mama Mahatma rising from her chair.

Father Fiasco offered to help me with the dessert and coffee. When we were in the kitchen, without thinking, I whispered, "Bernadone's figured out who killed Dio. That's what he's going to tell us!"

"Are you serious? You mean, he knows?"

"Yes, it came to him this afternoon after Mass. He told me as people were leaving. He was standing in front of your icon of the apocalyptic prophet when he suddenly realized who had killed Dio. He didn't tell me who it was, however. He said he needed some time alone to put all the pieces together."

We carried the trays with coffee and the cheesecake I had

baked into the living room. It was then that it occurred to me that telling Father Fiasco about the Inspector's discovery wasn't terribly prudent. After all, Father Fiasco still was a prime suspect. After everyone had been served, Bernadone slowly sipped his coffee. Setting his cup and saucer down, he began, "Friends, what I wanted to tell you is that I believe I know who killed Dio!" Everyone's eyes moved about the room from one person to the next.

"Which one of us struck the fatal blow?" asked Jon.

"The coroner's report revealed that Dio did not die from a blow to the head. He was squeezed to death! While his body had bruises, small cuts and a blow to the head, Dio's death was the result of suffocation. Someone very strong simply squeezed him to death."

"*Peine forte et dure!*" gasped Fiasco. "It was a form of execution in the Middle Ages. It means 'pain hard and long.' Being pressed to death was reserved for those who had committed an 'unnatural offense.' It was used on heretics but could be inflicted on anyone who had offended Church or State."

"If my memory serves me correctly, Father, *peine forte et dure* lasted for days," responded Bernadone. "Dio was killed in a matter of minutes—and by someone very strong."

Anxious glances shifted back and forth from Jon to Father Fiasco, they being the two strongest persons in the room. For their part, they shot quick glimpses at each another. That exchange between the two suggested that neither had murdered Dio or that one of them was a good actor.

"As regards the identity of the murderer, we know, Jon, that Maria said you were with her in her room at the time of the murder. While you have the physical strength to have killed Dio—and a good motive—it wasn't you. Father, you also were a suspect; you had both the capability and a reason. Mama Mahatma has testified, however, that she came to get you in the carriage house to give Dio absolution. You may have been able to return there after killing Dio, but you didn't kill him either. That leaves an unlikely but real suspect—Mama Mahatma herself!"

"What? That's impossible!" cried Maria. "Mama Mahatma is the only one in this room who treated Dio with any kindness."

"True, Maria, but she's a very strong woman, strong enough to have crushed the life out of him. She also had motivation: Dio's nailing you to the door and his refusal to let you be free – as well as his brutal killing of Fatima!"

"Dio killed Fatima?" asked Fiasco, surprised. "I've missed her around here, but I didn't know she had been killed."

"Yes, George saw Dio intentionally crush her to death by running over her in the driveway. It's possible that Mama Mahatma saw it as karmic justice for Dio also to meet his death by being crushed, right? He also took delight in squeezing Maria, pulling her around with his tight grip. We all witnessed that behavior at the dining room table. Furthermore, Mama Mahatma's explanation of her whereabouts at the time of the murder is, shall we say, weak? She told us she heard Gloria screaming and knew that Dio had been killed, correct? George also told us that she was in the hallway when he came downstairs to the kitchen and said she looked very disturbed."

The eyes of everyone in the room moved uneasily toward Mama Mahatma. Maria was shaking her head in non-verbal denial as Bernadone continued, "Mama Mahatma herself told us that when she heard Gloria scream she ran to get Father Fiasco. Now all of us, except for Mike, were gathered by the grandfather's clock in the hallway when the body was found. Not one of us, however, reported seeing Mama Mahatma leave by either the carriage entrance door or the side door. Since she couldn't have left by the kitchen door without passing through that hallway, the only other way is the front door. Why, friends, would she have gone out that door? It's the longest way to the carriage house! No, I'm sorry, but Mama Mahatma wasn't in her room when she said she heard Gloria scream."

"I never said that I was in my room, did I?"

"No, but we all supposed that you were, which is what you wanted us to think. The question is: where were you at the time of the murder?

"But there's another detail – small, yet important. That incident at the basement door when you led George, the Lieutenant and me down to the basement. As we came to the door, the lights went out, and we all were left standing in the darkness. When the lights in the house came on again, you had the door open. It would have been impossible for you to unlock that door in such a short time or to do so without making a sound. No, Mama, you didn't unlock that basement door because you knew that it was already unlocked! You yourself had unlocked it earlier but were unable to lock it again."

Mama Mahatma raised her coffee cup, took a long slow drink and set it down again in its saucer with dignity. With a calm smile she looked at Bernadone, who went on, "I believe – and will prove – that Dio was killed in the basement! I'm convinced, Mama, that you carried and dragged his body upstairs and laid it on the bench next to the grandfather's clock. I suspect your intention was to drag it outside and leave it somewhere in the yard. At that moment, however, as you were catching your breath, or perhaps preparing to lock the basement door, you heard Gloria coming down the front staircase. So you left Dio's body on the bench and fled out the west door. In your haste, though, you failed to close it completely. We found it slightly ajar as we were investigating the scene shortly after finding Dio's body. You then ran from the house to the carriage house to get Father Fiasco."

"Bernadone, this is crazy!" said Father Fiasco. "To think that Mama Mahatma is the murderer! I know the evidence may point to her, but I can't believe you would even pursue such a path of logic."

"It's painful for me as well, Father, but it's my business to consider everyone as a suspect. So far, however, I have not said that Mama Mahatma is guilty of the crime."

"If it's not her," said Jon, "the only one left is Lucien!"

"Yes, that's correct, Jon," replied the Inspector. "I propose that before anything else is said we all go down to the basement together."

"What?" cried Gloria. "What if he's down there? What if he's returned?" Her left leg was bobbing as she voiced the fears of each of us.

Mama Mahatma's face appeared aged and fearful. "Is that really necessary, Inspector? I don't think that Lucien has returned to his room yet."

"No, he hasn't, Mama Mahatma. To begin with, that isn't his room. It's yours! While he may have visited you there, it's not

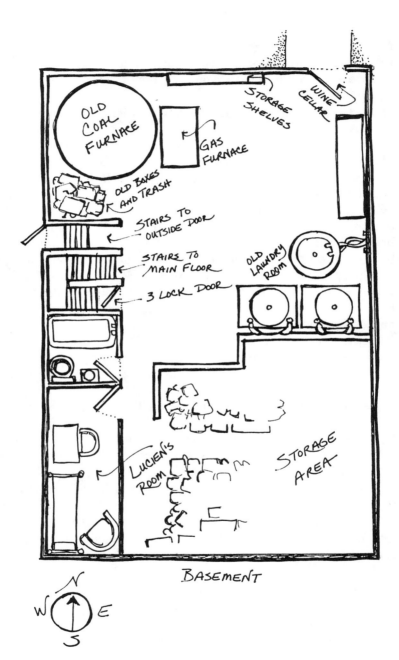

OLD COAL FURNACE

GAS FURNACE

STORAGE SHELVES

WINE CELLAR

OLD BOXES AND TRASH

STAIRS TO OUTSIDE DOOR

STAIRS TO MAIN FLOOR

3 LOCK DOOR

OLD LAUNDRY ROOM

LUCIEN'S ROOM

STORAGE AREA

BASEMENT

N
W E
S

his room. I believe Lucien is down there and that he's been down there all along. Come, everyone, there's nothing to fear, I assure you. It's time we settled this affair."

We descended single file into the basement and stood gathered together under the glare of the single bare light bulb that hung from the ceiling in the center of the first large room. Bernadone stood facing us with his back to the furnace and the old cupboard. "Last night when we came down to search, we did not find Lucien. Mama Mahatma took us down that hallway behind you to a room which we supposed was Lucien's. She didn't say it was his, but that was the implication. The room was, as I said, not Lucien's, but hers. It's your quiet place, Mama, your hermitage, correct?"

Mama Mahatma reluctantly nodded in agreement but didn't say a word. I trusted Bernadone's assurance that we had nothing to fear down here, but as with some Church dogmas, it was a belief that wasn't free of doubts. I also felt icy needles of fear being inserted one by one into my spine as I anticipated having to meet the mysterious Lucien. What would he look like? What would he do? Bernadone said there was nothing to fear, but I was afraid. Clearly, the others were just as fearful, even Jon. Bernadone walked around us and pointed to the large sinks and the old washing machine. "As you can see, this was once the laundry area for the old household." He pointed to the floor near the drain between the sinks: "Here, I believe, is where Dio met his death!"

"Inspector, here?" asked Jon. "How would he get down here? The basement door is always locked, and only Mama Mahatma has keys to those locks."

"He didn't come down the way we got here, Jon. He came down from up there." Bernadone was pointing up at the ceiling to a large, square hinged door. "I didn't see that opening when we were down here last night, but this afternoon I knew that it had to be there. Those benches by the grandfather's clock and on the second floor at the end of the hallway are directly overhead. They are actually old laundry chutes – large and tin-lined, rather common in old houses like this one. They were designed to save the labor of taking bed linen and clothing downstairs to be washed. George told me that he heard Dio

197

stumbling around in the hallway upstairs last night just before Jon came home. He said that Maria had pushed Dio out of her room fearful that Jon would kill Dio if he found him there. George also told me that Dio was very drunk and high on cocaine and was staggering around in the hallway. In his drunken stupor, Dio was searching quickly for someplace to hide. Thinking that the empty chest-like bench would serve that function, and not knowing it was actually a laundry chute, he climbed inside to escape from Jon."

"That was the sound Mama Mahatma asked me if I heard," I interrupted, "the sound of Dio crashing down from the second floor to the basement through the old laundry chute!"

"Correct, George. His fall down the laundry chute explains the numerous cuts and bruises on his hands and face and his snagged clothing. As he slid down the chute, its metal edges nicked him and tore his clothes. The bruise on his head must have been caused when he hit, head first, here on the basement floor. The fall wasn't enough to kill him, but it did stun him or perhaps temporarily rendered him unconscious.

"After talking with George in the hallway, Mama Mahatma realized that the sound of something large and heavy falling down the chute must have been Dio. She was anxious to get down here as soon as possible. When she left George, she only pretended to go to her room. As you went to the kitchen to fix your sandwich, George, she quickly returned and opened the basement door."

"Yes, I thought I had heard something, but dismissed it as the storm winds rattling something outside. So it was actually Mama Mahatma unlocking the door."

"Yes, George, that's right. Mama knew that Dio had fallen down into the basement, but she was too late. The delay caused by meeting you in the hallway, her return, unlocking the three locks on the door and coming down here was enough time for Lucien to kill Dio."

"Lucien? But why?" asked Father Fiasco. "What was his motive? And where is Lucien?"

"One question at a time, my friend. I believe the motive was self-defense. I also believe that Lucien was here, right where we are standing, when Dio came crashing out of the laundry chute. Lucien was frightened and did what we all do when we're frightened: he struck out at a supposed enemy. As to where Lucien is—he's right here! Remember, George, I asked you to pay attention when we came down here last night? I said it was important not only to see everything that was here, but also to see what wasn't here."

"Yes, and I thought we did that. We looked around this room and Mama's hermitage and even inspected the wine cellar, but I didn't see anything that was missing. What's absent that should be here?"

"I didn't see it either, last night. It was only this afternoon in the chapel that it came to me. I was standing at the icon of the prophet, the bottom of which is still unpainted. Then I realized that the missing piece both in the painting and in this unsolved case was down here in the basement.

"Look over there. See the gas furnace that heats this house, and beyond it is the original coal furnace. But where's the coal bin? Do you recall the old coal chute covering surrounded by a concrete pad at the back of the house? Fatima used to sit on it frequently. Question: where does the chute empty out down here? I believe that there are two underground rooms separate from this main area of the basement. One is the wine cellar over there on the east side of the house and the other is the coal bin!"

We all looked at one another with an "Aha!" glance of recognition, which quickly turned into one of bewilderment. True, if once the house had been heated by a coal furnace, the basement would have had a coal bin. But still, what did that have to do with the murder?

Seeing our confusion, Bernadone continued, "Let me go on. The coal bin is behind this old cupboard, right Mama Mahatma?" Pointing to the floor, he said, "Last night I saw this scratch by the door to the wine cellar. Something large and heavy must have been dragged across the floor, something like this old cupboard. I believe that when you arrived down here the other night, Mama, you discovered Lucien had killed Dio. You pulled this cupboard aside and hid Lucien in the old abandoned coal bin. Then you closed the door and hurriedly shoved the cupboard back into place. I suspect that you've hidden him in there before, perhaps when repair men had to come down here. With Lucien safely in his hiding place, you carried and dragged Dio upstairs. You laid him on the bench next to the clock and turned to lock the basement door. It was then that you heard Gloria coming downstairs, so you ran out the side door. If you hadn't been interrupted by Gloria, you would have dragged Dio outside the house so he'd be found in the yard. If that had happened, it's not likely your beloved Lucien would have been implicated."

"Very clever, Inspector. You're very good at your profession. Yes, you are correct. I didn't want poor Lucien blamed for this. It wasn't his fault. The poor child was frightened. He's not a violent or vicious child."

"I think we both know, Mama Mahatma, that Lucien is no child – but rather a mature adult – and more than capable of killing a man. I'm sorry, but I must push aside this cupboard to prove my theory so we can settle this case. Jon, please give me a hand."

Jon and the Inspector put their shoulders to the old cupboard and easily slid it along the floor toward the wine cellar door. In its vacated place another door was revealed in the north wall of the basement. Bernadone slowly opened the door and turned to Mama Mahatma. "Mama, would you please call Lucien out?"

"I can't. Lucien is...ah...hard of hearing."

"Yes, I know. Or at least let's say that I supposed he couldn't hear your voice." Then, strangely, Bernadone began to stomp his foot on the floor. Simultaneously he reached up and pulled down an extension cord wrapped around one of the pipes, switching on the large light bulb at the end of the cord. Taking the end near the lighted bulb in his right hand, he swung the cord like a cowboy in large arcs at the entrance of the coal bin.

We all stood in a half-circle behind Bernadone who was creating rapid figure eights with the swinging light. As he chanted, "Lucien, come out!" my heart was racing. I was magnetically drawn to whoever was hiding in the darkened coal bin. At the same time, I was equally repelled by a fear of the mysterious figure Bernadone was calling out to meet us. Like I did as a small child when something horrible was about to happen at the movies, I wanted to close my eyes. Then, suddenly out of the darkened hole, hissing and angry, leaped Lucien!

200

"O my God!"

"Look out, get back!"

Gloria began screaming hysterically. The fingers of fear grabbed me about the throat, cutting off my air. As if we had been one body, the whole group fell back in terror. A huge snake, a giant python, emerged from the coal bin. He must have been twenty feet long, his body as thick as a tree trunk. His head swayed from side to side and his forked tongue flicked outward as he hissed in anger at having been disturbed. Fearful of the unknown, the great snake began recoiling his long body, slithering back into the black hole of the coal bin.

Fiasco grabbed my arm, saying, "My God, look at that monster! He must weigh over two hundred pounds; he's enormous!"

"My Lucien, my poor gentle Lucien," wept Mama. "You were only frightened. You only attacked Dio in self-defense. O God, now what will become of you?"

Maria had sought refuge in Jon's arms, her face buried in his chest. Mike, having attempted to calm Gloria who had fled back toward the laundry sinks, shouted, "Bernadone, you didn't have to bring us down here for your cheap Italian theatrics just to prove something! Why did you expose us to such danger?"

"There's no danger to any of us! Everyone, please be calm. Lucien isn't going to harm us."

The giant python had coiled himself into the darkest corner of his place of refuge, but his head was still raised, his tongue hissing out a warning. Bernadone held the light overhead so we could see the coiled snake up against the back wall of the coal bin.

"Bernadone, you *knew* Lucien was a giant python, didn't you," I exclaimed, unable to take my eyes off the huge snake whose long, thick body was as beautiful as it was frightening. "But how? How did you figure it out?"

"Two things really haunted me. There was the bathtub full of water and those two empty cages we found last night over there by the old furnace. You told me, George, that twice you saw a farmer give Mama Mahatma some large rabbits in wire cages. There were no rabbits down here, however. Absent also was any sign that they had been kept as pets. I kept asking myself why Mama wanted rabbits if not for pets or food? In all my years here, we've never been served rabbit meat. I even considered the possibility that they were being used for some scientific experiments, but there was no sign of that anywhere here in the basement."

"Let's get out of here," cried Gloria. "Can't we discuss the fine points upstairs? That monster in there is dangerous. I hate snakes!"

"Really, Inspector, is it necessary that we remain down here. My wife is . . . ."

"Patience, friends, we're almost finished."

I was still intent on getting to the bottom of the mystery, so I asked, "Bernadone, why did you whirl that electric light in front of the coal bin?"

"Snakes, George, even very large ones like Lucien, have short-sighted vision but are attracted to moving objects, especially ones that emit warmth like this heat lamp. I stomped my foot because their hearing is sensitive only to vibrations."

While shaken by the experience, the group began to slowly gather in front of the coal bin. Father Fiasco even stuck his head into the open doorway for a better look at the huge snake, saying, " 'Now the serpent was the most cunning of all the animals that the Lord God had made . . . .' "

Bernadone returned the light to its place. "Thanks, Father, for the quote from Genesis. It's a good reminder. By the way, you're all quite safe in coming closer. Lucien is more afraid of us than we are of him. As I told you upstairs, you have nothing to fear — and I would now add — but your own fears!

"As I said, I was baffled about the cages till this evening after Mass. While standing in front of the icon of the prophet, I was looking at the stars falling from the heavens like luminous snowflakes. Of course, I had seen them many times before at Mass in the chapel. I had even seen the artist's penciled-in image of a great serpent. This afternoon, for some reason, I made the connection between those stars and the light. Light in Italian is *luce*. It was a quick jump from *luce* to *Lucien* and then to *Lucifer*. Yes, Lucifer, the Angel of Light, who when he fell from the heavens became the great serpent. The rabbits then made sense. They were the monthly diet of a large python."

"That's why Mama Mahatma kept the basement locked, why

only she came down here," said Fiasco. "It all makes sense now."

"But I don't understand the implication of the water in the bathtub," I interjected.

"All serpents in captivity need water, George. Very large ones like Lucien need a lot of water. They immerse themselves in it. The old bathtub was ideal for Lucien."

"That explains the empty soap dish! But, Inspector, how do you know so much about snakes?"

"First of all, George, you were observant to notice the empty soap dish – Lucien had no need of soap. As to my knowledge of snake lore – when I came home from Mass I went upstairs and looked in one of my books. As you know, I'm an animal lover, and I have several volumes on birds and other animals. What I found in a book on reptiles confirmed my intuition. Large pythons kill their prey by wrapping themselves around their victims. With each breath the victim takes, the python tightens its grip until it has completely cut off the victim's oxygen and blood flow."

"But what's to prevent it from attacking one of us?" asked Mike.

"No real danger of that, Mike. A snake, under normal circumstances, does not attack something larger than itself. However, if you handle it roughly, attack it or attempt to capture it, the snake will throw its coils around you and squeeze with all its strength. I suspect that Lucien was coiled up here in his usual place on the floor near the laundry sinks, directly below the heat lamp, when Dio fell through the chute and landed right next to him. Startled and frightened, Lucien coiled himself around Dio quick as lightning. Naturally Dio resisted his attacker, which only sealed his doom more quickly because it made Lucien tighten his grip. Lucien was probably still coiled around Dio when Mama Mahatma arrived. From my research I learned that she could have released Dio from Lucien's grip in a matter of moments by grabbing his tail and untangling it. Unfortunately, a serpent as large as Lucien would not have taken long to kill a man the size of Dio. Well, friends, that about wraps it up. Any more questions?"

I had a sense that there were a number of questions, but we all preferred to get out of the basement. Bernadone left the door to the coal bin open so that Lucien could come out when we were gone. He took Mama Mahatma's arm and led the way as the rest of us followed them upstairs.

As Mama Mahatma closed the door, she turned with tearful eyes to Bernadone and asked, "What will happen now to my poor Lucien?"

"I'll file my report tomorrow. I'll do everything in my power to see that you can keep him. You must have had him for many years, as large as he is."

"Yes, he's been with me for a long time. I want to thank you, Inspector, for your sensitivity in clearing up this affair. I'm glad that it's over and there's no need to hide Lucien any longer." Then, with a weary smile, she looked upon all of us. "Well, friends, I'm very tired and would like to go to bed. Good night to you all."

CHAPTER 13

Jon, Maria, Mike and Gloria excused themselves and went upstairs to their rooms. Bernadone, Father Fiasco and I went to the kitchen. In all the excitement I had forgotten that the dinner dishes were still stacked in the sink and on the table. Bernadone and Fiasco offered to help me clean up, and I readily accepted. As we washed and dried the dishes, we visited mostly about Mama and all the stress that this ordeal had placed on her. We all felt great relief at the outcome.

When we were finished with the dishes, I was still too energized to go to bed and proposed that we have a glass of wine as a nightcap. They both agreed, and as the three of us sat at the kitchen table Fiasco lit up a cigarette. "Excuse me, friends, for smoking, but I need a strong shot of the old drug after a night like this. God help us, when I saw that big python I thought my heart would jump out of my body. Great work, Bernadone, in solving the murder! George, you're not half-bad yourself as a detective."

"I agree, Fiasco," chimed in the Inspector. "He's become very observant, aware of how things fit together, one of the rewards for paying attention in life. Care for a job, George? We can always use another good detective."

"Thanks anyway, Inspector, sounds exciting, but I've got to get home. I only have a couple of days left in my sabbatical. It's time for me to return to a normal life again. I must confess that while I'm eager to get back to Martha and the kids, I hate to leave you two. You've become good friends – and teachers as well."

"A toast to friendship," said Fiasco, raising his glass. The three of us drank heartily. "You know, George, I've always wanted to take a sabbatical myself. And I know, Bernadone, that you've spoken of traveling to the Near East to learn more about...what's his name?"

"Najmuddin Kubra, 'the Greater.' Yes, you're right. It always has been a dream of mine to learn firsthand about his Sufi Order of the Greater Brethren, but . . . ."

"Dreams shouldn't end with a *but*," said Fiasco. "You're never too old or too busy to midwife a dream to life—even if you're as gray-headed as this old priest. Let's toast to unfulfilled dreams."

Again we toasted, laughing at the flair for life possessed by the pastor of the Lone Star Cathedral.

"George, are you sure you're ready to take on the quiet suburban life? Don't you have a hidden dream, one yet to be explored?" added Fiasco.

"Well, I have toyed with the idea of going to Tibet someday. That's insane, of course. The possibilities are about as remote as my going to the moon. There are the issues of getting free from work again, the cost of such a trip and my family responsibilities. Yet there has been a haunting sense that maybe in Tibet I might find what I'm searching for in my quest. For sure, I haven't found it here."

"What makes you say that, George?" said Bernadone. "I've seen a real change in you since you first came here six months ago. I know you're not having visions, but you are seeing things and people differently than when you arrived. To see life in a different light is at the heart of enlightenment! I know you're not glowing with extraterrestrial light, but you are more enlightened about how the ordinary is the workplace of the true quest. I plod along on my journey, working for the police department. Fiasco here does the same in his job at the freight company— which more than supplements his work as pastor of the Lone Star Cathedral. You can continue your quest in suburbia, just as we do ours here. Don't forget that good seekers never try to gauge their own progress on the path. Spiritual progress doesn't often come at a jackrabbit's pace. As my friends, the Moslems, say, 'Those who travel the path do so at a turtle's pace.' "

"Yeah, George, look at me. I'm a crawler too. While our lives may be—and that's only *may* be—a bit more adventuresome than yours, anyone's life can be filled with adventure, if one is seeking the Divine Mystery. Furthermore, I don't think it's the place one seeks as much as the company one keeps which holds the power to open the hidden doors. Bernadone is that for me – a door opener – and so is Mama Mahatma."

"A doorman, now there's a religious vocation!" quipped Bernadone. "Fiasco, I like the ring of it."

"In one way or another," continued Fiasco, "all the roomers here at the boarding house have been that for me. They come and go, yet each of them has in one way or another been a teacher for me. At times, an actual journey to someplace far from home has the magic power to speed up the process. It requires relating in new ways to resolve new issues. Yet every journey leads back home, and that's why I agree with Bernadone. Wherever you are is, or can be, the place of transformation. All that being true, I really believe that the three of us should go on an actual adventure. Think about it, wouldn't it be great to travel together, even if we only went to Cleveland?"

"Cleveland? You mean Cleveland, Ohio?" My voice was filled with disbelief.

"Sure, Cleveland, Cairo, Tibet or Timbuktu, the place isn't as important as the fact that you are on a journey that opens you to newness. You don't travel as a tourist but as a pilgrim. When you travel as a pilgrim, the world is crowded with hidden shrines and with teachers who don't even know that they're spiritual guides for others." After a pause that was pregnant with possibility for each of us, Fiasco continued. "Well, friends, we've finished our wine, and like Mama Mahatma I'm tired. I think I'll go upstairs to bed."

"Thanks, Father, for those pilgrimage seeds you planted," I said. "It's an exciting prospect, but it's a little too much to fully contemplate at this moment. Now that the mystery is solved, we can all go to bed and rest. This chapter of my life is about to end – only a couple of days before I leave."

"Good night to both of you," said Bernadone. "Yes, it's been a most eventful day, and I'm also beginning to feel very tired. I'll hate to see you leave, George. I've enjoyed living under the same roof with you, but I understand that you need to go. We all need to follow our hearts when it comes to the quest. I can tell that your heart's speaking to you, George, but are you sure that the mystery of this old house has been completely solved?"

Rinsing out the wine glasses and setting them on the edge of the sink, I smiled. "Of course, Lucien killed Dio. Maria and Jon are free to get married. Mama Mahatma trusts that you'll do everything you can so she won't have to part with her beloved Lucien."

We left the kitchen, climbed the stairs, said good night again and went to our rooms. I was ready to go to bed but felt a sudden urge to go up and turn on the old Magic Lantern. Even though it had been a very full evening already, I closed my door quietly and climbed up to my attic hermitage.

The house was silent except for the hum of the large electric bulb at the heart of the Magic Lantern machine. I fished around in the sack of boxes of slides until I found the "right" one. I carefully inserted the first slide in the machine and sat back to examine the image on the wall. It was a static image of a crowded road somewhere in the Orient, perhaps India. The roadway was jammed with men, women and children carrying what appeared to be their life possessions. On the outer edges of the river of people was an endless line of bicycle rickshaws. There was even a string of pack-laden camels plodding along the side of the road. As I stared at the image, the people, rickshaws and camels began moving, and the attic room became filled with sounds of humanity. I could actually smell the dust and sweat. The entire scene began to slowly flow around me as I became aware that I was viewing it from the back seat of a car. It was certainly the most direct of my Magic Lantern experiences.

"Be careful, Prasad. I would honk my horn more if I were you," came a voice from my far right. "The road is very crowded today, and we don't want an accident." While I could hear the voice, I couldn't clearly see who was speaking or who was driving. The driver followed the unseen person's instructions and the car's horn began bleating like a lost sheep. The river of poor, ragged people parted as we approached, but the crowds were so dense that the driver was forced to slow down to a speed of only a few miles an hour. Pressed against the windows of the car on my left and right were dark, foreign, angry faces. A few shook their fists at us as we passed them. I had a strong feeling of being different from them—and, for some reason, despised. To my surprise I heard my own voice saying, "I don't care for the way they're looking at us. Their faces are filled with hate. Are you sure we're safe?"

"Don't worry, chap, this is an embassy car. While there's a good deal of unrest among the populace, I don't think there will be any *real* trouble for now. However, there has been a rumor going around for days of an attack here in the city by that radical religious group, the Shivaites...watch out, man! For God's sake, Prasad, you almost hit that child!"

"Sorry, Sahib, she ran right out in front of us from the crowd. I didn't see her until the last moment." For the first time I had a clear view of the driver over the front seat. He wore a white turban, and his head almost touched the ceiling of the car. He had to be six-and-a-half feet tall. His large dark-skinned hands gripped the steering wheel, but he seemed as relaxed as a cat in a basket.

"Lay on the horn more and be careful, Prasad. I wouldn't want to have an accident and be stranded here in the middle of this hostile crowd. As I was saying, George, there shouldn't be any problems at customs — at least any more than usual. It's been a pleasure to be of some small assistance to you. It was great luck for you that you were a friend of one of our former embassy men. Always a pleasure to help out an American. I'll wager you're happy to be getting out of this country and on your way home again. We don't know when, but there's sure to be trouble soon. Ah, here we are at last."

The car pulled off the main road and entered the gates of an airfield. A stream of the river of people also branched off, and hundreds were pouring into the airport. At the main gate there was a large sign in both the native language and in English which read **Restricted Area!** The airport and surrounding area, however, didn't seem to be restricted. It was jammed with refugees, with countless people carrying bundles, old suitcases and boxes of possessions.

"Most unusual," said the man to my far right. "I mean, this crowd at the airport. They can't have the means to purchase air tickets. I wonder what . . . ."

"Sahib, here's the departure gate," said the driver in a crisp British accent.

"Good, good, we'll soon have you on your plane, George, and

safely headed for home. Why don't the police have better control of this mob?"

As I stepped from the car, I was caught off guard by the sudden press of native porters all grabbing for my suitcase and a half-dozen beggars crowding around the opened car door with outstretched hands. I suddenly felt a powerful grip on my right arm and my suitcase being taken from my hand. "Sahib, with your permission. Allow me."

"Go with him, George. He'll get you through that crowd. I'll be following up . . . ." His voice was drowned out by the sound of automatic weapon fire and the screams of the crowd. The masses gathered at the entrance of the airport ran in all directions or fell to the ground. The automatic rifle fire roared from both our front and rear. I could see uniformed police and soldiers in front of us firing weapons over our heads at terrorists somewhere behind us. As I was ready to dive for cover, I felt myself being lifted up and pulled to the right.

"Sahib, this way, quickly . . . ."

In that emotionally charged moment the face of the tall, muscular driver came strikingly into view. His white turban framed his dark face with its deep-brown eyes and half-moon-shaped black beard. Across his right cheek was a narrow scar. With amazing speed and strength, he led — almost carried me — through the entrance of the airport terminal. Inside, everything was chaos. Soldiers were firing their automatic weapons through windows and doorways at those attacking from the outside. Passengers were huddled under chairs and benches or clustered together near the ticket counters. Some were laying on the floor with their hands over their heads.

Prasad seemed unconcerned about his own safety as he spirited me toward the customs counter. The customs officials had either fled their posts or were hiding underneath the desks. He smiled a wide grin. "No customs today, Sahib. This way — hurry or we'll miss the plane!"

As we ran toward the exit door that opened to the landing strip, our departure was suddenly blocked. Into the doorway stepped a wild-eyed rebel with an automatic rifle aimed directly at us. He was shouting something, the only part of which I could make out was the name of Shiva.

With his left arm Prasad pushed me behind him, hurling my suitcase toward the doorway with his right hand. The heavy suitcase sailed through the air and struck the rebel just below the chin. His head jerked back as if his neck had been broken, and he was hurled against the wall.

"No time, Sahib, to get your suitcase. Hurry or you'll miss your plane," urged Prasad as he pushed me through the doorway.

"That's not my plane," I shouted over the racket of the gun-fire as I saw an ancient DC3 twin-engine plane slowly lumber-ing down the runway. My tickets were for the government airline plane to my left. I quickly noticed, however, that both of its front tires had been shot out.

"Hurry, Sahib, they're trying to escape before the terrorists stop them. No time . . . ."

"But where's it going?" I cried out as we ran after the plane.

"Can't be selective now, Sahib, it's the last plane out!"

The cabin door of the old, battered DC3 was still open, and I could see a figure waving us on as we ran to catch up with the plane. It was only now that I saw the name painted on the side of the plane: **Red Dragon Airlines**. By now the two of us were almost parallel with the DC3. I suddenly felt myself be-ing lifted off the ground. Prasad had grabbed me around the waist and was lifting me up toward the open cabin door where waiting arms reached out for me. With a powerful thrust, he half pushed and half threw me into the open doorway. As my head hit the floor, I heard a voice from the cockpit: "Shut that damn door. We gotta' get out of here!"

"Sahib, I am your servant . . . ." Prasad's resounding pledge followed me inside as the cabin door slammed shut, leaving everything in total darkness. Though I couldn't see anything, I could still feel the plane moving down the runway and could hear gunfire.

No other images appeared on the wall. I sat in the blackened attic room, my heart pounding, my hands sweaty. This was by far the most vivid and engaging of my Magic Lantern episodes. I had never been so completely caught up in it. I looked for another slide, but there was none. For whatever reason, this Magic Lantern experience was over. But what did it mean? As different as it was, it was as unexplainable as my first encounter, the scene of the Buddhist monk with the nail in his hand. I was totally drained – exhausted. I slowly stood up and left the attic for my bedroom.

I undressed and climbed into bed. Laying back on my pillow, I wondered if next door Maria and Jon were asleep in each other's arms. With the relief they must have felt at the mystery of Dio's death being solved, it seemed natural that they would make love together tonight. I was happy that nothing now stood in the way of them being married. All was quiet in the old house as my mind played tag with a collection of thoughts. My musings about Maria and Jon made me think of Martha, and I realized how eager I was to be home. The wine, the calm at the end of all the evening's excitement and the lateness of the hour all wove a spell around me that carried me to sleep in seconds.

I slept deeply until about 2:30 a.m. when I awoke with a start. I tossed and turned for some time without being able to return to sleep. A rush-hour trafficway of thoughts cloverleafed in my brain. The two lanes were crowded with memories of my time at Mama's boarding house and with images of my anticipated homecoming. Suddenly the cloverleaf of thoughts was transformed into a great coiling python. A shudder passed through my body as I thought of Lucien in the basement. Then, strangely, I felt an impulse to go down and look at Lucien.

Shaking my head, I tried to count backwards from a thousand, a technique I've used when trying to fall asleep. However, the urge to go down into the basement and see the huge serpent – even if it was after 3 o'clock in the morning – was strong. It came in waves of excitation, giving it almost a sexual quality. Finally, I got out of bed, put on my bathrobe and tiptoed out into the dark hallway. I climbed down the back stairs as quietly as possible so as not to awaken anyone. In the silence, the ticktock of the old clock on the first floor was accentuated, matching the beating of my heart.

The basement door was not locked. I had somehow hoped that it would be, a sign from God that I wasn't supposed to do this. I guess there was no longer a need to prevent anyone from going down to the basement since we all knew what was lurking down there. I opened the door and quietly closed it behind me before I turned on the stairwell light.

212

Like Dante descending into hell, I crept into the basement. My heart began pounding as if it were a tribal drum, the rhythm swirling me in a jungle of fear and attraction. Making the turn in the stairs, I stopped on the next-to-bottom step. The basement was barely illuminated by the light in the stairwell. At first I didn't see Lucien. Perhaps he was in the coal bin or back in the shadows of the dimly lit area. I gathered my bathrobe more tightly around me and was daring myself to step down into the basement when Lucien appeared.

He came slithering out of the bathroom, his shimmering scales dripping water. He turned his head and stared at me, his eyes as expressionless as those of the serpent coiled around the face of the clock upstairs. A shudder like cool lightning raced up my spine. Deliberating, I sat down on the second step of the stairway as Lucien coiled himself slowly and sensuously in the lighted area.

"You're evil," I thought, "the only creature that God ever cursed, at least according to the writers of Genesis. Why are you so attractive; why did I want to come here to visit you?" Lucien stared at me, his long body coiling upon itself in reptilian eroticism.

"You're also holy, aren't you, Lucien? The serpent is a symbol of health, healing and transformation, once a god of sexual pleasure and a goddess of fertility and enormous earth energy." Lucien raised his head slowly, his scales glistening in the light. We looked at one another, and I wondered if this was the way that Eve and the serpent began their conversation.

As if a claw rising out of the dark had grabbed my heart, I was terrified by the thought: "What if Lucien begins to speak?

"Yes, I'm afraid of you, Lucien, regardless of what Bernadone or Mama said. You were judge, jury and executioner for Dio. You aren't some cute little pet; your reptilian brain is your only brain! You're not disturbed by 'temptations' to forgive and forget or to peaceful non-violence. No conscience pricks you when you defend your territory against an invader. Your heart is frozen, deaf to all cries for mercy.

"Lucifer, fallen angel, I know what dragged me out of bed and down here—it was my fallen angel! Coiled deep inside me, its feather wings now moist with scales, my fallen angel lusted to look at you, Lucien. Since I came here, I've felt messages from my fallen angel locked in my reptilian brain. My intense anger at Dio, my feelings for Maria, perhaps even my desire for deep wisdom, are they not expressions of my fallen angel? Is not all passion a kind of possession?" Though I asked Lucien that question, he only stared silently at me. His silence was a relief since I was afraid that he would offer me, as the serpent offered Mother Eve, a way to be godlike.

The two of us sat facing each other in silence until I said aloud, "You know, Lucien – or Lucifer – you're a sign of self-growth, of self-determination, even if it was God whom you challenged in your quest for independence. As an American, I especially can't find the desire for self-determination and independent thinking to be all evil! What is evil anyway, and what is good? Was it evil of you to execute Dio by crushing him to death for sins that cried out to heaven for revenge? In a way, Lucien, you only did what religion, civilization or fear prevented us from doing to him. Yet we would have sanctioned the State to execute Dio. Aren't capital punishment, war and all such evils that are called 'necessary' or even 'good' expressions of stunted evolutionary growth, a failure to move beyond thinking with our reptile, fallen angel, brain?

"Why are you, even as a symbol for evil, more attractive, more magnetic, than some saints? Why must holiness have only one face – pious and plain – while evil has a thousand faces: cunning, adventuresome, aggressive, brutal, seductive, sensual, invigorating, throbbing with passion...? Share your wisdom with me, Lucien. Tell me if what's judged as evil today will be considered evil tomorrow." I directed those questions right into Lucien's deep, vacant eyes.

Then I reflected on Jesus' statement that just as Moses raised the serpent in the desert to heal the people, so Jesus had to be lifted up. Looking into those bottomless eyes, I wondered, "Is that how my reflections on the cross and surrender tie in with my reptilian, fallen-angel emotions: that somehow all my primal passions have to first be embraced and then lifted up?"

Lucien again raised his head and paused as if he were about to speak. Then he slowly slithered into the darkened shadows by the coal bin, perhaps weary of my reflections or perhaps just tired. Alone, I realized how late it was. Climbing the steps, I turned out the light, closed the door and ascended the back stairs to my room. My alarm clock showed 4:15 as I slipped into bed. I closed my eyes and fell asleep in minutes.

CHAPTER 14

The next couple of days disappeared like an egg in a magician's handkerchief as I packed and prepared to leave. How quickly the months had come and gone; it was already the morning of my departure. Last night after dinner, I had said my goodbyes to the others in the house – that is, everyone but Mike and Gloria who left suddenly yesterday. Their unexplained departure made me wonder about Dio's accusation regarding them.

I decided to make my farewells last night since I knew that the others would all be at work by the time I left in the morning. Maria had a new job working as a secretary and now left the house as early as the others.

Having packed my bag and stripped my bed linen, I stood at the north window of my room, absorbed in thought. Bernadone had told me yesterday that he was working on a way so that Mama wouldn't have to give up Lucien. He had applied to the city zoning commission for a permit to open a children's petting zoo!

It would be a fenced-in area with proper shelters for the animals. Besides Lucien, there would be a few small reptiles, a couple of pigs, goats, sheep and a llama. Bernadone also wanted to set up a small aviary. The plan was to locate the zoo on the west side of the house, using the front half of the area now occupied by Mama's flower garden. Bernadone felt that they had an excellent chance to be granted the permit. He was delighted because everyone would benefit. Lucien could live out the rest of his days here. Mama was greatly relieved that she would not have to give him up. She would also enjoy the presence of children around the place. And Bernadone, as well as the children, would derive great enjoyment from the presence of all the animals. It was also an opportunity for people to let some of their own primal pets out of the "basement" and, by playing with them, find a measure of healing.

I smiled to myself as Bernadone enthusiastically told me about his plan. As bizarre as this complex already was – with its eccentric roomers as well as the presence of Father Fiasco's strange chapel – all that Mama Mahatma's boarding house needed was a petting zoo! Looking out at the big gold star atop the Lone Star Cathedral, I laughed to myself: "I'll bet old Fiasco will hatch some really imaginary name for the petting zoo."

Piece by piece, each of the issues here in the house was being resolved for the good as I prepared to return home. I was surprised to find myself full of heartfelt emotion, tearful at the idea of leaving. Six months isn't very long, but in that time I had fallen in love. I surprised myself by using that expression, but, no doubt about it, that's how I do feel toward the people who live here. It occurred to me that while I may not have scaled the top of the crystal mountain of holiness on this sabbatical, I have become more human!

As I wiped my eyes, I reflected on the difference between myself today and six months ago. Tears as well as laughter were flowing much more easily now than before. It was as if some inner authority figure had given me permission to feel freely, to touch those rivers of emotion deep inside me, rivers of anger, love and joy. It was easier now to ignore that childhood echo in my head that sing-songed, "Don't be a cry baby," and to let my heart say whatever it wanted to say. An elementary truth had eluded me until now: when you shut down the expression of one emotion, deny it or repress it, you end up shutting down all of them!

While I still found it a bit embarrassing to be teary-eyed, especially at the thought of others seeing me, I didn't mind it. Moreover, I was surprised that others didn't seem to mind my tears either. Who knows, maybe becoming holy is really becoming more human – fully human as opposed to superhuman. Maybe I had made it higher on that crystal mountain than I thought.

I picked up my gear, left my room and closed the door with a real sense of closure. It was quiet in the old house. The only sound was the tick-tock of the old grandfather's clock downstairs.

I had a ticket reserved for the late-morning bus and was ready to go. I carried my Magic Lantern case in one hand and my suitcase in the other. As I came down the back stairs, I was struck by just how *magic* the old Lantern really was. It had been a real teacher for me. Perhaps it had more stories to share. The antique shop owner was right; I was lucky that it had chosen me. True, I still didn't understand some of its stories, but maybe their meanings would come with time.

I set down my suitcase and Magic Lantern box at the bottom of the steps. I had to smile – the basement door was ajar. I walked to the kitchen, taking one last fond look at the scene of so many of my culinary "crimes." Then I returned to my suitcase in the front of the house, calling out to Mama Mahatma. She emerged from her room. "Ah, George, you're leaving as you came, a case in each hand!"

"I may look the same, Mama, but the George you see this morning isn't the George who walked into your house months ago! I must confess, however, that I'm sneaking out with a treasure hidden in my suitcase – or rather, my heart."

"Stealing," came a voice from inside her room, "is a crime, a matter for the police." Bernadone stepped out of her room. "Put your hands up, George, you're under arrest!"

"Stealing," came another voice, "is a violation of the fourth, or is it the seventh, commandment and requires absolution by a priest!" Out came Fiasco wearing the same cowboy hat I had seen on him the day I arrived.

"Bernadone, Fiasco, at this time of day? You're supposed to be at work! We said goodbye last night. What are you two doing here?" I set my cases down and embraced my two friends.

"We wouldn't want this historical moment to be lost, so I'm taking notes," said Maria, her dictation notebook in hand as she stepped out of Mama's room. She gave me a moist kiss and embraced me. "George, we're back to Mama's cooking again – we won't need any diets now. We're going to miss you – and your marvelous dinners. If I were lucky enough to be your wife, I would make you do all the cooking."

"Watch your step, George," said Jon as he popped out of Mama's room, "that woman you're kissing is my future wife!" Jon stood squarely in front of me with one hand gripping each of my shoulders. "We're all going to miss you, George. Like the others, I couldn't let you leave without a proper send-off." He wrapped his arms around me and gave me a long bear hug.

"I...ah...I'm lost for words. Maria, Jon, and you, Bernadone and Fiasco, thank you all. I'm really touched by your love." Just then a car horn sounded out on the street.

"Your ride's here," said Fiasco. "We wanted you to go to the bus station in style, so we called you a cab. I'll go and tell the driver that you'll be out in a moment."

"Goodbye, George," said Mama Mahatma. "Come back and see us sometime, and bring Martha and your children. We'd love to meet them." It was her turn to hug me. As she pressed me tightly against her ample bosom, I felt as if Mother Earth herself had embraced me.

"We'll send you an invitation to our wedding. We hope you can come," said Jon, standing with his arm around Maria.

"Here, allow me," said Bernadone as he grabbed my suitcase and the Magic Lantern case. "I'll walk you down to the cab."

"Remember, George," said Mama with tears in her eyes, "pay attention to everything. If you understand the way the universe works, every point along the journey is the destination, all the way there is *there*, if you know what I mean!"

I kissed her farewell. "Thanks for everything, Mama, and give Lucien a hug—or I should say, a *pet*—for me." I turned and walked down the steps of the old house. My eyes were a bit misty, true, but I could still see that the vehicle at the curb was no cab. It was a long, white stretch limousine!

"George!" I turned around as Mama called after me from the porch, "Remember, 'Trust in Allah, but tie up your camel!' "

I waved to the three on the porch and turned toward my camel for the day.

"What do you think, Pilgrim?" laughed Bernadone. "Nothing like leaving in style!"

I shook my head and laughed as I replied, "I thought limousines were only for weddings or funerals! Isn't this a bit extravagant?"

"George," returned Bernadone, "the final stage of poverty is to give up poverty!"

Then, for some unexplained reason, I suddenly remembered Bernadone's question in the kitchen a couple of nights ago: "Are you sure, George, that the mystery of this old house has been solved?" I had thought he was referring to the mystery of Dio's murder and had answered, "Yes." Walking down the sidewalk with him, even with my recent sense of resolution, I now wasn't so sure of my answer. I wondered if there was some other mystery left unsolved.

"Inspector, what did you mean the other night when you hinted that a mystery still remained to be solved? If there is one, tell me what it is before I leave."

"Detective SenT George, if I recall correctly, you kept a journal of your stay here, right? Well, maybe you'll find the key to the unsolved mystery if you look back to what you wrote about a certain dinner conversation."

"Come on, Inspector, give this rookie a clue — at least a lead about where to look."

"All right, I'll give you a clue as a farewell gift. Look in your journal notes about the story that Maria told after supper one night."

"Maria's story? I can't recall it right now."

"It was several nights after the feast of the Purification, somewhere around the time you discovered that your meditation hourglass was really a stash for Dio's coke."

"Thanks, I'll look up what I wrote about that night and search for the unsolved mystery. Bernadone, I hope you know how much I've enjoyed our friendship, and I have a farewell gift for you. You like mysteries, and so I hand into your safe custody my Magic Lantern machine. I promise you, it will keep your wits sharpened. Who knows, maybe it even has some Islamic stories reserved just for you."

"Thank you, George, truly. I know this is no ordinary gift! I promise you that I shall care for it as a rare treasure."

We reached the street where Father Fiasco had opened the back door of the limousine. "Your carriage, sir," said Fiasco, bowing and making a low sweeping gesture with his cowboy hat. "Blessings on you, amigo. I'll miss you. Here's a wee parting gift." He handed me a brick from the wall of the Lone Star Cathedral.

"Thank you for this reminder of who I am. Thanks too for all the beautiful and challenging experiences you provided in your carriage house chapel. Who knows, I might even start going to church again if I can find one like yours back home.

"Thanks to both of you for those special sessions of dish washing and conversation we shared together. They were a rare collection of Ivory soap, a little wine, a dash of philosophy and theology and a beginner's course in crime investigation. It was like doing dishes with Sherlock Holmes and Bernard Shaw." I embraced both of them one last time. The only words I could get out were, "I'll miss you guys."

I climbed into the back seat, embarrassed by all the luxury. Fiasco and Bernadone bent over and peeked inside the door window. "Don't say goodbye for good, George," said Fiasco. "Remember my proposal that night in the kitchen. I envision the three of us together on a trip to the Near East, the Orient, maybe even Tibet!" Then, straightening up, he motioned to the driver and said, "To the bus station. Pronto, pronto!"

The long limousine slowly pulled away from the curb. Salty rain clouds filled my eyes as I looked out the back window. I waved to the two men on the curb and to Mama, Maria and Jon on the porch. As the car picked up speed, Mama Mahatma's boarding house grew smaller and smaller in the frame of the rear window till it was no more.

With tear-filled eyes, I turned to face the front. For the first time I noticed the limousine's driver. He was a large, dark-skinned man wearing a white turban. As I stared at the back of his head in disbelief, he turned around and smiled at me, his almost perfect white teeth framed by a coal-black beard. His large, intense brown eyes glistened, and the scar slanting across his right cheek provided an exclamation point. As I gasped, he made a slight bow of his head and said, "Sahib, at your service!"

THE END?

LISTING OF STORIES WITHIN THE STORY

ACKNOWLEDGEMENTS

Author is a singular noun, implying that one person wrote the text. In the case of some highly gifted authors, their touch alone was needed. With the book you are holding this is not the case. Many of the fingerprints on this final edition belong to the following friends:

I acknowledge and thank **Thomas Turkle**, the publisher and eagle-eyed editor, for his personal insights and his careful reading of the text.

I acknowledge and thank **Thomas Skorupa** for his creative editing, his patience and imagination in the preparation of this book. Without his creative assistance this book would have remained but a dream.

 My gratitude to **Paula Duke** and the members of the Shantivanam community to which I belong for their encouragement in writing this book as well as their proofreading skills.

I am also most grateful to **Michael Cipolla** for his enthusiastic assistance and insights in critiquing this book. I thank my friends **George Steger** and **Gerry Hanus** for their contributions. My gratitude also to **Dr. Robert Murphy** for his medical expertise and to **Captain Richard Chaminski** of the Kansas City, Kansas Police Department for his technical assistance.